LIGHTNING'S HONOR

THE VIRTUES BOOK VI

A.J. DOWNEY

COPYRIGHT

ISBN: 978-1-950222-42-1

Edited and book design by Maggie Kern at Ms.K Edits

Cover art by Dar Albert at Wicket Art Designs

DEDICATION

For Sarah G. You're welcome for all the stories. I hope you can keep up now that you can see again. We'll forever miss you. You were gone too soon.

PROLOGUE

Lightning...

Was I fucking crazy? Maybe, but I loved the thrill of it out here when it was like this. The charge in the air, the crackle of electricity through the clouds; that wild buildup that I swear I could feel right down to my core before *boom!* That glorious flash of light, as all of that fury gets expelled and channeled to a single point.

Man, the rush! There wasn't anything like it.

I stood well back from the rebar and their plastic tape markers fluttering in the stiff wind as the thunderstorm rumbled and choked overhead. I raked a hand back through my hair that was plastered to my skull.

I was after some fresh fulgurites in a deal I had with one of the gift shops in town. I had a corner on the market – for sure. I was the only bastard crazy enough to be out here during a storm.

Was it dangerous? Incredibly. Had I paid my price more than once being out here? Absolutely. Which is why Galahad and his woman, Charity, were up in the captain's house, looking on in case I got my ass crispy crittered again.

The sky grumbled and I got down a little lower, knowing that it didn't make much difference. If the electricity decided to source through me, my fuckin' goose was cooked, but I had shit out that was a much tastier target than I was for the crackling ozone layer around me.

I lived for that smell. Swear to God, it got me a little high, like a good spliff on a lazy Sunday afternoon. Only rather than mellow me out, the smell had me all kinds of jazzed and ready to go.

I don't know what it was that made me turn and look down the beach. I had to blink through the downpouring rain and the steamy atmosphere to be sure that I was genuinely seeing what I was seeing.

I got up from my crouch, shading my eyes from the rough stinging patter of the rain to, again, see if what I was seeing was really real. It didn't seem to matter how much I blinked – she was still there.

A woman was walking along the beach, at the waterline. Her body was lithe, like a dancer's, and the way she stepped along the sand at the water's edge just as graceful. She hugged a long brown loose-knit sweater beach coverup thing around her shoulders and wore a long, sheath-like wrap skirt in hippie-dippie earth tone colors that enveloped her from her hips to the tops of her feet, the material clinging wetly to her legs.

Her long dark hair was plastered to her skull, a piece artfully stuck to the side of her face, following the curve of her jaw as she gazed out over the churning sea.

I half expected her to walk into it, for her to bob along the surface for a second and then dip, and a fantastical fin would pop above the surface and she would disappear. She was that otherworldly and beautiful. I had to know if I was hallucinating or if she was real, so I started to jog in her direction.

I wasn't but four, maybe five paces from my miniature forest of rebar thrust into the sand when it hit. The last thing I remember was flying forward, my back arching painfully as I tried to fold my damn self in half backward with the force of the blast. Then it was cool wet sand in my face and lights out.

1

Lightning…

"Wow, that's crazy!" Amy's blue eyes were wide beneath her fringe of white bangs. She was older, in her sixties, and her skin was that deep, red-hued, speckled bronze that a lot of older Floridians sported from too much time in the sun.

"I know, right?" I asked.

"But you're alright?" she asked, her eyes narrowing with concern. I laughed.

"Oh, yeah! Hazzard of playing in a storm. Not my first time getting hit, and probably won't be the last," I said, leafing through the crisp bills she'd handed me.

"Well, don't you go and get yourself killed!" she admonished and I laughed, tucking the money into my front pocket.

"We all gotta die sometime, sweetheart," I told her with a wink. "What'd that one musician say? It's better to burn out than fade away?"

She rolled her eyes at me and tsked, crossing her arms under her small breasts, over her bright turquois tank top. She wore it well beneath her airy white linen jacket and matching white linen pants. She gave me a chiding look and I gave her a wink, even as the sunlight coming in the door from behind me winked off of her chunky silver-and-turquoise necklace.

Amy had class, came from rich parents, a rich husband, and was just a lonely widow by the sea, as she liked to call it.

In her late sixties, she ran a high-end gift shop here in town and was one of my best customers for the sturdier fulgurites I managed to produce.

She also wasn't a half bad lay, a total GILF, or *Grandma I'd Like to Fuck*. Well, she would be if she'd ever had any kids or grandkids. She hadn't, and we'd kept our flings on the down low. We had both been pretty liquored up on the occasions that they'd gone down.

She was a free spirit, that one, and had plenty of lovers of all ages and varieties. Some even younger than me – but she wouldn't think of ever getting married again. Hell, she remained steadfast in not making anything with any one of her "gentleman callers" a permanent deal. I don't think she would ever get over her husband and that was alright. I certainly wasn't interested in staking any kind of a claim on her.

Of course, thinking about claims, my thoughts went back to the mystery woman in the storm – about her ethereal beauty, her skirts flowing in the wind, her long dark hair lashing her cheek as she stared out over the waves. How she'd chased it back with an elegant hand.

The guys thought I was crazy. That the hit I'd taken had knocked me stupid… but I knew. I knew I'd seen her and I was a little desperate to see her again, to ask her why the hell she'd been braving the storm. I mean, it'd been a little more intense than I even tended to like, and I'd honestly never met anyone brave or stupid enough to go out for a fuckin' stroll in one. Not like she'd been.

My crazy sort of liked her crazy, and I wanted to know more. My curiosity about it had been insatiable ever since I'd woken up. Voracious in its intensity. Enough to eat me alive.

I left Amy's shop and walked back down the block. She was set back from the boulevard by half a block or so, but it didn't slow her stride. She was across the street from one of the fanciest and busiest restaurants in Ft. Royal.

I happened to look up from recounting what Amy had given me

and doing the math in my head for my bills and shit when I saw her. My mystery woman was drifting across the side street I was on just ahead, looking over some papers in her hand, a tote over her shoulder with some leafy greens poking out the top.

The Farmers' Market was happening in the marina's parking lot today. It happened every Thursday afternoon – mostly for the locals. I rushed myself up the sidewalk and turned the corner after her. She'd stopped, her back stiff, her black hair drifting on the wind, and she turned slowly, so agonizingly slowly, in my direction.

"Are you following me?" she asked and she looked perturbed.

Her voice was as beautiful as she was, clear and crystalline, hard, and yet soft at the same time. I was struck nearly dumb by it.

"N-n-no!" I stammered out like a lunatic.

She narrowed her deep brown eyes in suspicion.

"I saw you!" I blurted out, not helping my case in the slightest. "A while back, on the beach – i-in the storm." I put a hand to the back of my neck and tried to loosen it up by pulling on it, the tension something unexpected and fierce as I *felt* myself fucking this up! Thinking frantically to myself, *you have one shot, you dumbass! This one shot! You're scaring her. You're fucking this up! Stop it! Figure it out! Bow out! What the fuck?*

"That was you?" she asked. She shifted her weight from foot to foot beneath the long, fluttery, brightly colored wrap skirt that rode low on her hips, the hem of it barely a whisper above the ground.

The breeze gusted and whipped some of her long, long, straight black hair across her eyes. She reached up and ghosted her fingertips along it, pulling it down and away from her face. She cocked her head to keep it blowing in a more favorable direction. Her long skirt that was almost lighter than the muggy air out here plastered against her slender legs and left nothing about her form to the imagination. I swallowed hard and tried to keep my eyes on her face. Her light, thin tank top clung to her upper body and her nipples hardened beneath the cloth, her small but perfect tits having no need for a bra underneath.

"I thought you died," she said. "I saw you get hit."

"Ah, yeah, no… I do stupid shit like that all the time," I said, feeling the heat creep into my face. "Wasn't the first hit I took. Probably won't be my last."

"H-h-how could you do that?" she asked, bewildered. "I mean, how did you or do you survive something like that once, let alone multiple times?"

A moment of clarity hit me and I said, "Let me take you out to lunch or coffee or something and I'll tell you all about what it is I do out there."

She looked skeptical.

"Folks around here call me Lightning," I said, holding out my hand to shake. "Guess I need no explanation as to why."

She stared down at my hand for a long moment, then looked back up into my eyes. Whatever she saw there seemed to make up her mind. She took her hand from the corded cotton rope strap of her tote up over her shoulder and put it in mine. She said, "My name is Honor," she said. "Sounds like a nickname, but it isn't. It's the one I was born with."

I smiled, her hand soft in my own. "Would it make you feel better to know my government name?" I asked.

She cocked her head curiously and nodded. I felt my smile grow as I took back my hand before I lingered too long and gave her a reason to feel creeped out.

"It's Charlie," I said.

She smiled and laughed a little. I laughed too and said, "Now you know why I go by Lightning."

"What? There's nothing wrong with Charlie!" she cried, and I *felt* the ice break between us.

"You didn't have to!" I cried, "and it's all good." She bit her lips together and took a light half-step back, her hips turning in that way that said she had to get going.

"So… can I take you out sometime?" I asked, turning sideways to let her pass and continue in the direction that she had been heading.

"Um… I'll think about it?" she said, and her smile held something I didn't have a name for. Not quite apprehension, but something.

"How do I find you?" I asked. "Can I get your number?"

Her expression turned a bit enigmatic and her smile changed to something borderline mischievous.

"It's a small town," she said. "If it's meant to be, it's meant to be, and we'll run into each other again." She lifted the shoulder unburdened by her tote in a shrug and I scoffed and laughed. I mean, she wasn't wrong. I had a hardcore gut feeling that it was *definitely* meant to be, so I let her have her way.

I nodded and called out. "Alright, bet!"

Her smile turned into a grin, and she kept walking. I stood for a long time, rooted to the spot, watching her go.

I noted when she turned off the boulevard, way far up onto what looked like Neptune Avenue, and made a mental note to cruise through that way every so often. I mean, Nothing and Char lived in that neighborhood if you turned off to the right. It was a pretty big development…

"Hmm," I hummed to myself and turned in the opposite direction, up the boulevard, to get back to where I'd parked my little beater truck. I had church in an hour. We had a run up and across to Daytona and the Ormond Beach area to plan. Bike week was once again coming up fast and I couldn't wait.

I wondered if this was the year I'd finally have a woman on the back of my bike, up behind me.

I had less than a month to magic make it happen – but Honor was right about one thing. This *was* a small town and the Kraken MC's tentacles dug deep, forming its roots.

I'd find her again.

2

Honor...

I paused uneasily on the walkway up to the house... *my house,* I reminded myself. None of it still even seemed *real.* I didn't know the people who had owned it at all. I still didn't understand how and why it'd come to this that I stood on the sunny shores of *Florida,* living in this old couple's home whom I'd never met, surrounded by knickknacks and things that didn't belong to me. All because, once upon a time, they'd adopted my mother.

I sighed. The situation was no less complicated the more I thought about it. I stepped up the cracked sidewalk that was surprisingly weed free between the broken pieces.

The small bungalow was on Poseidon Drive in Fort Royal, Florida – a town that had, inexplicably, managed to avoid progress and high rises. Unlike the rest of the Florida coast, the beaches here weren't jam-packed with resorts and hotels. Just about everywhere else I'd seen on the drive down the Gulf Coast side of things on my way here had been, and it'd left a bitter taste in my mouth. I admit, I'd sort of counted my chickens before they'd hatched and had already made plans to sell this place if my views were going to consist of steel and glass rather than waving palms and blue sky. When I'd arrived, I'd been pleasantly surprised.

My mom's adoptive parents had both died and I'd never met them. It was their lawyer that I'd met in the driveway as I'd exited my beat-up, old-as-dirt, Honda that I swear had barely made the journey from New Mexico where I'd been born and had been living when the private investigator had found me.

Ruth and Mitch Pilchuck weren't *rich* by any means, but they'd been frugal and had quite the nest egg built up and remaining when they'd passed – apparently within a week of each other, leaving everything to my mother and then me.

Problem was that my mother had disappeared when I was sixteen and so that'd left just me.

I was still working with their lawyer now, almost three weeks later, finalizing all the inheritance things. I have to say, in some ways, I felt like some tragic Cinderella… a real rags-to-riches story except with no Prince Charming.

Charlie's handsome and chiseled features, yet still on the slightly scruffy side, flashed through my mind like, well, *lightning*.

I smiled to myself and thought about how he'd seemed so eager and sincere; excited like… like a Golden Retriever, almost. Pure and wholesome. You know?

It was that golden retriever energy that'd stayed my hand on being rude and just telling him to fuck off like I typically did with every creepy male who usually tried to hit on me.

Truthfully, I was glad to see him *alive.* I'd genuinely thought I'd seen him vaporized that day on the beach. The lightning had flashed so bright, it'd left spots in my vision and I'd felt all the hair on my head and body stand on end. When my vision had finally cleared, he'd been gone, a waft of smoke blowing down the beach where he'd stood.

I'd been scared and I'd run back here, soaking wet and shivering, to dive into a hot shower. I'd cried, genuinely thinking he'd died, watching the local news outlets on social media for any information about it, but there'd been none.

I got the mail from the letter box by the front door, all of it addressed to Ruth and Mitch Pilchuck, and went into the house.

It was almost chilly in here after the heat outside. Fearful of the electric bill, I went and turned the temperature up in the house by a few degrees and listened to the hum of the air unit click off.

An almost eerie quiet swept into the home's small space and I looked around.

The bungalow-style house was perfectly suited to the old couple who had lived here. Everything was done in peachy sunrise colors, which *almost* reminded me of a more muted color scheme that was popular in the southwest, particularly in New Mexico.

I set my tote of groceries down on the kitchen counter and sighed. Planting my hands on the counter, I looked out over the open floor plan of the house, into the peachy yellow pinks of the small living room, over the dining room table that was one of those light oak faux-wood things that old people seemed to like.

I tried to picture the smiling woman in the photo albums baking cookies with my equally White mother in this kitchen and failed. My mother wasn't the cookie baking type. She could honestly barely cook at all. Sometimes even Hamburger Helper was too much for her to handle. I'd even seen her ruin a box of Kraft macaroni and cheese.

I sighed.

My mother had run away from these people when she was between sixteen and seventeen. I hadn't seen her face since *I* was sixteen and she'd disappeared.

I sighed and flipped open the old photo album on the counter by my cold cup of coffee from that morning, my eyes skimming my mother's face when she was a child.

She was a miserable kid, and I didn't know why. The Pilchucks, by all accounts, were a lovely couple. I hadn't found *anything* in this house to contradict that.

I let my eyes skim the smiling faces of Mitch and Ruth Pilchuck, the blonde toddler on Ruth Pilchuck's lap, staring blankly into the camera with no smile on her face. Just these wide, somber brown eyes, her chubby little fist in her mouth as she slobbered all over it.

My mother had been adopted when she was two. It was a closed adoption. She'd never known her birth parents and that'd torn at her.

I sighed, closed the book and looked up, anywhere other than at the photos on its pages.

That rankled me.

My mother had had perfectly loving parents in the Pilchucks, by everything I had been able to find, and I had just *wished* I'd had the same in my mom. I mean, there were so many times in my childhood I had wished my mother had given me up and let me live with people who could actually take care of me.

As I said, my mother had run away from these good, kind, caring people and had offered sex for passage with a bunch of truckers. She'd wound up abandoned at a truck stop in New Mexico and had continued to turn tricks and worked there as a waitress, living in the dingy hotel there until she could rent an apartment.

That'd been her plan, anyway, until she'd met my father.

That was a whole other tragedy as far as the life of Rosemary Pilchuck was concerned.

I groaned and put my groceries away, thinking about it.

My dad had met and fallen in love with my mother. He was a truck driver and had driven regionally, back and forth, coming through the diner every two or three days. He talked to my mom, encouraging her, trying to get her straight, off the drugs, and out of the lot-lizard lifestyle and he'd been successful.

He had even gotten work that would take him off the road and would have him home every night – even if he had hated it.

My mom had been happy, right up until I was three and the accident had happened at my father's work. He'd died, my mom hadn't been able to cope, and she'd spiraled right back down into her drugs to forget.

We lost the house. She'd even lost custody of me for a while and I'd bounced in and out of foster care until I was almost five. But somehow she'd managed to pull herself together with my grandmother's help – that would be my father's mother. She'd held on by a thread until my grandmother had died when I was eight.

By then, I was old enough to lie to cover for my mom and I kept it up, afraid, and pretty much thrust into the role of household adult.

My mom met and married my stepdad when I was nine and *God* had that been a mess. He was a drunk and a bully, the absolute height of *loser* and I couldn't wait to be out from under his roof.

That came sooner, rather than later, when my mother disappeared when I was sixteen.

Ramone had kicked me out and I'd never looked back. I finished school and had gone straight to work as a waitress at the same truck stop, in the same lost town, at the edge of the reservation my daddy had been born on. I'd worked hard to climb out, but there was no climbing out in that area.

…and then the private investigator had shown up and everything had changed.

I looked around me at everything and felt no less confused about it all.

3

Lightning…

I must have had a bounce in my step or a stupid grin on my face when I got off my bike and went into the club because Cutter raised his chin from up there on his throne and asked me, “What’s got you in such a good mood?”

I grinned, took my seat at the table, and said, “I took the fulgurites from that day on the beach over to Amy’s and made a good bit off ‘em. Was heading back to my truck to take it home and grab the bike to come here and who should I run into?” I asked, dropping into my seat and leaning back.

“Well, don’t keep us in suspense,” Pyro grumped, and I flicked my gaze up to Cutter, who didn’t look too happy with his best friend and business partner.

“The girl from the beach?” Radar asked, raising an eyebrow.

“The girl from the beach.” I nodded, confirming, but Pyro’s attitude had taken some of the shine off things.

The aforementioned man scoffed and Cutter talked right over whatever negative obnoxious bullshit was fixing to come out of Pyro’s mouth.

“Who is she?” he asked.

"She said her name was Honor. Saw her heading up the boulevard from the farmers' market and got to talk to her for a second. She played it cool, didn't give me her number, but said it's a small town and if it was meant to be, we'd run into each other again." I grinned and I knew it looked a little feral. I mean, *challenge accepted,* am I right?

Pyro snorted.

"I'm just about sick of your bullshit, pissing on everyone else's parade, man. Cool it." Cutter glared at his best friend and Pyro put his hands up in surrender.

"You see where she went?" Cutter asked me and I nodded.

"I watched her go. She made a turn on Neptune. That's when I lost sight of her… What?" I was looking at Radar, who was grinning like the cat that'd got the fuckin' canary or whatever.

"You said her name was Honor?" he asked.

"Yeah, that's what she said," I told him.

"Did a skip trace for a local PI a while back on the adult daughter of the Pilchucks."

I frowned. "Honor isn't old enough to be the Pilchuck's kid," I said.

"No, you're right. The skip trace was for Rosemary Pilchuck, who disappeared in 2011 in New Mexico out near Shiprock. What I did find was *her* adult daughter, Honor. It *has* to be the same person," he said. "Honor isn't exactly a typical name."

"Well, shit. What were the Pilchucks using a PI for?" I frowned.

Radar lifted a shoulder in a shrug.

"They died not too long ago," Atlas said, slipping into his seat with a drink in his hand. "Ruth went first and Mitch went just a few hours later. They were both close to fuckin' ninety and had their health problems. Shit, not many around these parts even knew they had a kid. She was adopted and I guess a wild child. Ruth and Mitch loved her, constantly talked about her, but I guess she dipped when she was a teen and they never did find her again except for the occasional Christmas card or whatever. Last communication they had from her was a Christmas card and a few photos of her and her baby. No return address – it was before those times, but the PI said it had a New Mexico postmark."

"We do a lot of freelance shit for that dude," Radar cut in. "I found an Honor Deschene in New Mexico. Guess he found her for her inheritance."

I gave a low whistle. "Shit, thanks guys."

"Just do us a solid and don't let on we told you anything," Atlas said. "I'd rather not torpedo our working relationship with this PI He pays pretty decent when he farms some of his work out to us and it's always easy shit for Radar."

"Mm-hm," Radar agreed. "Ain't brought me anything even remotely challenging yet."

"Your secret is safe with me," I told them, filing the information away for later that she was at the Pilchuck's house.

"Go easy, brother," Atlas advised. "The whole thing sounds like a touchy and messy situation."

Radar nodded in agreement.

"Probably ain't worth it," Pyro said and got up to get himself a drink. "Half these females now ain't worth a damn."

"Hey, just because you and your former ol' lady were a toxic soup doesn't mean it's that way for the rest of us," Radar said pointedly, and his words were like jagged broken glass.

Justice, Radar's woman, was a sweet and different sort than Cutter's Hope and her two sisters. She'd hit it off best with Stoker's Serenity and Marlin's Faith. Still, when it came to Justice and Serenity, they were like two peas in a pod and friendship aside – when it came to their men? They were as loyal as could be.

Hell, I felt bad for Pyro, for sure. The fact his woman didn't stay true but holy shit, was he going rotten to the fuckin' core over her.

I didn't say anything. There wasn't really anything left *to* say about that whole situation. Seemed the more he drank, the angrier he got over it and honestly, it'd been a year or three and he was drinking *all the time.* That, and he just kept picking the wrong women.

Even Cutter couldn't talk any damn sense into him anymore and things were going to come to some kind of head eventually. We could all see the train wreck coming, but ain't none of us have a clue how to stop it or what form it was going to take when the derailment or crash finally did go down.

I traded looks with the guys that were around the table so far, and we could all see it written in each other's sour expressions. Something was going to have to happen, and soon.

"So, what're you going to do about her?" Marlin asked with a sigh once Pyro was completely out of earshot, over at the bar helping himself.

I shrugged and shook my head, spinning the Kraken challenge coin we all had on us when we couldn't fly our colors on the scarred wooden table.

"I'm going to play it cool," I said. "We're bound to run into each other sometime. Town ain't that big."

Atlas grinned. "I'd start by seeing about getting some more business with your main hustle on ol' Poseidon Drive. Maybe speed things along," he said with a wink.

I nodded.

I'd taken over Nothing's house-painting gig when he'd gone back to being a medic a few years back. That only went so far, so I'd gotten into lawn care and shit on the side, which had led into power washing and shit, and then had moved right on into just general handyman services.

I wasn't hurting for work by any means, but maybe it was time to take a couple of hours and tape some flyers to doors. It was a thought to maybe *speed things along,* as he put it. Maybe just a little bit.

4

Honor…

I didn't know what to do with myself. I found myself taking super long walks on the beach and just *thinking,* endlessly *thinking…*

Everything had ended up settled when it came to the Pilchuck's estate. All the fees and lawyers had been paid. All the money that was left from that had been transferred into my name, and the house's deed, bills, taxes, and everything else were in my name as well. I found it incredibly lonely, in addition to overwhelming.

I was in the process of selling or junking my old car. The Pilchuck's, much newer, much nicer Hyundai Tucson had been transferred into my name and I even had a Florida license now.

I guess this meant I was officially a Florida resident, and I didn't know how to feel about that.

I felt no connection here. I didn't honestly feel any connection to what was supposed to be *back home*, either. The blue and the water were soothing to the soul at least. I was absolutely in love with the water, over the arid dryness of the high desert; so I guess that was something.

There wasn't a lot when it came to the house. Everything in a month *did* come to more than I had paid in rent and bills back in Shiprock, but at the same time, every job that I applied for paid more than out in New Mexico, too.

I had more than enough in my bank accounts to live comfortably for up to three years if I was *very* careful and didn't eat much. But I kind of wanted to eat and so I looked for work.

Still, I'd never in my life had this much money at my disposal. As much as I wanted to spend a little and do some things to make the house my own, I was afraid to. At least until I found a job.

I'd put in a ton of applications around town for waitressing and hospitality industry jobs and I hoped against hope that someone would be calling me soon.

I had regrets about sending Lightning away like I had without contact information the week or two before. I mean, I hadn't at the time, but now that the overwhelmingness of it all had come down some and the loneliness had risen to near critical mass levels? I could use a friend, and Charlie, with his friendly smile and Golden Retriever boy energy, seemed like he could be a good friend to have. At least, the more I thought about it. Truth be told, I couldn't seem to get him out of my mind.

While I did have regrets, I wasn't too hard on the girl I'd been almost two weeks ago because it *was* indeed a small town and I was sure we would, at some point, cross paths again. As I turned off of the soft sand of the natural earth and onto the concrete of manmade structure, I found myself wishing he would cross my path sooner rather than later.

It was a long walk from the beach to Poseidon Drive. I crossed the boulevard and slipped down Neptune Avenue, turning left on Hibiscus, and marched steadily on to Poseidon. I was unused to the humidity along with the heat and felt like I was almost drowning on dry land with how thick the air was.

I worried about that, being that it was only March.

Just how much worse was it going to get with the real summer heat? I wondered.

I stopped at the end of the walkway up to my grandparents' house. *My house*, I corrected myself for the umpteenth time silently.

A man stood on my doorstep, taping something to my front door.

I swallowed hard and called out, "Can I help you?"

He froze, his tanned shoulders revealed by the cut-away sleeves of the tee he wore over his board shorts, stiffening then loosening back up as his head dropped and he turned slowly around.

"I don't know about you," Lightning called out. "But I sure think Fate just helped me out in a big way."

I couldn't help the grin that spread my lips.

"See," I called back. "I told you it was a small town and we were bound to run into each other sometime!"

"Yes, you did!" he said, putting his hands on his hips. His eyes, like the time I'd seen him on the boulevard, were hidden by his sunglasses again – these wraparound things with bright mirrored yellow-and-orange reflective lenses.

"What are you doing?" I asked him.

He turned to look back at his handiwork and the black-and-white photocopied flyer taped to the – *my* door.

"Uh, advertising for my business," he said, shading his eyes. "You related to the Pilchucks?" he asked.

"That's complicated," I answered, shading my own eyes against the glare from the white porch and the brightly painted aqua color of the house. "I'm their granddaughter… I guess."

"You guess?" he asked.

This was a little stupid. I gathered my skirt a bit and continued my walk up to the porch steps, my sandals slapping against the concrete path.

"It's a long story," I said.

"Want to tell me about it over dinner or a drink?" he asked. "My treat."

"Oh, yeah," I said. "You're probably busy now…"

"Nope," he said, gently folding the rest of his flyers longways and sticking them in one pocket while he slid his tape dispenser in the other. "Beauty of being the boss, I do what I want when I want."

I took the flyer off my door and read it.

Lawn Boy!

Here to take care of all of your lawn and landscaping needs. Licensed, Bonded, and Insured for:

- *Lawncare*
- *Landscaping*
- *House Painting (Interior and Exterior)*
- *Handiwork including most remodels*

Call Charlie Boyington at... and his number.

"Lawn *Boy*?" I asked, trying and failing to stifle my laugh. I looked up at him, raising my own aviators off of my face and up to hold my hair back.

"It was supposed to be a play on my last name," he said, shrugging lamely.

"Uh-huh," I said and he grinned, bouncing on the balls of his feet.

"Well, I'm stuck with it now," he said, laughing too. "Been established around here for a few years with it, and what can I say? It sounded good and funny when I was drunk and came up with it."

I laughed and said, "I can imagine. Um, I actually *could* use some help out here. How much do you charge?"

"Tell you what," he said, looking out over the yard. "You got something cold to drink in there? I'll do up a quote right here right now."

"Deal," I said, giving a nod, and pulling my house keys off my arm where I kept them on one of those coiled rubber arm or wrist bands. It was a habit I'd picked up with the till key at the truck stop diner I'd worked at for so many years.

"Alright, rock on," he said, and I let myself into the house while he stepped off the porch to look at the front lawn, which was getting in need of some TLC.

I keyed my way into the house but before I could go in, he called out, "Hey, is the gate to get around back locked? If not, cool. If so, I need to get a look at the backyard to do something about it."

I took my keys out of the door and tossed them to him without a second thought. Sometimes when you met people you just knew, you know? I had a good feeling about Lightning. Good enough that there was no hesitation. He smiled really big at me and called out, "Thanks!"

"Back in a sec!" I called, flipping the switch for the three ceiling fans out here on the front porch to get the air moving as I slipped into the air-conditioned hush of the house to get something cold to drink for the both of us.

I used the bathroom before I did anything, washing my hands and face, patting it dry and happy to be rid of the excessive sweat, dirt, and oils that'd accumulated on my walk. I stared into the mirror for a handful of seconds and realized just how deeply tanned I was getting. I was looking every bit like my father these days, with the deep bronze hue my skin was taking on.

I went into the kitchen and moved around efficiently. I was growing familiar with the house and its layout. I moved automatically to pull a serving tray from where Ruth Pilchuck kept them in the underneath cabinet along with the cookie sheets. Finding glasses, ice, a pitcher, I loaded the glasses with ice, the pitcher as well, and pulled the two-liter bottle of ginger ale from the fridge to fill the pitcher. I put it away and took a deep breath, my hands on the edge of the stone countertop, and stared down into the gently bubbling golden liquid on its white and light wood tray.

"Hope you like ginger ale," I muttered under my breath. It was really the only thing that I had with any kind of flavor to it other than just water.

I took up the tray and carried it to the front door and stepped out onto the porch.

The best way I had to describe the feeling of the humidity slapping you in the face out here was… well, it was like stepping out into somebody's used bathwater hitting you full in the face. Tepid and not at all *hot*, but clinging to you, damp and, and, *moist*. Uncomfortable and thick.

The movement the white ceiling fans on the porch provided was just enough to take it from downright unpleasant to just a notch below still disgusting but tolerable.

I sat down and relaxed in one of the two white rockers to the longer side of the porch after setting the tray on the table between them. The white gate to the fence that encircled the backyard stood open in front of my much newer car and *still* none of this seemed real.

I'd managed to find a scrapyard to come get my old one and they'd paid me almost three hundred dollars for it. That was honestly probably way more than it was worth for even scrap, but I took it and gladly.

I waited and tried to soak in the breeze from the fans and the quiet of the neighborhood, hoping that some of that quiet would seep through into my very disquieted soul. I opened my eyes at the sound of Lightning re-latching and locking up my grandparents' gate, and watched as he came up the steps.

It was hard to take my eyes off of him to pour the ginger ale into the waiting glasses. I handed him one and he took the other seat on the other side of the table, holding out my keys. I took them and looped them automatically on my wrist, setting down my glass on the tray long enough to shove them up my arm, leaving the warm metal to tap the back of my arm.

"Well?" I asked.

He smiled and took up his glass, taking a drink.

"Everything is in good shape still, just needing a mow. I can do it say… once every other week for forty bucks each time."

Eighty bucks a month? I thought about it…

"I think that's doable," I said, and he grinned and held out his glass. I clicked mine against it and he leaned back, taking a drink with a satisfied "ahhh."

"Haven't had much luck finding any work around here," I remarked.

"Depends. What kind of work are you looking for?" he asked.

"Waitressing is pretty much all I know," I said with a shrug.

"Ah, yeah, give it another couple of weeks and they'll be slammed for Spring Break. You'll be beating off offers with a stick. Most of these young things no-call and no-show or end up quitting from the stress. You'll be a shoo-in."

I mulled that over a bit and nodded.

"I mean, the diner I worked at got pretty busy, but Spring Break wasn't a thing where I'm from."

"Which is?" he asked.

"Shiprock area of New Mexico."

He nodded. "Dry out that way, ain't it?"

I nodded and swallowed the drink of ginger ale I'd taken and said, "Very. This is… a little… yikes. I mean, I don't know if I'll ever get used to it."

He made a face and pushed his sunglasses up on top of his head and holy shit, *those eyes…* They were beautiful and vibrant, shining out of his face. Clear windows to his soul which I was speechless in the beauty they held.

They were probably the most vibrant green I had ever seen set in anyone's face and, once they'd been revealed, I couldn't help but stare.

He smiled and showed very white and even teeth in his tanned face and said, "You said this whole thing was complicated." He waved his hand in an airy sort of gesture to take in the whole house and the yard. I rolled my lips together and nodded.

"I didn't know the Pilchucks. Like at all," I said.

"Really? Didn't meet them even once?"

I nodded.

"Interesting," he remarked and I had fully expected a judgy kind of thing like "that's weird" but it never came. He looked sincere in his troubled expression and it was clearly troubled on my behalf. I found that sweet.

"I can't honestly begin to tell you much about my mother," I said, sighing and leaning back.

"I don't think we every truly know our parents," he mused and I smiled at that. As true as that was, it didn't feel the same. At least not with my situation.

"If you don't want to talk about it, that's cool. I'm content to just sit here and drink… What is this? Ginger ale?" he asked, raising his glass to swirl the liquid and ice inside of it.

I smiled and nodded. "Yeah. The stress of all this got to me this last little while and gave me an upset stomach. My nan and my aunties all used to give it to me to settle it when I was sick."

"Your dad's siblings and mom?" he asked.

"Oh, my dad was an only child," I said laughing. "I mean, my grandma was my grandma on his side. His mom, but all the aunties, those were tribe. I'm half Navajo."

"Oh, wow." His eyebrows went up.

"My mom ran away from here when she was a teen. Met my dad, fell in love. They had me, but when I was three, he died in an accident at work. I never really got to meet him or have any memories of him. My mom was pretty messed up before him…" He frowned at that and I corrected quickly, "Although through no fault of the Pilchucks that I can see!"

"Yeah, see, because that wouldn't track. Mitch and Ruthie were good people."

"You… you knew them?" I asked.

"Small town," he said nodding. "The rest of the club and I would come around and batten down the hatches when a big storm would come through. Come check on 'em after and do any cleanup or repairs they needed. Mitch would always come out and try to help. We'd let him until he got too unsteady. Hell, he was one of the original guys to do that kind of volunteer work and got Cutter into it."

"Cutter?" I asked, shaking my head. He was going a bit fast for me. I didn't know anything about the name and I wasn't entirely sure what he meant by "club."

"Sorry," he said sheepishly and took another drink from his glass. Whistly sufficiently wetted, he went on…

"Cutter's the president of the local motorcycle club, of which I," he put his hand to his chest, "am a member. Well, not just a member. I'm its enforcer."

"Enforcer?" I asked.

"That means I enforce the rules, although I haven't had to do anything for a real long time. All the guys are pretty chill."

"What does your club do?" I asked, unsure about the purpose of the whole thing.

"Psht! A lot of things. We ride together, party together, help each other out when it's needed, help other clubs out when they ask, and help the community around here when we can."

"Like with storm cleanup and buttoning things up?" I asked.

"Exactly," he said brightly, his eyes sparkling.

"Okay, and back to the Pilchucks…" his smile diminished a little bit. I rushed out with, "Sorry, I don't mean… I just… You're the first person I've met since coming out here that knew them as people, you know? Not clients or… or…"

"Hey." He reached out a hand and gripped the arm of my chair, giving me a rock and said, "It's cool. You don't gotta explain anything to me. It's just, they really were nice people and we all miss 'em around here."

"See, yeah… that's what my mom used to say about them too, and I just don't get it! If they're so nice and so wonderful I don't get it. *Why did she leave?*"

Lightning looked thoughtful and shook his head and said, "What was your mom's story? I didn't really know the Pilchucks had any kids. I mean, it never came up."

I sighed, taking in a deep, deep, breath and letting it out in a cleansing rush. I said, "I mean, she wasn't theirs. She was adopted. It was closed and she couldn't get any info on her birth parents, but I mean, she would never talk about it. Like, she wouldn't say anything about it beyond that."

"So, it sounds like it was a 'your mom' thing and not anything the Pilchucks did."

"Exactly," I said and I knew it came out a little unhappy. "I just wish I knew anything about her from when she was younger."

"You make it sound like she's gone too," he said and his easy smile had been lost.

"Uh, you know, I'm sorry. I don't know why I'm telling you all of this. It's not like you're my therapist." I gave an uneasy laugh. "I shouldn't be dumping all of this out like a bucket of Legos."

He laughed.

"A bucket of Legos?" he asked.

I smiled and laughed tentatively.

"Yeah, a bunch of busted pieces that make something but worse than a puzzle because you have absolutely no clue on how they go together. Even if you *did* have a picture, it's not like it can help you make any sense of the mess in front of you."

He nodded slowly. "Wow. A bucket of Legos. I'm going to have to remember that one. That's a good one."

"Thanks," I murmured.

"I can tell this is all a lot and pretty painful, huh?" I nodded and he nodded too. "Like stepping on a Lego."

I laughed and nodded. "Sometimes, yeah."

He smiled and said, "So, how'd you get here?"

I thought about it a second, searching his face, and asked, "You really want to know? Like the whole story?" I asked.

He nodded. "Yeah, I really want to know. Hit me with it. The good, the bad, the ugly. Sounds like you could stand to talk it out and sort it out some. I'm here for it."

"Really?"

"Really."

I nodded and swallowed another mouthful of ginger ale and, with another sigh at the monumental task of breaking my life story down into one serving, I said, "Buckle up, this is going to take a while. But you're right. I could really use it."

He leaned back in his seat and swept a hand out in front of him and said, "You have the floor. Hit me with it."

…and so, I did.

5

Lightning…

Her mom was a shitshow. I maybe knew a thing or two about that, but god*damn*, I think if her mom and my mom were competing in the substance abuse Olympics, her mom was the one to take the fuckin' gold. My mom was bronze level at best compared to her mom but the jury was still out on the *piss-poor-choices* event.

"So let me get this straight," I said. "Your mom was adopted by the Pilchucks, like the *nicest* couple I think I've ever met, and she chose to fuck off across the country. Like, I mean that *literally*, and then she winds up with your dad – who by all accounts was also a great fucking human being. Then he died and she had you, who by all accounts is *also* a *great* fucking human being from what I can see, and she throws that away by getting with *that guy* next. She can't stay sober to save her life and just up and disappears and leaves you to fend for yourself?"

Her head slowly bobbed up and down in a nod at everything I was saying, tripping up only once when I got to the part where I called her a great fucking human being – which I call bullshit on that stutter. From everything I could tell, Honor *was* a righteously excellent human. She didn't go down the same path as her mom, despite the same amount, if not going through *more* tragedy than her mother. Shit. That said a whole fuck of a lot about her and her character, didn't it? I mean, it did to me.

The more she talked, the more I liked her and the more I wanted to learn about her. I wanted help in whatever way I could, untangling the mess that her mom had left in her lap to deal with because she seemingly couldn't be fucked to deal with on her own.

"That's about the size of it," she said after a moment.

"That's completely fucked. Like, I'm mad *for you.*"

She smiled, shook her head, and said, "People are people, all with their own feelings and thoughts. Everyone is different. I don't *blame* my mom anymore. I mean, I could, but she was lost and confused and couldn't cope. With all of this," she gestured out in front of her, "I can empathize. I can sort of relate. I mean, our situations aren't the same by any means, but the feelings are, I guess."

Holy shit... this woman was a fucking *saint.*

I scoffed a bit incredulous, sat back in my seat, and said as much. "Girl, you are a fucking *saint* with that outlook."

She laughed, a high and wild sound that reminded me of these wild horses I once saw up in the Carolinas when the brothers and I took a ride up that way once to go see 'em.

The sound was beautiful, wild, and *free*, and it made her an absolute *stunner.*

"Thanks, but I don't really think so," she said. "I just… I just try to show people the same grace I'd like to have shown to me. That's really all it is."

I laughed a stuttering sound of incredulity.

"You realize that makes you a really good person, right? You do know what a saint *is* and that's, like, pretty much one of the hallmarks of a saint or whatever."

"I'm not much up on my Catholicism but I thought it took more than just being *nice* to people to become a saint. I thought there were, like, miracles and shit—" She adorably covered her mouth at the expletive and immediately tried to apologize. "Sorry, I spent too much time around truckers."

I shook my head laughing. "Only thing swears more 'n a trucker is a fuckin' biker – or a sailor, and a bunch of the guys are both."

"What, a trucker and a biker?" she asked with a grin. I grinned back.

"Sailors," I said. "Actually, both our P and VP are sailors. Different rigs doing different things, but both out on the water when they aren't on two wheels. Both actually live on their boats for the most part."

"Really?" she asked and her eyes wandered in the direction of the water, as though she could see it through the tracts of houses between us and the boulevard. I nodded.

"Yeah, Cutter runs a maritime salvage business and Marlin does deep sea fishing tours."

"Maritime salvage?" she asked, looking back at me.

"Yeah, he raises boats that've sunk and keeps ones trying to sink up off the bottom and brings 'em in to junk 'em or whatever."

"Sounds interesting," she said thoughtfully.

"Oh yeah, never a boring day doing that – that's for sure."

"Sounds like you've done some with him?"

"Yeah, I've been a deckhand off and on when he needs someone reliable."

"Interesting," she said and she sounded like it. Like she was genuinely interested.

"You like learning about stuff, huh?" I asked.

"Does it show?"

I nodded. "You seem like one of those women who soak up knowledge like a sponge," he said.

I nodded. "My grandmother used to say that men hold the power and could and would take everything they could away from me. But the one thing no one could ever touch was my mind and that I needed to use it and never stop using it."

"Sounds like your grandma didn't have a very high opinion of dudes," I said. I think I had my first reservation, a yellow light, so to speak. It wasn't quite a red flag yet. I mean, I knew most dudes out there were trash. It didn't take a rocket scientist to figure that one out. In fact, you had to be blind to not recognize how much dudes generally put women through but still – I tried really hard not to be that guy and I know all the rest of the guys did too. I didn't want to hook up with a misandrist. I was hoping there was a good explanation coming and Honor? Honor didn't disappoint.

"She didn't have a high opinion of *white* dudes, but I honestly don't think she'd ever met one to disavow her of that notion. No, when she said it to me, she was talking about one dude in particular and that was my stepdad." She made a face. "I just learned through life experience that it definitely applied to more than just him and I'm glad that it stuck with me, honestly." She sighed. "Truthfully, it applies to women, too. You know, like the types who act and feel like you're constantly in some type of competition with them for like forever and always?" She rolled her eyes and I nodded.

"I know quite a few Beach Barbie bimbos that fit that kind of model. The catty ones who like to rag on the nerdy girls for being nerdy but in all actuality, I think that boils down to jealousy."

"Jealousy?" she asked.

"Well, yeah. They're dumb, but they're just smart enough to *know* they're dumb and that they'll never be able to keep up with the nerdy girls. That puts sand in their vag in a big way."

Honor laughed.

"I have *never* heard it put that way," she said. "The pretty girls seriously have no reason to be jealous that I can comprehend. I mean, they have the world as their oyster just by virtue of winning the genetic lottery. What on earth do they have to be jealous about?"

"Pretty ain't last forever, and deep down they know it. My question is why you're sitting there lookin' fly and yet talking like you aren't one of the pretty ones yourself?"

I think she blushed, her deep tan definitely hiding some of it and taking the edge off of it. She looked away and murmured softly, "Thanks, but I am definitely *not* one of the pretty girls. I don't even feel like I'm one of the brightest. I feel like I'm just average in just about every way and you know, I'm good with that."

I snorted.

"Humble, I'll give you. You're definitely humble, but you're also smart, *and* a total knockout. So do me a favor and the next time you look in the mirror try and think about it from where I'm sitting or from anyone else's point of view. I'm not sure who got to you and told you that you were just average but I'm here to tell you no – no you are not. Mm-kay?"

She stared at me, her eyes wide and the rest of her face slack with how stunned she was at what I'd just said. I shifted a bit in my seat and almost felt the need to say something stupid like *sorry, I can be brutally honest.*

Like the part about being brutally honest wasn't stupid, but the whole wanting to apologize for telling the truth? Yeah, that was dumb as hell, so I wasn't going to do it.

I split the difference and said, "Sorry if I made you feel uncomfortable. That was definitely *not* my goal there."

She shifted in her seat and set her sweating glass onto the tray on the little table between us.

"No, I appreciate your honesty. I just… I don't think anyone has ever given me a what-for before that left me feeling *good* about myself afterward! Like, how did you even do that?"

I laughed, shrugged and said, "I don't know. Natural talent?"

"Ha! That's a hell of a gift there, Lightning. Don't ever lose it, okay?"

"Promise," I said and she smiled big, capturing her bottom lip between her teeth. There was that shy look again that screamed she was blushing even though it was hard to tell otherwise.

"You got any plans for dinner?" I asked her.

"What? No… why?"

"You hungry?" I asked her.

"Um, I could eat," she said after a moment of thought.

"Bet," I said. "What do you have a taste for? It's on me. A belated welcome to the neighborhood."

She smiled and said, "Okay. They got any good burgers around here?"

"Shit yeah, a woman after my own heart, talkin' like that. You can never beat a good burger."

She smiled really big and got up.

I set my glass on the tray when she went to take it up.

"Let me clean this up, freshen up a little, and we can be on our way," she said.

"Sounds good," I told her, totally stoked she wanted to do dinner and spend more time with me. "I'll wait right here."

"I'll be right back," she said. I got up to hold the screen door and open the front door for her so she could pass through with her tray. I sat back down with a sigh, the excitement buzzing somewhere in the center of my chest like a swarm of bees had just moved in.

This was so totally cool.

6

Honor...

I freshened up and redressed in jeans and a different tank top. Instead of sandals, I went for more sensible walking shoes, this time having no idea what he might have in mind. I donned my southwestern felt hat to give myself a bit of a break from the sun and ran a finger along the beaded band.

I'd had the hat since early high school, one of my aunties having purchased it brand new and beading the band herself. The black was a touch faded now when it came to the felt, but the beading was as rich and vibrant in its traditional Navajo pattern as it had ever been.

I felt a sort of strange connected and yet at once disconnectedness to my heritage. The bane of having a white mother who'd at points kept me from my father's family and tribe for reasons unknown to me.

I sighed and tried to shake off the confusion and feelings of not belonging anywhere. I didn't know where I fit, but that was a trouble for another time. I couldn't keep worrying about it endlessly without taking a break. It just wasn't good for me.

I slipped back out onto the front porch with a soft sigh and locked up behind me. Lightning stood, his expression rendered unreadable by the orange mirrored wraparound sunglasses he'd put back over his eyes.

"You want to take my truck, your car, or walk?" he asked and I appreciated that. It took any unease off me and left me in control – made me feel a mite safer, which was nice.

"Um, how far is it?" I asked. "I mean, where are we even going?"

"The Plank," he said. "Other end of the boulevard." He gestured in a vague direction.

I said, "I'll drive if it's alright with you."

He grinned and his whole face transformed and lit up. That Golden Retriever boy energy that I found totally endearing was back.

"Bet," he said cheerfully and gestured grandly that I should precede him off the porch. I stepped down and he trailed right behind me, stepping up to my side and walking with an excited bounce in his step with me across the grass that was just starting to look overgrown.

He surprised me, jogging around the back of the car ahead of me as I hit the button on the key fob to unlock it. He hauled open my door for me and waiting patiently as my step faltered for a moment in my shock.

I don't think I had ever had anyone my age open a door for me – just older gentlemen and truckers at the truck stop, and certainly never my car door for me.

"Thank you," I said and slid into my seat. He double-checked to make sure that he was good to close it and that my extremities were out of his way before doing so.

He jogged around the hood of the car and got in beside me, reaching for his seatbelt and pulling it across himself.

"Head for the boulevard and where you can take a left, do it."

"Okay," I said, pushing the button to start the car.

It was strange to have a car that not only did I push a button to start it, but it started right away without the squealing belts. When I did turn it off, there was no knocking in the engine.

I didn't honestly ever picture myself in anything but old junkers and in some ways this whole thing was like a fairytale which messed with me in its own way. You know?

I followed Lightning's directions and he chatted amicably about the town, pointing out places that were good to eat at and that would be even better to work for. He also pointed out a few places that he said were good to hang if you were a customer but let me know that the management and some of the owners were creeps. It would be good if I steered clear of them for employment.

"Shit," I said. "I think I applied to that one."

"Yeah, if you get called up for an interview I wouldn't even bother to show up. Marty who runs that place is an absolute creep to the female staff. Like such a creep, I'm pretty sure I'd have to come bust him in the mouth before you even finished out your first shift."

I laughed. "What makes you say that?" I asked. "I mean, like, why would you do that?"

He lowered his sunglasses and winked at me over the top of them and said, "Because we're friends now and I don't let anybody fuck with my friends – especially the way I've heard Marty fucks with some of the girls who've gone to work for him."

My heart did a little bit of a flutter at that sexy-as-hell wink, but it was all butterflies and good vibes when he called me his friend. I felt myself go all gooey in the middle and probably blushed. Something on my face or in my posture certainly gave me away because Lightning's soft smile turned into a full-fledged grin. He put his sunglasses back up and turned to look out the window again, pointing out another place, saying something about definitely applying there.

"Good to know," I murmured. It wasn't but a scant moment or two later and we were just about out of road. He was telling me to turn right and find a place to park.

I slid into a spot at the curb, just after a line of bikes, and put the car in park, pressing the button to shut it off.

"Let me get your door," he said. Before I could do much more than let out a little laugh, he was out of the car and coming around the front to get it for me. I gathered up my purse and let him, because it was kind of nice. But it also didn't feel like something a friend did and I didn't quite know how I felt about that.

I mean, it was definitely nice to be hit on, and Lightning was drop-dead gorgeous. To be hit on by him? Why, yes, please! Still, I didn't know if I was honestly looking to go there right now with just *everything* and how topsy-turvy my life had gone.

It was just a lot. Like one more thing to add to the dogpile of just literally *everything else.*

Of course, I could also be overthinking and overanalyzing everything to death, too. He could just be being *nice* and here I was going buck wild with my imagination.

I paused and looked up over the door at the sign for the place.

The Plank burned into a polished piece of driftwood and underneath it in gilded script? *It's beachy, it's manly, it's made of hard wood.*

I snorted a laugh and asked Lightning, as he dragged open the big wooden door set in the face of the low, gray, cinderblock building, "Just what sort of a place is this?"

He stood aside and I let my eyes run over the length of the building with its giant, and I do mean *giant* reclaimed porthole windows on either side of the wooden door set with big brass rivets and a smaller porthole window in it.

"My favorite place," he answered with a shrug. "Just got done with a bit of a reno and we offer food now."

"Yeah?" I asked, slipping through the door into the dimly lit interior. "Who's 'we?'"

"That'd be *us*," a deep voice answered, and I turned my attention off of Lightning literally just in time to avoid running smack into the wall of a muscular chest framed in black leather and faded dirty patches in front of me.

I looked up into a pair of piercing blue eyes framed in shoulder-length blond beachy waves.

"Hey, Marlin," Lightning greeted the man cheerfully. Marlin smiled down at me, a toothy smile that was pretty jovial and full of even white teeth.

"Sup, Lightning?" Marlin asked. "Who you got here?"

I raised an eyebrow and said, "Honor, pleasure to meet you." I stuck out my hand and didn't let on that Marlin had unsettled me in the slightest.

Marlin's smile grew and he stuck out his big hand and engulfed mine in a firm, warm shake. Firm, yet gentle.

"Pleasure to meet you, Honor," he said. "I was just heading out to grab my girl. She should be pulling up with her sister any second now."

"Nice to meet you too," I said. I was a little surprised to realize I meant it. Marlin relinquished my hand and turned sideways to let me and Lightning past into the small bar.

"See you in a bit, man," Lightning said and Marlin nodded, his eyes lingering on me a moment, the curiosity in them unmistakable.

"You bet," Marlin said, disappearing out into the glaring sunshine outside.

"Come on back this way," Lightning said, jerking his head to the big wooden archway leading into a bigger looking back room than up here.

I trailed after him and blinked in surprise at the old electric chair on a dais, and the man sitting on it like it was some kind of a throne.

His hair was long and a dark brown, shaved up underneath to cut down on the thickness. His beard was trimmed close, and his dark eyes somehow sparked as he looked over the room. A woman brushed past me with a couple of beers in her hands and she went up to the man on his throne, handing him one.

At first I thought she could be the man's sister, having eyes just a shade or two darker than his and her hair a near perfect match in color; but then he pulled her down into his lap. The way his hand caressed her hip wasn't at all brotherly. I moved them to a different kind of "related" category in my mind and sped through the rest of my assessment. She and he held the same air of danger around them. An aura of tightly controlled movement that I recognized for the barely contained violence that it was. That, in and of itself, made me want to hang back and avoid them but for Lightning stepping up and greeting the man with respect.

"Ho, there, Captain! How's it going?" he asked jovially. The man's guarded look flicked from my face to Lightning's, and he broke into a genuine smile. His entire expression changed and went from thunderhead to clear skies and sunshine.

"Lightning, she with you?" he asked.

"Ah, yeah. Honor, I'd like you to meet Cutter and Hope. Cutter's the captain of this here crew and one of the best men you could possibly know here in Fort Royal."

"How do you do?" I asked coolly and Cutter looked me over.

"Nice to meet you, Honor," he said equally as cool as he appraised me.

"Honor was the one I was telling y'all about. Out there on the beach when I took that hit," Lightning declared.

Cutter's eyebrows went up at that and his look crossed somewhere into the boundaries of respect.

"Now what was a girl like you doing out in a storm like that?" he asked.

I shrugged but didn't say anything. Truthfully, I didn't know what I'd been thinking. Maybe I hadn't been thinking at all. It'd been dumb, I'll admit, but I was also struggling at the time and had been lost in my own little world.

"Didn't know it was as dangerous as it was, I guess," I said finally when they continued to wait for my explanation. It was as good as I was going to be able to give.

The group looked form one to the other, mollified, and Lightning took up for me.

"She's not from around here," he said with a shrug. "Not sure there are a lot of electrical storms in New Mexico." He looked at me.

I shook my head. "I mean, it doesn't rain there like it rains here. We get maybe a dozen days of rain spread out through the entire year. We sometimes would get a thunderstorm or two but not like here. It was different. Dry and high in the clouds. I don't know…" I shrugged lamely.

"What part of New Mexico you from?" Cutter asked.

"Shiprock," I answered.

"Shiprock," he repeated to himself, "never heard of it." his girlfriend leaned down and said something quietly in his ear. He looked me up and down and said, "That tracks."

I raised an eyebrow and smiled faintly as she quickly filled in, "I've been. It's beautiful there in its strange sort of way. Navajo reservation is…" she groped for a polite word and I felt my smile water down with a deep and aching sadness for my father's people.

"Depressing as fuck when you're an outsider looking at it, I know. But it isn't about the lack of money or how barren it is. I promise, the people are rich there in a way that most couldn't understand."

"You miss it?" Lightning asked hesitantly.

I turned, smiled, and nodded. "In some ways. I mean, it's the only home I've ever known. In others? I don't really know how to explain it. I guess I've never really felt like I belonged."

"Well, I think *that* is something we can *all* relate to," Cutter said, leaning back, Hope shifting on his lap. "So, what brings you out around here?"

Lightning's hand fell gently to my lower back and I jumped. He gestured out with an apologetic look, his sunglasses up on his head and those green eyes of his kind and jovial once more. He steered me with that gentle touch that raised goosebumps on my skin over to a chair he pulled out at a four-person table. I took the seat offered closer to Cutter and Hope, like they were holding some modern version of a medieval court, as Lightning took a seat across from me and handed me a laminated single sheet of a menu stiffly folded into thirds.

I pressed my lips together and Lightning, taking the seat across from me, caught my eye and asked silently with his eyes if it was okay if he went ahead. I gave him a barely perceptible nod and he answered for me, which was a relief.

"The Pilchucks, actually," he said.

"The Pilchucks?" Cutter echoed in confusion.

"Honor is their granddaughter," he said. "They left their place and everything to her."

"Huh," Cutter said. "I'll be damned. I didn't know they even had any kids, let alone grandkids."

"My mother was adopted," I said quietly.

"Sorry, darlin', I didn't catch that," Cutter said kindly. Whatever stiffness and mistrust he and Hope had held had seemingly melted away in the last few minutes. More like the last few seconds... like me somehow being related to the Pilchucks had made all the difference from being an outsider here to… I don't know, like I was suddenly and, as if by magic, moved from the "other" or "outsider" category to "local" or even, dare I say, "family" which was so very strange to me.

"She said her mom was adopted, but maybe now's not the time, eh, Cap?" Lightning looked at me from over the menu I found I had become interested in hiding behind.

"Sure, sure," Cutter said and saluted with his beer before taking a pull. That was when Marlin and a petite, slight blonde woman slid into the other two vacant seats at our table. Marlin sat next to me and what I presumed to be his woman slid in beside Lightning.

"Hey there," Marlin said with a nod.

"Hey," I murmured back, straightening up in my seat some.

"This here is my woman, Faith. Faith, this is Honor. She's Lightning's guest."

"Hi," Faith said in my direction.

"Nice to meet you, Faith," I said and stuck my hand across the table to shake. Her hand was soft and limp in mine, like she'd never been taught to properly shake a hand.

"So, you're Lightning's mystery woman from the beach?" she asked. I raised an eyebrow and tilted my head down, hiding under the brim of my hat and stared back down at the menu without reading it.

I was starting to feel like a curiosity or a… a specimen to be examined.

"I guess so," I said and felt bad that it came out tart, at least to me. I glanced at Faith but her expression didn't say that she'd taken any offense. She simply leaned her chin on her hand, her elbow on the table, and looked at me, interested.

"Nice!" she said with a slight laugh. I glanced at Lightning who was laid back, leaning in his seat with an arm hooked over the back, grinning at me gently.

I couldn't help but smile back. I honestly couldn't tell you why I was so uncomfortable with all the attention other than it somehow felt like this ragtag bunch of bikers knew way more about me than I did them and yet without *really* knowing anything about me at all.

"So, what's good?" I asked the table and Faith laughed.

"Everything," she said without a hint of sarcasm or dryness.

"Yeah, Zach has been doing us proud," Marlin remarked.

"Us?" I asked, glancing at Lightning whose grin only grew.

"Club owns this place," Cutter interjected.

"We didn't serve food up until a few months ago," Lightning said. "Remember that place I told you to avoid putting in apps at?" I nodded, setting down the menu I had yet to actually read to give him my full attention. "Zach used to be the head cook there, but the owner pissed him off one too many times."

"His loss, our gain," Cutter said, taking a pull off of his beer.

"Yeah," Lightning said. "Zach convinced us to redo the old, out-of-code kitchen here. Get it up and running for him. Said he'd revamp this place and make it into something more than the dive bar at the edge of town nobody wanted to come to because it happened to be our club's."

"Apparently, we're scary for the tourists." Marlin flashed teeth in an almost savage grin and Faith giggled.

"You are scary if you aren't one of the fold," Faith quipped.

I laughed a little nervously and said, "Bikers and truckers are some of the most reliable people I've ever met."

"I'll be damned," Cutter said. "Ain't get many citizens through here with that kind of attitude."

"Honor's not your average citizen," Lightning said with a wink. I smiled and shook my head.

"I don't know about all that," I said. "Has it been worth it? Fixing the kitchen and doing food in addition to the liquor?"

"So far? Fuck yeah," Cutter declared.

"Could use a waitress," Lightning said slyly.

"'I see,' said the blind man as he peed into the wind, 'it's all coming back to me now!'" I grinned.

"You a waitress?" Marlin asked.

"I am," I said nodding.

"Well hell," Cutter said. "You're hired."

I blinked.

"Just like that?" I asked.

"If you want it," he said.

I narrowed my eyes and asked, "What's the pay?"

He grinned. "A fuck of a lot better than you're gonna find anywhere on the boulevard. Fair warning, it can get a little rough around here sometimes, though."

Lightning cut in, "We don't tolerate shit and when someone wants to try and dish it, we aren't afraid to quash it."

"Some dumb fuckers come in here looking to start shit," Marlin declared with a gusty sigh.

"Yeah, but we finish it," Hope said with a wink.

"Always a pleasure watching you work, baby," Cutter said, looking up at her and she smiled.

"Aw, you always say the sweetest things," she said and kissed him. I blushed and looked away when the making out got a little hot and heavy for, ah, public consumption?

"I think Honor can handle it," Lightning declared.

I gave him a crooked smile. "You might have a little too much faith in me there. You barely know me."

"You said you worked a truck stop diner and the night shift to boot. I think if you can handle that, you can handle a biker bar," he said.

"Two very different animals!" I declared laughing. "Truck stops practically in the middle of *nowhere,*" I said, raising one hand like I was hefting something. "Biker bar at the edge of a tourist town," I said, weighing the other like it was heavy.

"Saying you don't want the job?" Cutter asked and he had a teasing light to his warm brown eyes.

I shook my head. "I am not agreeing nor disagreeing to anything until I hear the actual rate of pay," I said.

"Sixteen dollars an hour to start, plus tips – medical, dental, and two weeks of paid vacation a year."

I stared at him for several heartbeats, trying to decide if he was joking. When the "*nah, just fucking with you*" didn't come… I coughed my tongue that I was certain I'd just swallowed back into my mouth so that I could speak with it and said, "When do I start?"

Cutter leaned back, rocking Hope in his lap and said, "When's good for you?"

"Tomorrow," I said without hesitation.

"Tomorrow it is," he said. "Thank you, Lightning."

"Don't mention it, P. I love it when shit works out."

I looked across at him and said, "Why does it sound like you all had this all planned out or something?"

Lightning shook his head but his smile was super huge. "I swear, I didn't, but when you said you were a waitress looking for work, it got my wheels turning. I wasn't going to say anything, but the more I talked with you, the more I realized you'd be a good fit. Just had to bring you around to see if the vibe was right and if you'd gel with the boss." He tossed his head in Cutter's direction who inclined his head.

I leaned back in my seat and said, "This whole thing, this place, this town – all of it is a major trip."

Lightning nodded. "I can dig it," he said.

"Why is it such a trip?" Faith asked.

I debated for a minute and spilled, but just the Cliff's Notes version about how I'd come here.

"So, if the Pilchucks are your grandparents, why'd your mom get skipped?" Marlin asked.

I met Lightning's eyes whose expression had turned to something bordering on concern. I didn't speak right away and, to his credit, he seemed to understand without me having to say anything out loud.

"Let's maybe spare Honor having to spill her *whole* life story in one sitting, yeah?" he asked and Marlin nodded.

"Respect," he said. "Sorry if it sounded like I was prying. Curiosity sometimes gets the better of me."

"You know what they say," I said with a smile to take any of the sting out of what I said next. "Curiosity killed the cat."

"Yeah," Faith said and her smile was made out of solid gold. "But satisfaction brought it back!" she and Hope echoed at the same time.

"Death by stereo," I muttered, and Lightning lit up with a thousand-watt smile.

"She likes *The Lost Boys*!" he crowed. "She's one of us!"

I laughed along with everyone else and it was like all remaining, I don't know, just *heaviness* dissipated and things just got *comfortable* after that.

It was nice, and for the first time, I felt like maybe there was something to this town. That maybe a misfit like me had found a tribe of misfits. That I maybe found a place to fit in after all.

Wouldn't that be nice?

7

Lightning…

We had a good evening. laughing and talking. Honor got to meet most of the boys and their ol' ladies. She missed out on Galahad and Charity who were on duty, but that was okay. We'd catch up with them eventually.

We ended up going for a walk on the beach to sober up some after a couple too many and it was nice being back to just me and her.

I worked up the nerve to ask her, now that she seemed infinitely more relaxed, and hoped it didn't ruin her good mood.

"So, I hate to ask, but you're killing me about the whole mom thing. What's there?" I asked.

She wobbled a bit, her shoulder knocking into mine and I braced in the sand so she could get her balance back. Her ankle boots were in her hand away from me, her socks tucked into them. I just dealt with walking along in the soft sand in my flip-flops.

"She disappeared when I was sixteen," she said finally. "No one knows what happened to her."

"Oh, shit," I said. "That's heavy."

She nodded, the wind whipping her long hair back from her face and she quickly put a hand atop her hat with its beaded band that was just *fire.* She looked so damn good in it.

"My stepfather kicked me out right after and I had a hard time for a while. Being homeless, no mom, finishing school… it was a lot, but I managed to keep the school and shit from finding out. I got my diploma and my own place and yeah… still don't know what happened to her, though. I think my stepdad knows, or that he did something to her, but there's no proving anything. It's a really sore spot."

"I can't even imagine," I told her.

She shrugged her slim shoulders and said, "That's life. Not just on the rez, but in the big city, small town, just anywhere America really." She gave a gusty sigh.

"Your whole world turned upside down and went inside out on you, didn't it?" I asked.

She nodded, smiled wistfully and said, "Yeah. I'm grateful for all this though," she said, waving her free hand after taking it off of her head.

Her timing wasn't the greatest because it was just as the wind blew again, sweeping her hat off her head.

"I got it!" I cried and took off back the way we'd come, losing my flip-flops as I jogged after her hat, which was moving pretty quick. I caught up to it and snatched it up.

She called out, "Yay!" and cheered me. I came back, shrugging my feet back into my thongs, first one, a few awkward steps, then the other, and met up with her as she strolled back my way.

"Thank you," she said as she took the hat back. "My auntie beaded it and I saved for it forever. I would have cried if I'd lost it."

"Hey, it's no problem. I think I secretly like being a white knight on my iron horse." She laughed and I smiled. I asked, "Speaking of, you ever ride?"

"What, on a motorcycle?" she asked.

"Yeah."

"Does a dirt bike count?" she asked and made a face.

"Not hardly," I said laughing.

"Then no."

"You should come take a ride with me sometime."

She cocked her head and searched my face and nodded.

"I think I'd like that," she said.

I felt my smile, which I swear to God had permanently etched itself onto my face in her presence, grow even wider and I said, "It's a date."

She nodded and said, "I guess it is."

"Head back?" I asked and she nodded.

"Yeah, it's getting past breezy and is getting just plain windy to be pleasant anymore."

"It's going to rain," I told her. "You can smell it."

"I swear, I have never seen so much rain since I moved here."

"Aw yeah?"

"I wasn't kidding when I said it only rains like a dozen days out of the year where I'm from. The rest of the time it's arid and as dry as dry could be. I can't get over how lush and green and colorful it is everywhere else in the country. I think that might be a big part of the reason I like walking on the beach so much. All the water, but at the same time, the sand is the closest thing to home too."

"You get real homesick?" I asked.

She thought about it and said, "I don't honestly know how to answer that."

"How do you mean?" I asked.

"I don't miss the desert," she said. "I don't miss the shacks or the struggle or the stray dogs that are, swear to God, *everywhere* – their ribs showing. I don't miss the truckers or the greasy spoon I used to work at. I don't miss my gross old studio apartment that used to be a motel room. I don't miss my old boss who was kind of an asshole. I definitely don't miss my stepdad or being so poor I could only have a meal a day and that was the meal I got at a discount at work."

"Okay," I said carefully. "When you put it like that, you paint a bleak picture."

I nodded.

"I know, and it's not totally fair, either." She sighed.

"What do you miss?" I asked.

"I miss the aunties. I miss the frybread and the beading circles. I miss hunting for turquoise for some of the aunties to make turquoise and silver jewelry for the tourists. I miss the dancing and the singing and feeling like for just a moment I belonged somewhere – even if I didn't ever really feel like I was *home*. You know?"

I shook my head on that last one. "You said you lived there all your life. If it wasn't home, then where is?"

She looked sad for a moment and said, "I don't know. I don't know if home even is a place or what. I've always felt out of place and like I didn't belong, you know? I'm too Indian to be white but at the same time, I'm too white to be Indian." She shrugged. "That's always the way I've felt about it anyway, even when the aunties would argue with me that it wasn't true."

She broke her gaze from mine and looked over her shoulder, down the beach, her hair picked up and wildly lashing in the wind. I knew that as much as I wanted to empathize on this, I don't think I would ever fully understand and I said as much.

"This is why I try not to talk about these kinds of things," she said. "I feel like I always sort of upset someone."

"Oh, hey, I'm not upset," I said, reaching out and lightly grasping her wrist since her hand was full of her boots and her hat. I gave it a reassuring light squeeze and said, "I just wish I could magic make it not hurt or whatever."

She smiled at me and it was a warm thing.

"Thank you," she said. "That has to be one of the kindest things anyone has ever said to me."

I smiled back and jerked my head back in the direction of The Plank and we picked up walking again.

"It's no problem," I said.

I opened her car door for her again and went around, getting in on the passenger side. I took her boots and hat from her and told her to shut the door just as it started to rain, and I mean *rain*. One of those squalls that came down in a hard microburst that should peter out before too long.

I tucked her boots and hat down on the floorboard at my feet as the pounding rain engulfed the car. We laughed and looked at each other. I don't know of a more magical fucking moment. One of those times that time itself stood still and you were just so keenly aware of the woman in front of you. Of how beautiful and strong a creature she was. Like something straight out of myth or fantasy.

Her smile slipped at the same time I felt mine flee in the face of just the awesome power of *her* set against the backdrop of the element raging outside the closed space we found ourselves in.

"Can I kiss you?" I asked, not wanting to push my luck. I mean, for as strong as she was, she was holding up *a lot.* I didn't really want to do something that was the right moment for me but the wrong one for her and fuck everything up.

"Please." Her voice was soft and nearly drowned out by the sound of the pulsing pounding rain. She leaned in at the same time I did, the moment drawn out so long the anticipation making my heart pound in my chest, as we both moved so carefully and slowly as though each of us was afraid of spooking the other.

Her breath was warm and sweet as it blushed across my lips and then hers touched mine. Fuck, *yes*. Her lips were softer than silk and the feeling of them against my own was nothing short of fucking *electric*. My desire for her only intensified. My body jolted by a shot of adrenaline that speared me through my chest and spread throughout it, zinging down my limbs in this sweet, sweet, fucking cacophony of all good things.

I felt my tense muscles loosen and my body go lax in this natural high that I didn't want to trade for the world.

She pulled back slightly, hesitating, and my hand went up, my thumb gently grazing her jaw, chasing back some of her hair. She whimpered so goddamned seductively against my mouth, the hum dangerous, like I was holding a live wire that threatened to arc and destroy me completely, and I didn't care. I welcomed that fiery rush through my body, that searing sensation that'd like to cook me from the inside out.

I wanted it from her so fucking bad, but somewhere in the back of my mind, the warning bells started to rustle, not quite clanging, but gently starting to jangle as she sucked in a sharp shuddering breath.

Her mouth opened to my inquisitive dart of my tongue to the seam of her lips and, with a groan, her tongue slipped out and crashed into mine.

We kissed each other breathless in the next moment, her hands finding the sides of my face and pulling me to her even as my other arm snaked around her back, locking there and half pulling her over the center console.

She made a startled "mm!" sound and her hands drifted from my face to my shoulders, then drifted lower, palms flat against my chest. While there was no push, no resistance, I could tell she might be getting overwhelmed and so I stopped.

It took everything in me to tear my mouth from hers and relinquish my hold, letting my hand slide around her waist, along her ribs as she mutually pushed back from me, both of us gasping and panting with our mutual passion.

"It's alright," I told her before she could get any words out. Her mouth closed from where she'd been about to speak and her eyes flashed some sort of emotion that was a strange mix of sorrow and anxiety.

"Holy shit, your kiss is amazing," I told her, leaning back against my seat, swiping my thumb against my bottom lip as though I could rub the sensation of her mouth on mine deeper into my core memory.

"Right back at you," she said breathlessly, holding on to the wheel of her car with both hands in a white-knuckled grip.

"I'm so sorry," she said and her voice tremored with emotion. "I don't know that I'm ready, that I should have done that, I'm so sorry—"

"Stop," I told her and I reached over and put my hand over her own where it gripped the wheel closest to me. "It's okay. It's alright. Just breathe."

She was dragging in breaths too fast; faster than when we'd initially broken our kiss, and I feared she was on the verge of a good-sized panic attack. I'd seen them before, out of Faith, and out of Serenity once. I knew the trick was to be steady as a rock and to keep everything on an even keel until she could get a better handle on things.

"Shhh, it's alright. Just keep breathing. Look at me."

She looked and I breathed with her, exaggerated like – like I'd seen the guys do with their girls, and even Galahad did it a time or two. In through my nose, hold it a few seconds, and out through my mouth. She caught on and did the slow breathing with me, and both of us calmed and steadied.

"I-I-I don't know if I'm ready for this. So much has changed, so much has happened in such a short amount of time. I feel like I'm falling and there's nothing to grab on to."

I pried her hand off the wheel of the car and gripped her fingers, curling mine under hers, letting her grip my fingertips as I gripped hers.

"Hey, it's okay," I told her again and I meant it. "You're all good, and you're right. You have had a lot of intense things happen in a very short amount of time and here I am just pouring gasoline on the fire. I'm sorry. I can totally curb my enthusiasm."

She pulled her other hand off the wheel and covered her mouth with it as her eyes welled.

"Hey, hey, hey! I'm not saying I'm going anywhere! Oh, honey!" I laughed and pulled her into a hug. "Bad choice of words," I said around my self-deprecating laughter. "I can pump the brakes. Seems to me you just need a friend right now, yeah?"

She nodded against my shoulder with a bit of a strangled sob.

"I'm sorry!" she choked out.

"Nope, no way, don't be. I got you. I mean it. It's okay."

She sniffed, nodded, and sat back, dashing at the tears just cresting her lower lashes before they could fall completely.

"I'll take you back to your truck," she said.

I told her, "Only if you're sure you're ready. You steady?"

She nodded.

"Okay, try to take it easy," I told her.

She pulled her seatbelt on and I did the same. She pressed the brake and pushed the button to start the car. The lights and automatic wipers turned on.

"When you're ready," I told her when she sat for a moment or two longer.

"I'm afraid I've embarrassed myself to the point I won't see you again," she said, and I had to laugh at that.

"Not a chance, sweetheart. You work at my favorite bar now, remember?"

She laughed then and nodded.

"In fact, I'll make you a deal. I'll come pick you up and drive you to your first day. Take you on your first ride. I won't hang out for like your whole shift, but I'll make sure you get home. How's that?"

She nodded and said, "You know, it's weird, but I think I'd really like that."

"Bet," I told her. "I got you."

She smiled and looking a lot stronger than she had the moment before, she checked herself in the rearview mirror and took a deep breath. The rain letting up just a bit, she put the car in gear and got us out onto the street.

"Atta girl," I told her and she laughed.

"Suddenly I feel like one of those stray dogs I told you about."

I shook my head. "Maybe a half-drowned cat by the time you make it from your car to your porch, but I don't picture you as a dog person. Too sleek. A lean, mean, hunting machine. Yeah, you give panther or cat vibes to me."

She laughed at me then and shook her head.

"You're too much," she said.

"Yeah, maybe," I told her, watching the darkened and shuttered town slide past my window behind the rain bands as we crept down the boulevard. "But I made you smile."

She grinned and nodded, concentrating hard on getting us from point A to point B through the downpour.

"That you did," she agreed.

"Then mission accomplished."

8

Honor...

I sighed and stood back, looking at myself in the mirror. I was nervously getting ready for my first day at work and kept checking my watch because Lightning still wasn't here. I was getting dangerously close to *having to go.*

I took stock of my appearance – hair in a braid down my back, white tank top – I'd been told a tee shirt for the bar would be ready for me in my size when I got there, and tight-fitting mid-rise dark jeans that terminated in a boot cut. I had on my good cowboy boots. The ones that had the really good insoles and were as comfortable as a pair of tennis shoes. For personal flare, I had on my Concho belt that'd been made by my dad's father's cousin – a man who'd been older than the grandfather on my dad's side. I'd never gotten to meet my dad's dad, but Tsela, his cousin, had made so many beautiful things that had been gifted to me after he had gone, for my graduation from high school. The aunties having kept them safe for me.

I clasped on my necklace and thought about my bracelet but decided against it. I didn't want the laden tray to make it dig into my wrist.

I picked a slim silver watch that'd belonged to my great-grandmother. As my grandmother had put it, it had been her pride from the Sears and Roebuck. I knew about Sears, but did they even really exist anymore?

I twisted this way and that and sighed out breezily. I went back out into the bedroom, taking up my small, hand-tooled leather purse and sliding its slim strap over my head and across my body. I snatched the key fob to the car and the key to the house on the ring that bound them up off the dresser as I passed and went out the front door.

I was sad and irritated with myself. All of the building storm of negative emotions melted away in an instant in the face of my astonishment as I turned around to bound off the porch. There, at the end of the walkway, just off the curb, sat Lightning, leaning his butt against the seat of a beautiful softly gleaming Harley-Davidson. His arms were crossed and he had a smile on his generous lips that'd kissed me with such a passion the night before.

"You came," I blurted with surprise and his smile grew.

"Sorry I'm late," he said, pushing up off the bike and holding out a hand, waving me toward him. "I got held up at my last job. Let's get you to yours. Don't want you to be late your first day, but if we are, I'll take the fall as it'd really be my fault."

"I don't think we'll be late if this thing can go fast," I said grinning, and he took my hand and laughed.

"I'd like you to ride with me again, so I don't want to scare you the first time out."

"I can't imagine riding an iron horse is too terribly different from riding a real one," I said dryly.

"Oh, I'm sure it's *very* different from an animal of flesh and bone. I just don't know which is scarier, to be honest," he said, getting onto the machine. I got on behind him without hesitation.

"Hold on, lean with me, and watch yourself and the pipes."

I nodded and he fired it up. I jumped at the sudden loud and violent noise. I couldn't help myself. But after that initial startlement, I settled in.

"Feels a lot more stable than a dirt bike!" I called out, grinning, and he handed me his wraparound sunglasses over his shoulder. I took them and slid them over my eyes. He pulled a pair of clear lensed safety glasses off of a spot near the controls, the arm of them hooked over a cable, and slid them onto his face.

"Just hang on to me!" he called back, and I snuggled up to his back, my arms around his trim waist.

He revved the engine once, checked over his shoulder, and pulled us into a smooth arc around and onto the street, going in the opposite direction than he'd been initially pointed.

The wind smoothed over my exposed skin and wrapped around the cobwebs in my soul. As we picked up speed out of the housing tract my mother's adoptive parents had their home in, I felt like the dust was starting to pick up off of me and blow free.

This was *exhilarating*! And we weren't even going all that fast yet.

Sadly, we didn't get to go as fast as I would have liked. The ride to The Plank was all too short. Before I could get into the groove of things, we were pulling up outside of the bar turned restaurant.

"That wasn't nearly long enough," I complained as I dismounted the bike from behind him.

"There's always tonight," he said. "If you're not too tired. I can tell you there's something magical about a night ride. Music up loud, wind carrying all sorts of troubles away. I'd actually love to share that with you."

I smiled and felt myself blush. It was hard to look at him, so I dipped my head and simply nodded as I put the key and fob I'd had looped around my finger into my purse, saying almost shyly, "I'd really like that."

"Good, it's a date, then. If not tonight, then for sure at some point in the future, yeah?"

"Yeah," I agreed.

I finally looked at him and he was grinning. I handed him back his sunglasses and he took them, putting them onto his face and folding up the clear safety glasses in his strong hands.

"Go get 'em, Tiger. I'll see you tonight."

"Thanks," I said with a wry smile and inside I went.

"Hey! You the new waitress?" a male voice called off to my right as I went through the door. I looked past the pool table at the kitchen window and the man resting his forearms at the inside edge of it.

"Yeah, you Zach?" I asked.

"That'd be me. Come on back this way. Rocco's got it for a minute from the bar."

I looked to my left at the man behind the bar who gave me a stiff nod.

"Cool," I said and I went back to the hall by the kitchen. The bathrooms were down that way, past the kitchen entrance, which was narrow as hell but a serviceable space for up to two people. It looked like Zach was a one man show back here. The kitchen, while narrow, opened up into a back area with a cooler. By the back door, out to the side alley of the building, held hooks and a bank of four banged-up old lockers.

"This one's yours. There are a couple of shirts and an apron inside. No need for a lock but if it makes you feel better to get one, go ahead." He rattled off all kinds of information quick and efficiently, and I nodded along. Finally, he said, "Welcome aboard. Hopefully I don't run you off."

I grinned.

"Highly doubt it. You haven't insulted me yet which is more than I can say for my last job."

He huffed a laugh, shook his head, and said, "No promises it won't happen but as long as you can hold your own, we'll do fine."

"Table map?" I asked.

"At the bar. We're going to get rolling for lunch here soon, but it's after hours that gets crazy. We'll see if you make it through the entire shift."

"For this kind of money? I can put up with a lot."

"You don't have to. Always remember that. Just find someone in a Kraken tee or one of their cuts and tell 'em what the problem is. We'll get it handled. I mean that."

"I hear you," I said.

"Okay, off you fuck. Let's see how you do."

I laughed at how he put that. "Off you fuck." That was good.

I got with Rocco who despite his dour expression was pretty nice. He was a big intimidating looking guy and I guess had come with Zach when they'd both quit wherever they'd been.

He gave me the laminated table map and I went over it. People were to just seat themselves and I was just sort of expected to keep up. That was okay by me. The place wasn't that big, just tables at the back room, most of which was taken up by a dance floor, and then the back patio. It wasn't laid out very waitress friendly, but that was alright. It was still early in the week which was good. It gave me a couple of shifts to ease into things. Cutter had said that it was busiest on Friday and Saturday nights and that I would have Sunday and Monday off when the bar was closed except for club.

I was good with that. I found it interesting that this club ran their clubhouse as an open-to-the-public type of deal. I didn't know much if anything about MCs but I did know enough to know that wasn't common at all. It actually made me feel better about them as a whole. I mean, how illicit could they be having everything out in the open like this?

I got into the groove of things pretty quickly and easily. Lunch wasn't overly busy, just a few tourists here and there. It was such a nice day, everyone opted to sit out on the patio which helped.

I wasn't used to serving alcohol, but Rocco was fast and efficient at slinging drinks. I would drop off people's orders to him first and by the time I got done putting in their orders with Zach in the kitchen, Rocco had the drinks up and waiting for me.

It was somewhere between lunch and dinner that Cutter arrived. He nodded at me as I got my tray of drinks for a table of four out on the patio, and he went right on by into the back room to drop into his seat in the electric chair. Rocco gave me a look and pulled up another tray. He made a whiskey sour and put it on there and said, "Captain first, always."

I nodded, took up the tray, and went over to Cutter while Rocco finished up the tray of drinks for my table outside.

He didn't look like he was having a good day. He was slouched in his seat, his elbow on one of the wide flat arms of the chair, rubbing his forehead with his hand as though he had a headache. The other one gripped the end of the chair's other arm as he huffed a sigh of what sounded like pure frustration.

"This might ease your troubles, Boss," I told him, and I set a napkin on the arm of the chair he rested his elbow on and deposited his drink on top of it.

He took up the glass, raised it in salute, and took a sip, closing his eyes, his jaw working as he swallowed under his dark, trim beard.

"Unfortunately, what's in this glass is a big attributing factor as to what my problem is."

"Should I get you something else?" I asked.

He shook his head. "No, I need the drink after today. It's my best friend who needs to lay off the fucking sauce."

"Ah." I leaned the edge of the empty tray into my hip and hung onto it with both hands, giving my shoulders a bit of a stretch.

"How's your first day?" he asked me.

I smiled. "Oh, well, you know. I've been at it a while, but it's really only just getting started." He nodded.

"Food stops at ten, bar's open until midnight during the week, two on Friday and Saturday nights. Doesn't look like it's going to get that busy tonight. Should stay—" He grinned at my glower.

"Don't you dare say it, or I swear to God, I'll quit right here and right now."

"Superstitious one, eh?" he asked.

"You served. You said so yourself! And having served in the military, you already know. Don't pretend you don't. It literally applies anywhere and to any blue-collar job. You never ever say the 'q' word or that it's…" I looked around. "That 's' word that means, uh, deceleration or essentially the same thing as the 'q' word."

He was laughing at me a little and he nodded.

"Point taken. Anything else I should know? Got any other pro tips?"

I lifted a shoulder in a shrug and said, "Not that I know that applies to Florida. Got all sorts of old tales that'd like to raise your hair from back on the rez."

"Oh yeah?"

"Yeah," I said. "Nothing I have time for right now, and definitely not anything I'd speak of after dark, but I have a few."

"Good to know."

"I've gotta go. I have a table waiting. You hungry?"

"I am," he said.

"Can it wait until after I've deposited the drinks the people on the patio are waiting on?"

He gave a nod and said, "It surely can."

"Okay, great."

I went and grabbed the tray of drinks and took care of my table, put in Cutter's order to the kitchen, and with everyone pretty much taken care of for the time being, did a little side work at the bussing station, rolling silverware into napkins while Zach bustled in the kitchen and made small talk with me.

It was nice, but it was also the calm before a bit of a storm. Dinner ended up being a bit mad.

It wasn't anything I couldn't handle. There was one Karen but Cutter put her in her place and all but kicked her ass out. It was actually quite impressive to watch.

It was so busy by the time the kitchen started shutting down that I hadn't even noticed Lightning had snuck in until I skirted by a Kraken bent over the pool table. When he straightened from taking his shot, I realized it was him.

"Oh! Hey!" I cried, laughing over the music blaring.

"Hey, you! How's it going?" he asked.

"Busy but I like it!" I declared and went into the back to hand the bus station's tub to the dishwasher in the back.

"Go on and get out of here," Zach declared. "Kitchen is officially closed. Anyone wants anything else, they can take their asses to the bar and get it themselves."

I nodded. "I'll just tell my tables and sneak back through to grab my stuff," I said.

"Good deal. You did good, Honor. I'll see you tomorrow."

I smiled. "See, now you're absolutely *nothing* like my old boss," I said.

"Good, the dude sounds like a miserable prick," Zach said. I laughed and zipped back out to my tables out on the patio, touching Lightning lightly on the hip as I breezed past and calling out, "Just a few last things!"

"Take your time!" he called over his shoulder.

I didn't. I absolutely rushed through the rest of things but that's not to say I didn't do them right. I absolutely did. I just tried to accomplish them with as much speed and efficiency that I knew I possessed.

When I came back out from the kitchen, purse slung over me cross-ways, Lightning was waiting for me.

"Awesome," he said. "Stoker, meet Honor. Honor, this is one of the other club brother's Stoker. His girl is Serenity."

"Hi, nice to meet you." I stuck out my hand and Stoker shook it with a firm but still gentle grip.

"Nice to meet you, too," he said.

"We're gonna hit it, man. It was good talking with you," Lightning said.

"Sure, I'll see you around," Stoker declared. He gave me a polite nod, some of his long, low ponytail sliding over his shoulder as he turned to bend to take his shot.

He was hot. Whoever Serenity was, she did good for herself. My attention was already back on Lightning and those green eyes of his and the firm grip he had on my hand as we trailed through the crowd lined up at the bar and slipped out The Plank's front doors and into the muggy Florida night.

"Whew!" I said, waving my hand in front of me at the oppressive weight of the air.

"Oh, you think this is bad? Wait until Summer," he said laughing, as he towed me gently down the row of motorcycles toward his.

"I bet! I'm used to high temperatures, but this humidity is killer."

"Well, let's get your knees in the breeze and cool us both off," he said and the look he gave me made me shimmer like heat coming off the land under the punishing sun of high noon.

"Keep looking at me like that," I said blushing. "I'm going to need more than a motorcycle ride to cool off."

He grinned and got onto his bike, pulling it up onto its two wheels from where it rested on its stand. I got on behind him and wrapped my arms around him, keenly aware of how I smelled of restaurant kitchen and all the unpleasantness that came with it.

"I could definitely use a shower and some clean clothes," I complained as he fired up the bike. I jumped again.

He laughed and called out over his shoulder, "That makes two of us!"

"Where are we going, anyway?" I called back as he went to pull out onto the street.

"You'll see!"

I huddled against his back, my arms around his solid waist, and my hands against his stomach. I couldn't help but notice that it was decidedly – ah, well, let's just say, a cobblestone street had nothing on him.

I tried with a heroic amount of effort to keep my mind off what my hands felt as we lurched forward and he made for the freeway.

So much for a shower and a change of clothes before our… *date?*

Oh, shit... is that what we were on? Was this our first date? Did he think that? Did I think that?

I swallowed hard as we hit the freeway on-ramp and he poured on the power and speed. Any sorts of anxiety riddled thoughts were blown off and behind me as we screamed up the concrete lane and into the unknown.

At least for me. I guess it said something about how comfortable a presence Lightning was that I wasn't the least bit concerned with *where* we were going versus was this a date or not. I just didn't know if I was ready for that sort of thing on top of, well, *everything* else!

I mean, I was all for a life-changing event or two to get me out of Shiprock but hoo boy – I felt like everything was hitting me all at once. I had absolutely no control over any of it and I was just… along for the ride.

That didn't sit well with me.

I would much rather be in full control over my destiny; the main character of my own story rather than just a passive… I don't know. Whatever it was that I was feeling now, I felt like a fish out of water, flailing and gasping most of the time.

I'd left Shiprock, gladly might I add, but at the same time, I'd also left so many unanswered questions.

"You alright back there?" he shouted as we came to the end of the exit, only about four exits up.

"Yeah, why?" I called back.

"Just looking mighty thoughtful back there. You sure you're good?"

"I'm good!" I crowed as the light turned green.

"Almost there!" he called back and off we went again, the wind drowning any possibility of conversing out as we made the turn and rode along perfectly manicured and edged streets and business fronts that looked as polished and professional as could be.

This town was much bigger than Ft. Royal, but at the same time, it was also *money,* comparatively. As in they had far more of it than little Ft. Royal.

We slowed and joined the flow of traffic, curving to the south along yet another boulevard. Only this one was two lanes in either direction versus Ft. Royal's which was only one lane each way.

A Ferris wheel lit up the night sky up ahead, and it looked as though we were working our way down a boardwalk of sorts.

Lightning pulled into a small parking lot and had me jump off so he could back the bike into a stall next to another that'd left room. The lot was jam-packed and was a pay lot. Except it appeared that three spots were designated for motorcycles and that motorcycles paid a sort of half rate which was nice, I guess.

He used his phone to scan a QR code on the sign and to enter his plate and the parking stall number. A few button presses later and he looked up at me with that smile that made my stomach flutter and the burden of my past traumas and the fresh new ones of moving across the country by myself seem lighter than air as compared to only a moment before.

When Lightning smiled at me like that, it was easy to forget everything bad.

He held out his hand and I took it, his smile growing. He swung our hands between us playfully and towed me to the lit-up food booth or whatever. It looked like something you'd find at a carnival or even at a state fair, only bigger and more permanent, the upkeep well done to the point it looked brand new.

"What is this place?" I asked, laughing as he towed me into line.

"Figured some dessert was in order," he said. "That, and this is a test."

"A test?" I asked.

"A test," he affirmed.

"What kind of test?" I asked.

"To see if we can remain friends," he said deadpanned. I cocked my head, a smile tracing my lips.

"That sounds ominous," I said.

He grinned, and I felt my own smile grow.

"All you gotta do is order and we'll see."

"No pressure!" I said sarcastically, rolling my eyes.

"What looks good?" he asked.

I turned my attention off him and up to the menu behind the teens and early twenty-somethings in their vertically red-and-white striped shirts. They had on white paper boat hats with a red stripe down the side, and they looked super retro and super cute.

It was an ice cream stand, by all appearances, but also specialized in floats, malts, and shakes. They had a good variety of flavors but oh, this was going to be tough.

"I don't know what I'm in the mood for!" I cried. "Like, chocolaty or fruity."

"I can't make up your mind for you," he said and his grin grew.

"The pressure is real now," I said. I hummed, poring over the menu, knowing I was on a clock. There were only a few people ahead of us in line.

"Vanilla is a highly underrated flavor," I said and Lightning's smile which had settled, came back to full force.

"It is," he agreed.

"I think I'm feeling fruity so… what type of fruit is the question." I rubbed my chin and made a great show of my decision-making process.

"Okay, but what's your usual go-to ice cream flavor?" he asked.

"Chocolate chip cookie dough," I answered immediately.

He nodded. "Chocolate chip mint," he said.

"Also worthy." I nodded.

"You pass," he said and I felt my shoulders drop in mock-relief.

"I'm so glad!" I cried. Rolling my eyes, I stepped up to order a banana shake with an orange sherbet and vanilla ice cream base.

Lightning ordered his chocolate chip mint cone and we were on our way; but where, I didn't know. Just up the boardwalk, I guess.

We walked along laughing and enjoying our treats, which Lightning insisted on paying for since he'd invited *me* out, and we settled into a very comfortable silence as we strolled.

It was nice.

9

Lightning…

She was beautiful, and I couldn't take my eyes off her. I didn't want to stare either, so I tried focusing on my fucking ice cream and just kept stealing looks and glances where I could and stared when I knew she wasn't looking at me.

We wandered up the boardwalk in the direction of the giant beacon that was the Ferris Wheel and threaded our way through the mounting crowd that was leaving for the night.

It was late, but this place stayed hopping until the wee hours, so most of the folks we saw leaving were punk-ass teenagers at this point. Maybe a few college bros that'd tied one on a little too early. They steered clear of me – what with my cut on. While I saw a few of them give Honor some lingering looks to her ass or whatever, when they caught me looking back, they scurried like the little fuckboi cockroaches they were into the dark.

"Thanks," she said softly.

I turned back to look at her and gave her a crooked smile. "For what?" I asked.

"Whatever it was you just did to get that literal *child* to fuck off," she answered and I laughed.

"You caught me," I said and took a lick from the cool, minty ice cream in my cone.

"I'm pretty much used to it," she said, sipping on her drink. "The leering and shit, but when dude's young like that? It's so fucking creepy to the max. If I didn't need a shower before…" she made a face and I laughed.

"I mean, it's not like you're old enough to be his *mom*," I said, trying to make her feel better.

She looked down and away and said, "Maybe not if I'd grown up out here… but back where I'm from? It wasn't anything for a girl to be pregnant at twelve or thirteen sometimes." She sighed. "My mom was barely out of her teens when she had me. Poverty does a number on folks. A lot of women like me got pregnant young. If they weren't ready, they'd go to a clinic, you know? Except it was a rule that they didn't get a second chance. For a long time."

"What do you mean?" I asked.

"They would sterilize us… the government."

"Shit." I reeled back and before I could stop myself it was out. "That didn't happen to you, did it?"

"No!" she cried. "No, but it could have."

"What does that mean?" I asked.

She looked away and sighing said, "I don't talk about it…"

"Oh, shit, hey. I'm sorry. It's honestly none of my business. I don't even know why I'm being so fucking nosey."

"No, it's okay – I mean, shit, I'm kind of inviting the attention to it. I guess I'm comfortable with you but I'm not sure I'm ready to talk about that one yet."

"Bet," I said. "Change of subject. What did you think of the ride?"

The way she lit up told me everything I needed to know, honestly. She was the one. For sure. There wasn't any way I could ignore the feeling I had in my gut. The way her lighting up at the mere mention of the ride made the butterflies take off in my stomach and told me everything.

She'd had a hard life up to this point. Been through way more than anyone like her should go through. I was glad I kept putting these smiles onto her lush lips and that I could keep bringing such a brightness into her dark eyes.

"That good, huh?" I asked laughing.

"Riding with you is almost better than sex," she said with an arched brow. The way she nibbled the red straw of her shake made me go from zero to rock fucking hard in point two seconds.

The words were out of my mouth before I could stop them and I said, "You haven't ridden me yet to know that for sure."

She threw back her head and laughed. When she brought her chin down, her eyes sparkling, to take me in again, she said "I walked into that one, I'll admit it, but all in good time, yeah?"

I grinned and nodded. I couldn't help myself, and I pulled the proverbial carpet out from under her again, saying, "It's been a few seconds, how about now?" But I softened my pushiness with a wink to let her know I was absolutely joking.

She laughed again, and that peal of laughter was everything as I picked up where we'd stalled out in our stroll and got us moving in the direction of the Ferris wheel again.

"You aren't afraid of heights, are you?" I asked and she shook her head.

"I'm not afraid of much of anything," she answered, and I thought to myself, *that's my girl.*

Out loud I said, "Hell, yeah, lady!" and held out my hand for her to give me five. She did and turned her hand. I clapped mine down on hers, and then took it and towed her along a little faster, excited to get into one of the gondolas – just me and just her and that spectacular view out over the Gulf.

We finished our ice cream as we waited in line after I bought our tickets, and I tossed the wrapper from my cone and her cup in one of the trash bins nearby before jogging back to her and casually taking her hand. She swung our linked hands between us and I smiled. We just stood in this comfortable silence, man. Like I don't even know… It was the coolest fucking thing, just standing there with her, looking at her, our hands playfully swinging between us, not saying a fucking word, but feeling like it was the best fucking conversation of my life all the same.

"Music," I said and she glanced over at me.

"Like what music do I like?" she asked.

"Yeah," I said.

"Hmmm," she hummed and I waited her out.

"I like a lot of old stuff," she said.

"Like nineties?" I asked.

"Bite your tongue! More like the sixties," she answered.

"Who do you like from the sixties?" I asked, my eyes narrowing in suspicion.

"Good 'ol Credence Clearwater Revival," she declared.

"No shit?" I asked.

"My grandma and a lot of the aunties listened to them and others like Jimi Hendrix and The Doors. I grew up with it. It has a bunch of nostalgia to it, I guess," she said and she sounded a little defensive.

"It's cool, it's cool, I'm not judging. Quite the opposite actually. I love me some CCR. It's a biker bar staple. A lot of the old shit like that is."

"Yeah?" she asked.

"Yeah. A lot of the old-timers, that was their heyday, man. It's good stuff. Sixties and seventies really gave rise to the biker way of life. A lot of the guys coming back from Vietnam and shit – drafted, or joining up, thinking it was the right thing to do, all on some bullshit the US Government cooked up. They came back home to a bunch of ungrateful jack wagons calling them baby killers and all sorts of shit. They made their own pockets of brotherhood and family when their country hung 'em out to dry and the people brought out the pitchforks and torches on 'em rather than welcome 'em home. A lot of guys got severely disenfranchised and the biker life gave 'em back the structure they craved and the welcoming family they desperately missed and needed, all while still letting 'em give a one-fingered salute to all the haters."

"That's—" she stopped, staring at me silently for a moment before starting up with whatever she was going to say. "You sound like you have a personal stake in what went down back then."

I nodded.

"My dad was a Vietnam vet," I told her. "He and his buddies all signed up for it after the whole Gulf of Tonkin thing came out – which was a lie. The president *knew* it was a lie, but he pushed it as the truth and so my dad and all his buddies joined up. My dad was the only one of them to make it home and then come to find out it was all bullshit. So, yeah, he was double betrayed. He ended up joining up with a club and lived the club life. Had me super fucking late with my mom who was half his age – but God*damn*, did he love her. Died of cancer in *his* seventies about fifteen years back. Married to my mom right up to the bitter end. As soon as I was old enough, I joined the local MC – I mean, I learned how to ride a bike before I learned how to drive a car."

"Wow," she said as we moved up in line.

"Yeah." I nodded.

"Mom still alive?" she asked.

"Eh." I lifted a shoulder in a shrug. "After a fashion, I guess. My mom and dad may have been married to the bitter end, but I tell you it wasn't always good. My mom's a drunk and did a lot of drugs. My dad loved her like nobody's business but they could be hella toxic together. He was definitely the more stable parent, but at the same time, that's not saying much. I love my dad, but my mom?" I shook my head. "Not a whole lot left there *to* love if you know what I mean."

She shook her head. "Not really. I mean, I'd sort of give anything to be able to throttle my mom but… yeah." She huffed out a breath. "She was a shitshow, but she was also the only parent I really had. My stepdad had no interest in being one and barely tolerated my presence, but that just made it easier when he kicked me out. I don't think I felt one way or the other about him by then. I just wanted to know what he did with her because I don't believe she just up and left. I don't *want* to believe she would do that to me. We were *kind of* close, as in that whole my mom tried really hard to be my best friend rather than my mom, and I ended up taking care of her more than she took care of me, but still…"

I put my arm around her and gave her a sort of sideways hug. She laid her head on my shoulder briefly, her arm around my waist, giving me a squeeze back.

"I'm okay," she said with a shaky laugh. "Thank you, though."

"No problem," I said.

"You're very easy to talk to," she said. "I feel bad for trauma dumping."

I laughed and shook my head. "You're not. Or, if you are, I just sort of did too."

She laughed and said, "Boy, don't we make a pair?"

"Sort of like it was meant to be or something, right?" I asked and gave her a wink.

She smiled a little serenely and turned to look anywhere but at me for a moment, but finally, she laid her head back on my shoulder and gave me another squeeze. I put my other arm around her, turning her so she could hug me for real, which she did.

We stood there, sort of holding each other for a long minute before a voice called and we realized we were up.

"All aboard," I said and she laughed a little as we went up the metal steps to our waiting pod thing and got inside.

It rocked gently, swaying as we got situated and the ride operator closed the door. It wasn't like the old-school Ferris wheels with the bar across the lap and the open car. No, nowadays, it was like this oval pod thing with a 360-degree view, the windows tinted and cool air blowing from fans beneath the seats. Yeah, the thing was air-conditioned and cool as a cucumber in here. It was nice. I guess they needed to do something to justify the almost twenty-dollar per-person price tag for something like only five or ten minutes of action.

I wasn't looking at the view, though. As the door shut, the light went out inside of the pod. We began to lift as the wheel went around, and we were treated to the view of the expansive Gulf in front of us. I put my arm around her and she automatically rested her head on my shoulder, but while she was captivated by the view out the bank of curving windows surrounding us, I was captivated by *her*.

As we rose into the air and she sucked in a breath at the reflection of the wheel's lights and the moonlight on the water's surface, I felt the same sense of wonder and delight at those same lights reflected in her eyes.

She turned to look at me excitedly, and her face took on a look of soft wonder when she caught me looking at her the way she was looking out over that view.

I know I promised to go easy and to keep it to just friends, but I couldn't help myself. I think that the magnetism went both ways, though, because as I lowered my lips to hers? Hers rose to meet mine and was joined by her hand, softly cupping the side of my face and drawing me in.

It was fucking wonderful, and the sensation couldn't be beat. As we rose into the air, the temperature between us rose too. It had nothing to do with the muggy Florida night outside the capsule we found ourselves in.

Her lips were soft against my own, trembling gently, and her breath hesitant. I was careful, matching her energy and her movements, mirroring her hesitation until she felt solid in what she wanted.

I groaned against her mouth when her tongue slipped out to touch my bottom lip, and she pressed her mouth to mine more forcefully.

I was so relieved that she couldn't seem to resist me as much as I couldn't resist her. The fact that the feeling was mutual was just something fucking *phenomenal.* I didn't know where this would lead, but I had a solid feeling that it was going somewhere *good;* and I think I needed it almost as much as she did.

She practically crawled into my lap as our kiss deepened, and I reveled in that. I loved it so hard, and I couldn't wait to get her somewhere alone that was out of the public eye to where I could give her the full attention she deserved.

They say time flies when you're having fun, and this was no exception. Before I even had a chance to register that we'd made our number of revolutions around the wheel and that we were coming to a stop, the door to our capsule opened and Honor yipped in surprise, burying her face into the side of my neck.

I belted out a laugh as the ride operator mumbled something about being sorry but the ride was over and *oh*, he had no idea… the ride was honestly just beginning just as soon as I could get her back to my bike.

She clambered off my lap and went out and I followed her, taking her proffered hand as she red-faced led us down the gangplank thing back to the boardwalk.

"Oh my God," she muttered. I laughed and put my arm around her shoulders as she leaned into my side, putting her arms around me.

We walked along and she eyed some of the carnival games, lingering at the skeet ball machines and I slowed.

"Balls in holes?" I asked, raising an eyebrow and making a face.

She laughed and said, "Maybe *your balls* in *my* hole if you're down for that. I mean, I know what I said but…"

"Say no more!" I said in a booming superhero-like voice and towed her quickly in the direction of the bike to her wild peal of laughter.

She ran with me and we got back to the parking lot and she looked both giddy and nervous as I backed the bike out of the parking stall and got turned around to where we could leave. She mounted up behind me and I gave her leg a squeeze as she cuddled up to my back, twining her arms around me and pressing a kiss over my tee shirt to the back of my shoulder.

"Your place or mine?" I called out over the chugging of my bike.

"Mine!" she called back.

"Thank fuck for that. My place is ugly!" I called back at her, and she laughed as I twisted the throttle and moved us out of the lot and onto the street.

The ride back to Ft. Royal and to Poseidon Drive was a swift one, even if it did feel like it was taking for-fucking-ever. All I knew was that I was going to get Honor in the shower and give her every opportunity to stand down if she wanted to. I hoped like hell she didn't, but after both of us put in a hard day's work? Yeah, there wasn't any way I was going to try and make love to her until I was clean. She didn't need to be subjected to my funk.

The headlamp on my bike swept over the sleepy houses of Honor's neighborhood, and I had to admit to feeling some type of way when I pulled up against the curb in front of the Pilchuck's house. They were a nice old couple, and I'd always thought of them as couples' goals. They'd lived long and well together and I just hoped against hope that I could find the same someday.

As I leaned the bike onto its stand and Honor smoothed her hands over my body through my tee as she went to dismount, I felt that flutter in my gut that told me *she was the one.*

I got off the bike and went to her, towing her in slightly by the waist and kissing her soundly, breaking the contact reluctantly with my mouth and taking a half-step back, my hands resting on her jeans-clad hips as I looked her in the eyes and asked the hard question.

"We leaving this here, or am I coming inside?" I asked softly and I couldn't deny the catch in my throat.

Her dark eyes warmed and she smiled and said, "I would really like for you to come inside, but thank you for asking, knowing what I said before. I'm sorry I'm so wishy-washy and inconsistent right now."

"Hey, no, it's completely understandable. I want to do what's comfortable for you. I can be patient. I don't` want to fuck this up, Honor."

Her smile grew and she darted forward, pressing her mouth to mine enthusiastically, her lithe body pressing against mine as I wound my arms around her and hoisted her up tight as tight could be against me.

She hummed in appreciation into my mouth as my tongue stroked hers and I liked that. I liked that a lot. Almost as much as I liked the feel of the globes of her ass under my kneading hands as I slid them into her back pockets, even as her arms twined around my neck like delicate vines.

I held her and she held me. It was one of those perfect moments that you knew you only got a few times in a lifetime. I held onto her and it with everything I was worth for just about as long as possible.

When she finally tugged back from me, it was with this sweetly solemn look, a smile on her lips bordering on shy. She was disappearing into her head a little, her insecurities bubbling back up. I touched the side of her face lightly, resting the pad of my thumb on her chin. I stared into those liquid dark eyes of hers and said, "Let's go in and take things nice and slow."

She tilted her head slightly, turning her cheek into my hand, the question in her eyes and on her lips like I knew it would be.

"What do you have in mind?"

"I'm thinking a nice hot shower for the both of us, then see where it goes."

"I'd like that very much," she murmured and I smiled and gave her a wink, taking her hand and leading her up the walk to her front porch.

She keyed our way into the house, and I threw the lock behind us as she took my hand and led me through the quiet hush to the master bedroom. She didn't bother to hit the light in the bedroom, but definitely hit the light just inside the bathroom door.

I had to laugh a little softly. The bathroom had grab bars and a stand-up shower with a low profile to step into it. The tub was one of those old people getups that had a swinging door and let you sit on a high bench.

"At least I'm set when I get ancient," she said with a soft smile.

"True enough," I replied and towed her into me once more. I did as I promised out on the street. I took things nice and slow, kissing her sweetly, languorously, until the tension left her body and she melted into me.

I broke first this time, gripping the hem of her tee and lifting it carefully over her head. She raised her arms and let me take it and I took the tank she had on underneath by accident. I hadn't meant to go that quickly on things – they just sort of stuck. I didn't apologize or even make it a thing, I just looked over her bronze skin, her black bra against it making her skin practically glow. She reached into the shower and turned it on. Then, with a carefully questioning look, she gripped the hem of *my* tee.

Tit for tat, I liked it… and that's just what we did. Undressed each other one piece at a time, her and then me, her and then me. But being that she was a woman and had a few more pieces of clothing than me, I ended up nude first and that was okay.

She still had on her panties and her bra. I didn't wear underwear often unless I needed to for something. I stood hard and ready while she looked me over and *fuck,* the way she looked at me sent an ache through my cock and balls with the desire to slide inside her.

She looked at me like I was a work of art and that had one hell of an aphrodisiac of an effect on me.

"Shit, the way you look at me is fucking hot," I whispered and she smiled at me, a glint in her eyes that I liked *very* much.

She stepped back into me and I reveled in the feel of her soft skin against mine. I unhooked her bra with one hand behind her back, and she giggled into my mouth. I slipped her panties down her long legs and drew her into the shower with me.

It was a tight fit, but that was alright.

I turned her into the warmth of the spray and what followed was a good half hour to forty-five minutes of us just kissing and taking our time washing each other, hands slicked with soap traveling over every inch of each other's bodies. She gave more generously than she got from me.

She wrapped her fingers firmly around my cock and with her gaze fixed on mine, stroked me root to tip, giving things a little twist around the head and *ah,* that felt good.

I put a hand to the wall over her shoulder and leaned heavily on it, closing my eyes, bowing my head, gasping, and stifling a groan as she worked me.

"Fuck, you keep doing that much longer, you're gonna make me go," I said, my voice shaky with the effort it was taking to contain myself.

"Then let's get out of here and take me to bed," she murmured, her voice husky with her desire as she kissed me, letting my cock go.

"Yes, my lady," I murmured back playfully, nipping her bottom lip.

She chuckled and reached behind her to shut off the water.

I got out first, handing her a towel that she promptly dried her face with and wrapped up her hair. I dried off cursory and quickly, wrapping a towel around my waist, and grabbed a third to dry the rest of her with.

She smiled at me, and her eyes closed as she soaked up the attention. I loved that I could do that for her.

I took her to her bed, covered in a traditional southwest-patterned blanket that was a bit much for the Florida heat, but appeared to be the only blanket aside from the top sheet that she had on her bed. It looked soft, that faux fur microfiber texture that was nice against the skin. I didn't hesitate to lay her down on it, losing my towel and stretching out beside her.

She hooked a leg over my top hip as I cradled her against me and we resumed kissing.

Like, *shit* – we made out like a couple of youngins and it was fucking *hot*. She whimpered into my mouth and writhed against me, and I pulled back.

"Shit, you don't have a condom, do you?" I asked and she shook her head.

"I get the shot, but no, I didn't anticipate having sex. I don't mind if you don't but I also get it if you don't trust—" I silenced her with my mouth on hers again and writhed back against her, my cock slipping between those sweet pussy lips of hers, not penetrating, not yet, but *fuck,* I wanted to.

"Mm, *yes*," she moaned, and I obliged her, sinking into her softly, slowly, curbing my enthusiasm to do things right and savor this first moment with her. You only got the first time one time and I wanted to make it count.

She cried out into my mouth and I swallowed the sound, rolling over her leg that was against the mattress. Getting between her thighs, I drove slow and arduously deep, trying not to let my fucking eyes roll into the back of my head at how fucking heavenly she felt wrapped around me. So hot, so wet, so fucking tight and soft. Everything about her was perfect as though our bodies had been made to fit together.

I could die, right here, right now, just like this, and I would die the happiest man to have ever lived.

10

Honor...

I lay back and put my arms above my head, arching my back and pressing my hands against the headboard, so that every thrust he made hit *deep*. He was so fucking *beautiful* above me, his hair wild and his green eyes brilliant and as hard as pale emeralds as they looked down at me. I closed my eyes briefly to lose myself in the feel of his body against and inside mine, and *oh God,* the sensations!

Every stroke sent ripples of pleasure through my whole being in such a way I had *never* experienced before. I loved it, the chemistry between us off the charts. I wrapped my legs around him and he groaned, collapsing over me to put his lips against mine. I swear, I would *never* get tired of kissing this man! He was delectable in just about every sense of the word, a feast for all of the senses – from the way he looked, to the way he felt, and even to the way he tasted. His feral moaning and breathless panting served to take me higher. I'd never felt so… so *elevated* by a man before.

I felt as though Lightning had placed me high up on a pedestal. While the feeling was wonderful and I had never felt so revered or cherished, it was also intimidating and felt like a lot to live up to.

I banished the niggling insecurities at the back of my mind and tried my hardest to fully engage in the moment, leaving the past behind and leaving the future and the unknown too. But the latter was hard.

I was seriously into Charlie, and I didn't want to be hurt. It was a lot, but it also wasn't for right now. For right now, I reveled in the feeling of his hard body against mine, his cock thrusting carefully and deep, at the way he gave his hips this wiggle and twist as he drove into me. Oh *shit*, how that motion seemed to do some miraculous things to my body.

I was practically drowning in the sheer, unadulterated pleasure of it, and the intensity was something else – the sensations building and rumbling through my body in a building crescendo like thunder. Every motion he made flickered through me like heat lightning through the clouds, bright and vivid, absolutely intense, and so incredibly, maddeningly, and so *briefly short-lived.*

I would have given *anything* to hit that pinnacle and yet, at the same time, I was warring with that because everything he was doing to me, *with me*, felt so damn fucking *good* right now. Like he knew just how to move, just where to kiss, just how to hold me as he slid in and out of my hot, wet, grasping cunt, to keep me right on that plateau heading up into the stratosphere. It was such a wonderful place to be.

It was wholly someplace where I could have just *lived* forever, but for that maddening *itch* to go up and over and hit that gold standard that would leave me arching and screaming his name.

He seemed content to leave me on this precipice, however, and I was content to ride it out right up until I couldn't. It felt like playing chicken with a bout of madness, though. Like flirting with an unknown danger that tempted from the dark – only without it at all being a bad thing.

In fact, being with Lightning like this felt indescribably *safe* and *good,* the likes I had never experienced before. I was so intent, so hyper focused on that, it wasn't even funny. It was to the point that voice in the back of my mind, the one I correlated with the powers that be, the ancestors, or whatever you wanted to call it, kept whispering to me, *think about what it could mean...*

Except for right now, I didn't want to. I didn't want to think at all. I just wanted desperately to *feel* and to be one with this beautiful man above me, who went to great lengths to make me feel *so good.*

His arms curved around my back and his lips touched over my heart as he awkwardly, yet successfully, moved inside me. I gasped and drowned in all of the sensations he wrought at once with me. I felt so incredible. It was as though micro explosions of light went off inside me, echoed by the thunder of my heart which I felt in my back and pounding against the inside of my ribs, swelling with something undefinable.

"That's it, baby," Lightning growled against my skin, before he released me and got up onto his knees, looking down at me. I looked up at him, fisting the bed covers at each of my hips as he bent me back on myself, raising my legs to put them against his chest, kissing the side of my calf, his shoulders and chest swelling with a deep, deep, breath as he drove into me that much harder, hitting points that I didn't think possible. The pleasure crashed into me harder than even before.

"Play with yourself, yeah," he grunted when my fingertips found my clit.

Sparks lit, flitting along nerves and fibers as I pressed my fingertips to myself, pressing just like I liked, making frenetic circles, the desperation to come overriding. I tipped full on into that delicious place of madness and I didn't care if I honestly ever came back from it as long as he was along for the ride.

Exhilaration crashed into me like a bolt from the blue. I felt myself drawn, arching as if pulled by strings, my body tight and tingling, bursts of color going off in my vision, everything coiled and bright for that one shining moment that seemed to go on forever before I crashed back to earth and writhed with the furor that he caused within me.

I was only vaguely aware of his panting groan of satisfaction as he collapsed over me, his arms holding me tight, his lips playing along the side of my neck and across my collarbone as he tried to regain his own composure.

"Wow…" was all I could manage when I regained my own.

"You can say that again," he said, pushing up off the bed so he wouldn't crush me.

"Wow," I muttered and he laughed a little, running his hands over my skin from my breasts to my hips. He stared down at me with such admiration.

"Do you have to go?" I asked timidly. "Or can you stay?"

"Hmm, baby, there's no place I'd rather be than right here with you," he said, and I couldn't help my smile.

He winced with his oversensitivity as he pulled out of me and I sucked in a sharp breath.

He winked at me and said, "Stay right here." He gave me a pat on the hip as he crawled backward off the bed and went into the bathroom again. The sound of running water hit my ears and honestly, I couldn't go anywhere even if I wanted to. I simply lay back and finished catching my breath, riding the tide of afterglow.

No, I wasn't going anywhere. I was going to lay right here and enjoy this.

LIGHTNING and I made plans to see each other the next night, but life got in the way. He had to work faster and harder the next day for the late start he got because of our, ah, escapades the night before. I felt bad about that. So, when the time came, he ran me back home, but he just looked *exhausted.* So, I kissed him a fair few times and sent him home to rest.

He texted me that he got home safe and said goodnight. I didn't hear from him again until morning. When I got up, there was a *good morning, beautiful* text waiting for me and that he'd see me when I got into work. He was sorry he couldn't give me a ride in but there was club business going on that was keeping him from it.

I showered, dressed, and decided against walking, unsure if I could get a ride home and knowing that I would *definitely* be too tired after having been on my feet all day to make that trek back.

When I went into the bar from the kitchen after having parked out back, Zach called out, "Stay back here a minute and let the guys finish up church."

"Church?" I asked, quizzically.

"It's what they call their club meeting. They'll send a signal when they're through and you can go out to prep your tables. In the meantime, you can do some side work if you got any."

"Oh, okay, cool," I said, looking out over the pool table at the bar where Rocco gave me a nod. I gave him a smile and a wave and did what I could to help Zach out until he said I was good to go out and the bar was officially open.

All of my curiosity evaporated when I saw Lightning come around the corner and head back for the kitchen from the archway leading back to Cutter's throne room.

"Hey, beautiful!" he crowed and I felt my face light up.

"Same to you," I said.

Marlin rounded the archway right behind him and said, "Aww, she thinks you're beautiful."

"Man, shut up." Lightning laughed and gave Marlin a playful shove.

"She here?" A man with dark hair leaned around the corner.

"Yeah, man, c'mon! Honor, I'd like you to meet Galahad. He's my best friend out of any of this pack of assholes," Lightning declared.

"You only say that 'cause I gave you my business." Galahad laughed.

I grinned and said, "It's nice to meet you." I stuck out my hand as I went forward to meet him. He shook my hand and looked me over.

"Nice to meet you too," he declared.

"You gotta go," Lightning declared. "You got a shift with Charity, don't you?"

"Ah, yeah," he said.

"What charity?" I asked and the guys laughed.

"Charity is my wife. We're paramedics and right now, we happen to be partnered up. We have a shift running emergencies here in the county – and yeah, I gotta go. Meet up with you later?" he asked Lightning.

"Yeah, yeah!" Lightning declared.

"It was nice to meet you, Honor."

"Yeah, you, too!" I called as he jogged to the door and out into the bright sunshine.

"He seems nice," I said and Lightning nodded.

"He's a genuinely good dude," he said. "More now that he's out of his depression, but even when he was in it, he was a good person. Just melancholy."

"Sounds like there's a whole lot of story there," I said as he snaked an arm around my waist.

"Oh, there is," he said and he leaned in and kissed me.

Sparks of joy fizzled in me as I returned the kiss. Cutter called out, "Hey, don't you be mackin' on my waitress when she's on the clock, now."

I jerked back and felt myself flush but when I turned my eyes to Cutter, his brown eyes sparkled with merriment and he gave me a wink, his grin telling me all I needed to know. I could relax and he was just yanking my chain.

I was good with that.

"Need to talk with you about next week," he said.

"What about it?" I asked.

"It's bike week," Lightning said. "And *we* need to talk to you about it. Him about here and me about there."

He gave me a wink and I frowned and said, "Okay, here first…"

"Bar's going to be closed. You have the week off," Cutter declared. "I'd pay you for it but you've only been here a week and while I'm generous, it ain't to a fault. You're here next year, though? You'll have it off paid," he said.

"Oh, I couldn't expect you to pay me a week's vacation after only a week of being here! I'll be fine. I wasn't exactly expecting to be employed this soon or what have you, and I had enough set aside for a while."

"Which leads me to *there,*" Lightning said as Cutter gave a nod and walked away to leave us to it.

"Okaaaay?" I drew the word out and he grinned.

"Come with me, as my guest. Room and shit is all paid for and I promise, it'll be the ride of your life."

He twisted us back and forth like we were dancing almost, his body pressed to mine. I couldn't help but smile.

"Where is 'here' supposed to be?" I asked.

"Across the state and up the coast. Only about four hours or so. We like to hit Ormond Beach and the Iron Steed," he said.

"What, like a ride? Like a *real* ride?" I perked up.

"A *real* ride, with the whole club," he said. "Hotel on the beach overlooking the water and meeting up with other bikers and other clubs. Most importantly – you don't have to serve anybody but yourself. We go to lighthouses and there's live music. we go to the flea market out by the track in Daytona and get up to all sorts of shit all week long."

"Flea market?" I perked up some at that.

"Uh-huh," he said.

"I mean, you had me at lighthouses. I've never seen one, but the flea market definitely seals the deal for me."

"Awesome!"

He darted forward and smacked a kiss to my lips as I laughed and then asked, "You walk or drive?"

"Oh, I drove today," I said.

"Cool. How about I see you when you get home since I feel real bad about last night? I can go through your underwear drawer, sniff your panties, and help you pack."

I laughed at his outrageous audacity and he let me go, bouncing his eyebrows and backing for the door, making finger guns at me.

"It's a date!" I called out to him, and he winked before jerking his head forward to make his sunglasses come off the top of his head to cover his eyes.

I shook my head and caught Rocco polishing the bar and shaking his head, his big shoulders shaking with silent laughter at our exchange.

"He's something else," I declared and Rocco nodded – a man of few words.

It was a bit of a slog knowing that Lightning would be waiting at home for me, but I made it through and relatively unscathed at that.

But boy was I *tired.* Like I was next-level exhausted. The bar was absolutely *hopping* and it *stayed* busy from an hour after opening to the kitchen closing. Like, holy fuck, standing-room-only level of busy.

Zach told me good work as I went out the back door. All I could manage was a nod and a wave as I slipped out into the lot and went for my car.

Every step was a tough one. My feet were not just tired, they *hurt*, but Lightning waited and I really wanted to see him.

When I pulled into my driveway, I found his truck and trailer at the curb in front of my place and him sitting on the front porch in the dark, raising a beer bottle up to take a drink, his face lit by his phone as he scrolled.

I shut my car door and he watched me carefully as I limped across my freshly cut grass past my maintained garden beds and up the low front porch steps.

"You look *rough*, baby. You okay?"

"Oh yeah," I declared, dropping into the porch chair next to his as he reached down into the cooler and handed me a wine cooler.

"What the fuck is this shit?" I asked, laughing.

"Bitch beer," he said. "I guessed. Looks like I guessed wrong." He handed me a real beer and I handed him back the bitch one, and he lowered it back into the cooler.

"Well ain't this like having sex in a rowboat?" I asked as he used the ring on his hand to pop the top for me?

"What's that?" he asked.

I washed some into my mouth and swallowed it down and said, "Fucking close to water."

Lightning had some of his own beer shoot out his nose and I laughed hysterically at him even as I reached out to rub his back.

"I ain't ever heard that one," he said laughing as soon as he finished coughing.

"I don't even remember where I heard it," I said.

"So, what kind of beer do you like?" he asked.

"Any," I answered honestly. "This is fine, really. Hell, the wine cooler probably would have been fine, too. I just wasn't in the mood for sweet right now. I ain't usually picky."

He nodded and took another drink, giving me this look before he swallowed to make sure I wasn't going to say something to make him laugh again. I chuckled and swallowed another mouthful of the Mexican import beer he'd handed me and said, "Sorry not sorry," before I toed off my sneakers.

"Hey, we're outside," he said with a wink and I nodded.

"I can't argue with you there," I said.

"Want some light out here?" he asked.

"Yeah," I said.

"Keys." He held out his hand and I gave them to him.

"Usually, I remember to leave it on," I said.

He keyed open the front door and said, "Ahhh, shit. You did. Bulb's burned out."

"I think there's more in the pantry, but don't worry about it now," I said.

"Nah, it ain't no thing. Best do it now." He popped out the door and unscrewed the porch lightbulb and went inside. A moment or two later, he came back out with a new one and screwed it in.

"Whoa!" I squinted.

"Shit, yeah, that's a bit much but if you're good, it'll have to do for now."

"It's fine, what is that? A hundred watts?"

"Eh, like sixty-five, I think. Really just needs a forty or something."

"Yeah… I thought it might be nice to put the string lights out here, around the whole edge, but I don't know. You don't think it'd look trashy, do you?"

"Fuck no," he said, dropping back down into the seat he'd been occupying when I came home.

"Should get that kind that you can change the color with a remote. Come Christmas, all you gotta do is change the color."

"Ooo, maybe two strands then. That way every other light come

Christmas time or any other holiday and all I have to do is screw in a colored lightbulb for the porch light to really make it festive."

He chuckled and said, "Now you're talkin'." We sat in silence for a little while and he asked me finally, "What other changes are you ready to make to this place? You know, make it your own."

"I don't know," I said. "Every time I think about it, it just feels really disrespectful, you know?"

He shook his head. "No, why would it feel disrespectful?" he asked. "They wanted you to have it. They left it to you."

"I don't know," I said. "Feels like I'd be erasing their memory or something."

"Nah." He shook his head.

"I don't know!" I cried. "I mean, I didn't know them so maybe you have a better idea than I do."

"Oh, hey, that's fair. I keep forgetting that you didn't really know the Pilchucks while they were alive. All you've got is a house full of ghosts and memories but no real context of how they were."

"Exactly," I said with a frustrated sigh.

"Hey." He reached out, took my hand, and gave it a little jiggle between our seats. "I'm sorry."

"No, it's okay," I said. "I'm not mad. I'm not really even annoyed. I'm just really tired. Today ended up kicking my ass."

"Yeah," he said and I looked over and he was eyeing me. "I can see that now."

"Sorry," I muttered a little defeated. "I didn't mean to bite your head off if I did."

"No, you didn't," he said. "Tell you what, how about we sit here and finish our beers, maybe have a second one if you're so inclined? I'll head in just a little before you and draw you a nice hot Epsom salt bath and we'll just go to bed. No need for sex or anything else, just some good old-fashioned cuddles and sleep."

"But I like having sex with you," I said back with a grin and a wink.

"Hey! I like having sex with you, too!" he cried. "In fact…" he dug around in his bag sitting beside his cooler that was further back and out of my sight, but that I'd spotted when he'd gotten up and the porch light had come on.

He tossed a cardboard box into his lap and I laughed at the condoms in it.

"The super big jumbo pack to save the day, huh?" I asked.

"Hey, birth control isn't one hundred percent, but I'll tell you something – we would make some pretty fuckin' babies. If it does happen to go down that way? That I put a bun in your oven? Well, here's to breaking generational curses. Even if we don't wind up sticking it out together, I vow to you to be the best damn co-parent you ever asked for if you decide you want to keep it. I get that it's your body and your choice and I'm cool with whatever you decide."

I felt the shock hit my face and freeze it unnaturally as he clicked the neck of his bottle against mine. I watched him in stunned silence as he took a drink of his beer. I shakily brought the neck of my bottle to my lips and took a drink, mechanically, but I didn't really taste it. His words felt like a cold bucket of water thrown on me, but at the same time, I felt wrapped in a warm, soft cloud. It was both delightful and confusing but—

"I think I just fell hopelessly in love with you," I said, deliberately looking away from him as tears stung my eyes.

"Oh, hey now," he said with a nervous laugh. "Are these good tears or bad tears?"

I sniffed and wiped under my suddenly running nose with the back of my hand.

"Ah, good I think. That was a very real, honest, and beautiful thing for you to say."

"Oh, babe. It's cool. I meant every word of it. I'm all about breaking generational curses. I swore up and down and side to side, if I ever did the kid thing, that I wouldn't raise that kid anything like my parents raised me. Just by virtue of that alone, I think that covers your mom, too."

"Yeah, it does," I said shakily. "But I don't think it was *all* her fault, you know?"

"Oh, hey, no… I didn't say that. C'mere." He got up, came over, and wrapped his arms around me. I wrapped mine around him and sort of cried into his loose-fitting tee shirt against his stomach.

"Weirdly, that hit different, you know?" I asked and I felt him nod, his fingers working at the hair tie holding my hair up into its ponytail, slipping it down the long strands in such a way that it hardly pulled. I sat cuddled into him while he lovingly combed fingers through my hair and gave me the space to feel all of these really big and overwhelming things. Let me tell you, it was a *moment.*

I was certain I wasn't pregnant, like *really* certain. My birth control had never failed me before but suddenly, the nervousness or fears of whether or not I could be were gone.

I wholeheartedly believed him when he said he would step up.

I'd never had that with any romantic partner before, and it was really something.

"Come on, baby. Let me get that bath going for us, huh?"

I nodded and reluctantly let him go. He was warm, and I liked that.

He took me by the hand and led me into the house, and back into the bathroom off the main bedroom beyond. He undressed me sweetly and made absolutely zero comment about my smelly socks, which I loved him for, too. He rooted around in the bathroom cabinets and made a triumphant sound when he came up with a blue-and-white bag accented with purple.

"I knew she'd have it."

"Who, Ruthie?" I asked.

"Yeah, how did you know that's what Mitch called her?"

I gave a shrug. "She kept all his letters from when he was off in the Korean War."

"Ah." He nodded. "Those two were something else," he said.

"Tell me about them?" I asked, and there must have been something on my face as he opened up the bathtub's door and ushered me in. I went in and sat on the cold material of the seat as he dumped a healthy amount of the white crystalline powder from the bag into the bottom of the tub and swiftly undressed.

"They were nuts about each other," he said. "Real couples' goals, or whatever. Just as in love with each other the day they died as they were every day that they were alive. They were the kind of couple that talked about each other with just the same amount of enthusiasm as the week they'd met. It didn't matter how many years had passed."

"Wow," I uttered faintly, trying to wrap my brain around the whole concept. I just didn't understand. It sounded like they were a loving family and I couldn't imagine what'd made my mother run from them.

Lightning got into the bath with me and took the other seat, getting the water going after latching the side of the tub.

"This whole setup is so weird," I said. "Like we're going to have to sit here and let it drain before we get out."

"Yeah," he agreed. "I guess it has its drawbacks, but just think about how good it'll feel to soak."

"Think Mitch and Ruthie ever got freaky in here?" I asked, making a freaked-out face.

Lightning laughed and nodded. "Absolutely I do," he said.

I gave a bit of a shudder and said, "Good thing I cleaned this place top to bottom."

He laughed again and bent at the waist, touching the back of my calf in a bid for me to raise my leg and hand my foot over. The water was filling fast, already up to my ankles, and the heat had worked a little magic already, but I still wasn't about to argue. I raised my heel to perch it atop his thigh.

He dug thumbs gently into the tender ball of my foot and I groaned in appreciation.

"Shit, that sounded like we skipped the damn foreplay and went directly into the hottest sex of your life!" he declared.

"You aren't wrong," I said and practically melted back into the tub's curved backing.

"Mmm," he said and the tone of it made me smile. Even with my eyes closed, I could tell he was looking at me with appreciation. I could almost feel the weight of his gaze along my skin like the caress of sable soft fur.

We were silent for a long time, the soothing rush of the water the only sound in the bathroom as he worked my muscles with even pressure and played the pad of his fingers atop my instep like my foot was a flute.

"Back to an earlier subject," he said.

"Mm-hm?" I murmured.

"Since I asked, you put any thought into small or subtle changes you'd like to make to this place to make it yours?"

I breathed in slowly, opened my eyes and said, "I suppose the easiest place to start would be paint."

He nodded slowly and said, "What else do you wish you could change?"

I thought about it…

"Furniture is expensive, otherwise I would consider redoing the living room."

"Furniture *is* expensive," he said. "But fabric isn't as bad and Stoker's girl flips furniture and gives it new life with new finishes, paint, and even upholstery. Maybe she could help in this situation."

"You know, I never even thought of that. I wonder how much she would charge for something like that?"

"Probably as much as I'm going to charge you for the yards," he said with a shrug. I could feel the shrug by the way his hands moved along my foot. I opened my eyes.

"Forty dollars every other week?" I asked and he grinned.

"Nah," he said. "I'm just going to take care of it for you, now."

"You don't have to do that!" I said quickly.

"You're right, I don't, but your money's no good here."

"Ah!" the sound came out indignant and he smiled at me. I heaved a big sigh and shook my head.

"I like the outside of the house, but I do wish it had more flowers," I confessed.

"Easy enough," he told me. "You come up with the money to buy 'em and I'll get you some Hibiscus plants. They're pretty affordable around this time of year at the local Wally World and I can keep 'em alive easy. You don't have to go to a nursery and break the bank."

"Really?" I cocked my head. "How affordable is your version of affordable?"

He raised his shoulder in a half-shrug and said, "Like thirteen bucks or less. When it gets toward the end of the season, they have 'em when they go on clearance."

"Really?"

"Yeah, they're like max thirty when they're fresh and flowering."

"That's not bad at all," I said thoughtfully.

"No, not really. Nurseries charge way too fucking much, that's for sure."

I rolled my eyes. "Tell me about it. I happened into one, thinking about getting a cactus or two and yikes. They wanted way too much for me to justify that cost."

He smiled and said, "There are always ways around that kind of shit if you've got the patience and time to nurse 'em into growing right. That's another thing I've got in common with Serenity – that's Stoker's girl. She raises orchids and she's a hell of a green thumb. I've learned a lot from her."

"Nice." I smiled faintly and took it for the green flag that it was that he could simply be friends with women and not anything more. I'd lie if I didn't say there was a fizzle of insecurity there on my part, though. Maybe even a hint of jealousy. I squashed it, though. Jealousy, to me, wasn't anything other than about *control,* and I wasn't in any way that kind of person. I had no interest in controlling anyone else's actions – simply my own, which is as it should be.

"Changing the subject," I said. "Tell me more about this bike week."

"What do you want to know?" he asked.

"How about when do we leave?"

He smiled at that, and I smiled too, as he released my foot and asked for the other one.

11

Lightning…

It was Friday and we were heading out across the great state of Florida and north to around forty-five minutes south of St. Augustine. We had all sorts of plans and with Pyro being so far out of pocket and unreliable lately, Atlas had been saddled with the busy work of road captain and planning this year's adventure. He'd taken it on gladly. He hadn't really enjoyed giving up the position of road captain back when he had, but had done so of his own volition when his day job had taken up a lot of his planning and brain power.

Now, he'd taken it back when asked, but I could tell it was a bitter-sweet thing for him as this time around, it wasn't because Pyro had abdicated the position like Atlas had. It was because Pyro had been stripped of it in hopes it would wake his ass up. You know, a wake-up call that he needed desperately to get his fucking shit together.

I sighed, looking across the marina's lot that we were using as our jumping off point in his direction. He was already sweating and had his sunglasses on. He looked *rough* under the black bandanna that was keeping his platinum blond puffball of a hairstyle under control.

Like, he had probably done a hell of a lot more than just tie one on last night. I wasn't sure what drugs he'd dipped into, but it was plain to any of us, just looking at him, it was a hell of a lot harder core than just some Mary Jane.

"You okay, baby?" Honor asked, hefting her backpack up onto her slim shoulders.

"Yeah, just worried about Pyro," I told her and she followed my gaze, shielded by my own wraparounds in his direction. The look on her face, even from behind her mirrored aviators, pretty much told me she knew something.

"Talk to me," I said, but I dropped my voice so just she and I could hear.

She worried her top and bottom lips between her teeth, switching between top then bottom, then top again, and finally heaved a big sigh.

"I saw him snorting something last night at the bar," she said under her breath. "Off his hand, as he was coming out of the bathroom. He told me I didn't see shit and sort of half-lunged at me like he'd beat my ass if I told anybody."

"He did what?" I demanded and she sighed, her shoulders dropping sort of defeat.

She said, "I didn't tell you last night because I'd honestly forgotten about it until just now but—"

"No, hey, it's fine."

"I'm so used to that kind of showboating and shit from the truck stop that I *really* didn't think about it," she said.

"I meant it, Honor. It's fine. I'm glad you told me, though." I reached out and took her hand and gave it a little wiggle between us.

"Told you what?" Radar asked, and I jumped slightly. I turned, saying, "Don't sneak up on a motherfucker like that!"

"Sorry, bro," he said with a laugh, and then followed Honor's gaze up over in the direction of Pyro, his shoulders dropping. I looked too, and Cutter had his hand on the back of Pyro's neck, hooking him in close and talking to him real low like. The way he did whenever he was checking in with a brother having a hard time. I mean, how many times had I seen him do the same fucking thing with Galahad.

"There are no secrets among brothers, especially when it's *about* what another brother is doing," I told Honor, giving her hand a squeeze. She nodded to me and I looked back to Radar and told him what she told me.

Radar swore.

"Right, keep it under your lid for now. I'll handle it," Radar declared.

I nodded. He was our SAA and part of the chain of command. "You taking it to Marlin or Cutter himself?" I asked.

"Both at the same time, if I can help it," Radar declared.

I nodded.

"Won't be until after we get there, though, if we're going to stay on schedule. You good with that?" he asked.

"Yeah," I said. "I don't want it weighing on the captain's mind for the ride." I looked back over to Cutter who had let Pyro go. Hope was by his side and they were both looking in Pyro's direction worried, and fuck if I weren't worried too, and pissed, but mostly worried.

Dude was absolutely out of his fucking gourd and none of us could understand it. It's not like his ex was particularly worth all this fucking drama… *damn.*

"I feel like I shouldn't have said anything," Honor said, wiping her hands on her jeans self-consciously.

"No, you were right to. You absolutely *need* to tell us things like that. It's not like we can help him if we don't know what's going on. It's also not like I can protect you if I don't know something is happening or fix it if I don't know what's happened. It's our job to hold each other accountable. What Pyro pulled is *definitely* not okay, baby. Anything that happens now? That's all on him, not on you, okay?"

She looked worried still and I said, "C'mere." I towed her into my arms and wrapped them around her, looking up at her from where I sat against my bike, waiting on shit to happen.

"You didn't do anything wrong."

"I thought snitches got stitches," she said with a tense smirk that didn't have any humor to it.

"That's not this," I declared. "That whole notion is sort of bullshit. I'm not going to lie. It's how problems don't get solved as they happen. There are no secrets when it comes to *inside* the club. You go talking out of turn to cops or citizens about club things, *that's* when there's a problem? Okay?"

She looked thoughtful and nodded before she gave me a look and said, "I don't talk to cops about *anything*. Pack of pig's assholes. *Especially* the white ones," she said. "We don't call them the Federal Bureau of Intimidation for nothing back on the rez."

I smiled at that and nodded. "See, you get it."

"I'm just trying to color inside the lines when it comes to your world, honey. Just like I know you'd be a fish out of water if you ever came to mine."

I nodded at that. "Mad respect," I said. "That's what it's about in both scenarios. Respect. Always. Pyro disrespected you in a big way, and he disrespected me by default. When you disrespect *any* of the brothers, you disrespect *all* of them."

She nodded.

"So, what happens now, in a case like this?" she asked.

"Depends on the club's bylaws, but what happens now is it gets taken care of – between brothers. It's not for you to know, just for you to trust me when I come to you and say it's been handled that it's been handled."

She nodded and lowered her mouth to mine and we kissed.

"Thank you for the crash course," she murmured against my lips and I smiled.

We'd talked about some of these kinds of things before – about club business and what was and wasn't hers and the like. She knew a lot of it, but some specific scenarios? Like this one? We just had to take them one at a time. Easy does it.

"C'mon, baby. Time to go," I said, catching Cutter raising his arm in the signal to mount up out of the corner of my eye.

Honor quickly climbed on behind me and as one, the club fired up their bikes. Hope was riding with the captain this time rather than her own bike, and that was cool. I'd honestly expected her to ride on her own for bike week. It was also nice to see that Galahad and Charity had somehow worked some magic to both get the week off at the same time. Marlin had Faith with him, and Stoker had Serenity. Then there was Justice, climbing on behind Radar beside us.

I looked into my side view down the line and nodded.

We were all accounted for – Hoss riding with Gator, and Rocco bringing up the rear behind Atlas as our rudder at the back, with Zach riding beside him as our friend of the club. He hadn't really made the leap on whether or not he wanted to become an official hang around or prospect. Honestly, though? I both hoped he did and didn't. Yeah, he was definitely a cool enough dude, but it would fuck up the flow for him at The Plank in the kitchen if he did.

We all followed Cutter out onto the boulevard and I took one last look at Pyro, just in front of Atlas and Zach, riding next to Gator and Hossler. I swear to God, if he did anything to fuck up this ride or get anyone hurt, I was going to go own fucking program and put him out of his misery.

Yeah, the anger was definitely building, not diminishing on that front.

But then something interesting happened.

Honor wrapped her arms around me and snuggled up to my back. That buildup of static electricity in my veins failed to manifest into that bolt from the ground to the sky that usually happened when the anger had an opportunity to build.

Instead, it dissipated into the ether.

It was hard to fuckin' be mad when you were grinning from ear to ear. I pulled up my orange bandanna to cover my nose and mouth before I managed to catch any bugs in my damn teeth.

THE RIDE COULDN'T HAVE BEEN PLANNED for a better day. There wasn't a cloud in the sky, as far as Radar could tell with his gadgets and widgets. He'd pre-gamed this shit. He said there wouldn't be any foul weather the whole way there and most of the trip. There were supposed to be some spotty thunder showers mid-week, and you fucking *know* I had my rebar packed in the crash truck and ready to go for it.

We were in a beach-front hotel and the Sacred Hearts were supposed to be meeting up with us. You abso-fucking-lutely know I had to show off some.

Speaking of showing off… I couldn't tell you how many fucking trucks we passed with bikes on trailers. It left a bad fuckin' taste in my mouth to be sure, the way a lot of bike week was being co-opted by these fuckin' RUBs or Rich Urban Bikers. Doctors and lawyers and shit who wanted to play bad boy for the week, who didn't even have the fuckin' nuts to *ride* their shit here, but rather towed it in with their big, overpriced trucks.

Was I bitter about it? Hell fuckin' yeah. Mostly because a lot of these fucks drove their cages like fuckin' idiots and didn't look out for shit for those of us who knew how to treat our bikes right. Those same fuckin' idiots I knew for a fact would be bitching and complaining about other cagers just as soon as they deigned to get their asses out of their climate control and up on their own two wheels.

Fuckin' posers…

We did our best to ride past 'em like they were standing still, throwing a few one-fingered salutes at 'em as we went by. We knew that one or two might try to nut up on us but that most, if not all of them, were too pussy to say somethin' once they were on what they thought was equal footing with us.

We stopped every once in a while, to let the girls have a break and for those of us that needed to, to tap a kidney. There was this relatively new phenomenon out there that was this wild fucking gas station that was like if a Wally World and a truck stop had this unholy love child. We're talking like over a hundred gas pumps only for cars and motorcycles, and if you went inside? It was *definitely* a Wally World of gas stations.

Brisket sandwiches, a bakery, fresh hot cinnamon roasted nuts, chips, drinks, and candy galore. A whole ass fucking *wall* of different beef jerky and absolutely *palatial* bathrooms. It was a cool joint and had a big fuckin' beaver on the sign. Everything in there was branded with the same buck-toothed motherfucker in his red baseball hat with his own face on it like some kind of mascot inception or whatever.

The only thing better than stopping at one was watching Honor fucking light up with glee while she loaded up on these big round chocolate bars that were like a quarter pound each for stupid cheap.

"We *are* on a bike, you know," I told her.

"I know!" she said, rolling her eyes. "I can keep the bag around my wrist. We're only like fifteen minutes from our hotel. I heard Radar say so to Jussy."

I laughed and Atlas clapped both of his hands down onto my shoulders and shook me some.

"Man, if you don't have a passenger comin' out the gas station on a road trip like someone sent an eight-year-old in unsupervised with a hundred dollars, are they even doing it right?" he asked.

"That's in a *cage*," I corrected him and he laughed at me.

"I will magic make this work," Honor declared, and she sounded straight up like the challenge had been put forth and it was fucking accepted.

I shook my head and said, "Fine, fine, it's fine." I held up my hands in defeat.

She ended up holding two bags, because I loaded up on some sport's drinks and jerky for when we got back to the hotel lit. Sober me was tryin' to help drunk me out, man. Both with the impending hangover and in case he got to feeling snacky in the middle of the night.

I tell you what, I was so looking forward to it being just me and just Honor for the whole fucking week when it came to our hotel room. I was super stoked to be able to make love to her every night so long as she was up for it, and we didn't break her vag with too much fuckin'. Hell, I wasn't entirely sure that would even stop her. She was almost more insatiable than I was.

We matched up perfectly in the sack for all we'd only done it a couple of times now and we hadn't even gotten all that adventurous yet.

We wound through surface streets toward our hotel and crossed the bridge over the inlet separating the mainland from the outer spit of land that the hotel sat on. The Atlantic stretched as far as the fuckin' eye could see beyond that.

I was stoked. I loved the rush of a good thunderstorm on the shores of the Atlantic. There was just something wilder about it than the Gulf. I didn't know how to describe or explain that one. It was just something you had to experience to understand.

I was looking forward to that shit like nobody's business.

The hotel we were at was this tall-ass fuckin' tower that had these rounded balconies that faced the beach. We pulled into the lot and backed our bikes in a line of parking spots, four deep to a space, trying to be remotely considerate and not take up any more than we fuckin' needed to. We had that shit down, the back of the line parking in such a way that when we went to pull back out to go do our thing that we just sort of naturally fell out into formation.

We piled up into line at the hotel's front desk and chatted, waiting on them to check us into our reservations. We got all squared away relatively quickly.

Honor and I got our room key and headed for the elevators, the whole club's rooms were all on the twelfth floor, which was pretty much two from the top and that was cool with us. It meant we almost all got a spectacular fuckin' view.

I swiped our key card into the lock and pushed the door open. Honor hefted our haul from Bucktooth Bonanza and we headed inside.

I set the majority of our luggage, such as it was, on the desk and looked at the two beds in our room.

"Could have sworn I booked a fucking king," I said, only slightly disgruntled.

"Doesn't matter. We only have to use one of them," she said, flouncing down onto the Queen furthest from the window.

"Don't want the view?" I asked.

"I don't want the sun beaming in my eyes just as soon as it comes up," she said with a laugh.

"Fuckin' A, you're one smart bitch," I said with a wink and a grin.

She grinned back and crooked her finger at me to come to her. It was a siren's call I wasn't about to fucking resist.

I leaped for her, snarling, and she squealed and giggled, high and bright, as I attacked the side of her neck with kisses and little love nips and bites. I put my hands to work tickling her ribs as she shrieked with laughter.

We were just shifting gears from playful to serious, the touching and kissing growing hotter and heavier, when a knock fell at the door.

"Lightning!" Marlin called through the wood. I groaned.

"To be continued," I growled and I crawled back off of her and went for the door, opening it up for my VP.

"This better be good," I said archly.

"Trouble in paradise, I'm afraid," Marlin said.

"What kind of trouble?" I asked and Marlin peered around me.

"The kind you can help fix, I'm afraid."

I narrowed my eyes. "How's that?"

"Half the Sacred Hearts got fucked by the hotel. They double booked. We need some of us to double up."

"Aw, man, c'mon!" I said and Marlin grinned.

"Got some good news for yah," he said.

"What's that?" I demanded.

"Pairing enforcer with enforcer? Alright!" I heard from behind Marlin and I dragged open the door.

"Yeah, okay," I said, my face splitting into a wide grin. "You should have said it was gonna be Reaver. What's up, buddy?" I crowed.

Marlin stepped aside to reveal the enforcer for the Sacred Hearts MC and his diminutive lady, Doll.

"Ahhhhh!" Reaver cried happily and reached out to hug me. I clapped him on the back and none too gently, either, but that was alright. I knew the crazy bastard could take it.

"Guess the captain got one of the rooms with a king?" I asked and Marlin nodded.

"That's one down, only four more to go."

I saluted and called back to Honor, "Babe, sorry to say—"

"Yeah, no, I heard!" she called from around the corner in the room and I stood back to let Reaver and Doll in.

"Damn, girl, you grew out your hair," I said to Doll, bending to kiss her on the cheek and accept her hug.

"I did!" she cried back jovially, all smiles. It was good to see her smile. I mean, it'd been years and years since the Sacred Hearts had all that trouble and their women were on like an extended stay with us – but, hey. That was ancient history and Doll looked a world away from the ghost of the woman she'd been when she'd thought Reaver was deader 'n a doornail.

"Come on in," I told her.

"Honor, meet Reaver and Doll. Guys, this is Honor. She's my new…" I kind of looked to her to fill in the blank and she smiled, her eyes meeting mine.

She said, "Girlfriend. It's like hella new, but I'm his new girlfriend."

"Yessss!" I made a fist and jerked my elbow back, and Reaver laughed.

"You're such a fuckin' nerd, man," he said.

He gave Honor a hug who said, "Oh!" in surprise and Doll came in right behind him for hers.

"Sorry not sorry," Doll quipped. "We're huggers."

Honor laughed.

"You better get cool with a lot of shit real quick, rooming with these two," I told her with a wink, and she widened her dark eyes and nodded, saving her questions for later.

"Sorry to crash your party, man," Reaver said.

"Hey, shit happens," I declared. "Not like you could help it. Just, if we get back here before y'all, and there's a Do Not Disturb on the door, go fuck off and find a drink or something, would yah?"

"Done deal," Reaver said, nodding judiciously. "Least we can do."

"Thanks," I said as Doll laughed at the expression on Honor's face.

"Oh, you poor thing," Doll said. "You really *are* new."

"I live and die by crash courses and figuring it out, so I guess this'll be an immersive experience so to speak."

Reaver eyed her. "Depends," he said. "How immersive you wanna get?"

Doll smacked him in the chest and rolled her eyes. "Don't scare her," she said pointedly.

"Hedonists," Honor murmured. "Got it."

Doll wrinkled her nose cutely and Reaver and I chuckled.

"Smart girl," Reaver said. "I'm sure you'll do just fine."

"It gets too wild, I told her she can tap out at any time and we can come back here."

"Good plan." Reaver nodded.

"What's your safe word?" Doll asked, grinning.

"Oh, I'm not like that…" Honor said, blushing.

"You don't have to be," Reaver declared, flopping down on the bed by the window and putting his hands under his chin, kicking his feet just like he was one of the girls.

I laughed at him, silently, my shoulders shaking as I tried to suppress it.

Honor looked to me and grinning, she asked, "Just how nuts is this supposed to get?"

"We'll just have to see," I said.

"No telling when it's bike week," Doll said with a shrug, sitting down beside Reaver with a gusty sigh.

"You seen the captain, yet?" I asked.

"No, not yet," Reaver said with a gusty sigh. "He's in some kind of closed-door meeting with one of your other leadership, doing king shit."

Ah, fuck. I knew what that meant.

"So, what's the big plan from here?" Doll asked.

"That's a good question," Honor said, leaning back on her hands and all eyes turned on me.

"What're you looking at me for?" I demanded.

"Fuck if I know. It's your turf and your room. I guess we all just sort of decided you're the de facto leader of this fucked up little cadre," Reaver said with a blasé little shrug.

"Oh, great. Because you know *that's* going to go well," I said and I was shaking with repressed laughter all over again.

"Meh." He shrugged and, with a spectacular grin, laced his long fingers together and rested his chin on the back of them, his elbows planted to the bed as he looked to Honor with a twinkle in his ice-blue eyes. He asked, "So, tell us all about yourself. Where you from? How you doin'?"

Honor laughed and said, "Uhhh… where do I even start?"

That was a good question. I couldn't help her, really. It was all about what she was comfortable sharing.

I said as much, looking to her and telling her, "I'm going to follow your lead on this one, babe."

She smiled in appreciation at that and rolled her eyes some, saying, "Oh great, that helps a lot."

I smiled back when yet *another* knock fell at the door and Doll went to go answer it.

"Need Lightning," I heard Galahad say.

"Yeah, right here, bud." I stopped before I went anywhere. "You good?" I asked Honor. She hesitated which told me, not really, but Galahad came to the rescue.

"Need your lady, too. Captain wants to see you briefly."

"Well, fuck!" Reaver said bounding up. "Let's all go! We'll say 'hi' and fuck off and leave y'all to it."

"Sounds good," I said, knowing the captain wouldn't be pissed about it in the slightest.

"Cool." Honor nodded.

I handed Doll one of the two keys that'd been given to me for the room. "Because I know if I give it to him, he'll fuckin' lose it," I said.

"Goddamn right I will. I can't even keep my mind. I lose that shit all the time," Reaver said and went out the door first. Honor laughed and shook her head, and Doll just rolled her eyes.

"He ain't lying," she said, tossing her long black hair off her shoulder. It was just below them now.

The hall was sorta half packed with Kraken and the other half Sacred Hearts as Marlin tried to find space for everyone. It was slow going, it seemed, but it also looked like it was working out.

Shit, we were mostly just using this place as a crash pad anyway. Not like we were going to be spending oodles of fucking time here.

Radar was standing outside the door to the captain's room and gave me a nod, using the key to open 'er up. Reaver said, "Ooo, that serious? I was gonna say 'hi' before y'all got to it."

"Yeah, bud—" Radar started, but the captain called out, "Reaver, that you, bud?"

"Sure the fuck is, man. Need me to come back later?"

"Nah, git in here. I got a little time to say hi."

"Knew that was coming," I said under my breath, and Radar grinned at me.

I stood back while Reaver and Doll went inside, and I held Honor's hand.

Galahad leaned against the wall outside the door on the other side of Radar and said, "This is a whole lotta cagey to start the trip. I don't like it."

"Ain't none of us like it," Radar said with a shrug. "You know how it is, though. No trip ever goes off without some kind of drama or a hitch. Best to get these speed bumps outta the way fast when they do come up, so we don't ruin the whole vacation."

I nodded in agreement but I was looking at Honor who was looking just miserable, staring at the closed door. I shook her hand and said, "Hey, you did the right thing."

She pursed her lips and nodded but didn't look so sure.

"Then why do I feel just like I did when I had a bunch of white girls bullying me at the school and I got called to the principal's office and got in-school suspension for bullying one of them?"

Radar huffed a laugh. "How'd that turn out?" he asked.

"The next one that opened their mouth, I shut it for her," she said with a shrug. "I figured if I was going to be in trouble for something then I might as well do it. I opened up a low-key reign of terror with a bunch of the other girls from the rez on them for the rest of the school year. We didn't play that shit."

"Well, this is definitely not that, but good job," Radar said, and Honor stood a little straighter.

We waited only a minute or two more and the door opened again. Reaver and Doll came out, blue and green eyes sparkling, and smiles on their faces, and we were ushered in, Radar bringing up the rear and coming in behind us.

Marlin, Hope, and Cutter waited inside and it was cramped – standing room only for sure.

I stood beside Honor and put a reassuring hand to her lower back as Cutter looked her over. She swallowed but raised her chin sorta defiantly, and Cutter's face split into a wide grin.

I just waited to see how this was gonna go.

12

Honor…

"Why don't you tell me in your own words what went down at the clubhouse with Pyro, sweetheart?"

I licked my lips and told the truth. The only time it hadn't served me well was with people who didn't want to hear it. If Cutter didn't want to hear it, which was a likely scenario given that Pyro was his friend, then there wasn't anything I could do, really. Still, I wasn't exactly thrilled at the prospect of getting on the club's bad side with having just relocated to Ft. Royal; but here we were and here I was, once again thinking I should have just kept my big mouth shut. Too late for that now, and so the truth was what I would tell. I would just have to hope for the best.

"I was coming away from the kitchen window after putting in and order and I happened to look at the archway leading back to the bathrooms as Pyro was coming out, sniffing something off of his hand, here." I balled up my fist and indicated the space just above the thumb where it made sort of a flat platform.

Cutter leaned back and nodded. "Go on," he said, crossing his arms over his big chest. He looked mad, and I was almost afraid to, but

Lightning put a little more pressure on my back, silently urging me to keep talking, and so I did.

"He got one look at me, started mean mugging me, and did one of these at me." I lunged like Pyro had, that sort of intimidating fists at the side, moving head and shoulders Cutter's way, like I was going to do something. "And then he told me, 'You didn't see anything, bitch. You say you did and you're fucking in for it.' And then he kept walking back on toward the throne room."

Cutter huffed a little laugh and said, "The throne room? Is that what we're calling it nowadays?"

Hope shrugged. "If the shoe fits, but don't get off topic, lover."

"You're right, you're right," he said with a heavy sigh.

"Anyone else see this?" he asked.

I shook my head and said, "Zach might've if he was turned around facing the kitchen window when it happened. *Maybe* Rocco if he saw it from the bar?"

Marlin shook his head. "Rocco didn't see it."

"How do you know?" Hope asked, frowning.

"Because he would have thrown Pyro out the front door by the back of his cut and the seat of his pants if he had," Cutter said. "He's got seven sisters and a strong Italian mamma who raised all of them by herself. Like *literally* by herself. Ain't none of her kids raised the younger ones. She ain't like that. Rocco doesn't put up with any kind of shit toward women."

"Oh," Hope said faintly. "I didn't know that about him."

"Today I learned," Radar said, exchanging a grin with Lightning.

"I knew I liked Rocco for all that he seemed like the Silent fucking Bob type which sometimes got on my nerves," Lightning declared.

"Find Zach. See if we can get some corroboration," Cutter said. Radar nodded and immediately went for the door.

"You don't believe me," I said, and I felt my shoulders drop with defeat.

"No, that's the rough part. I absolutely do," Cutter said. "Still, it's always good to get some corroboration. Mostly so Pyro can't weasel his way out of any consequences by sowing doubt with any of the other guys. If Zach saw it, he wouldn't speak up about it – but he *would* if he's asked directly about it. That's the kind of guy he is."

"I wish I'd have torn that play out of his playbook," I muttered, and Lightning again gave me a reassuring squeeze.

Hope sighed. "Pyro's been on this track for a long time," she said. "It was only a matter of time. Honestly, if he's so comfortable doing it, what's to say he wouldn't do it to a customer or even one of the other ol' ladies? No, we're glad you spoke up. We'd like to deal with this quickly and judiciously."

"In any case, how do you want to deal with it?" Cutter asked. "Now, or after the trip, back in Ft. Royal?"

"If you don't mind, I'd rather not put a pall on the whole trip for everyone. Back in Ft. Royal is just fine with me if it's fine with Honor," Lightning said.

I nodded quickly.

"I would rather not be any more drama," I said.

"Hey," Cutter said sharply.

"It's Pyro that's the drama, not you," Hope said and her voice was steel. I met her eyes and she gave me a look that *clearly* translated – *fucking men.*

I had to smile at that. She wasn't wrong. Men could be way more drama than they would ever admit to.

Radar came back after a minute or two with Zach in tow, and Cutter raised his chin and asked point blank as soon as the door was shut, "Hey, man, you see anything go down between Pyro and Honor last night?"

Zach nodded. "I saw Honor flinch for half a sec and then Pyro went walking by, why?"

Cutter bowed his head, shook it, and said, "Nothing, thanks, man."

"No problem," Zach said. He looked at me. "You good?"

I nodded, relieved he *had* seen something and said, "Yeah, I'm good."

"That it?" he asked Cutter.

"Yeah, that's it, man."

"Cool. Natives are getting restless out there, man."

I scoffed and rolled my eyes, and Zach gave me an apologetic grin. "Shit, sorry," he said.

I gave him a half-smile and nodded. He went out, Radar holding the door for him.

"Right, I guess that's it for now, then," Cutter declared.

"Sorry, man," Lightning said.

"Yeah, me too," Cutter declared.

"So what happens now?" I asked.

"Nothing, baby. We drop it and we get it dealt with when we get back home," Lightning declared.

"You did good bringing it up," Cutter said. "Anyone makes you uncomfortable or does some shit like that, you bring it up right away to any one of us. If it's a club brother, take it to Lightning, Radar, me, or Marlin."

"Or me," Hope said.

Cutter nodded. "Or my queen," he agreed. "If it's someone *outside* the club tryin' to give you that kind of grief, you bring it up to any one of us nearby and we'll quash that attitude right then and there. You feel me?"

I nodded.

"Good girl," he said, and I blinked rapidly, feeling like the color both rose and drained out of my face at the same time. Lightning laughed.

"I'll have to remember that one," he said.

"Don't you dare!" I quipped and Cutter grinned.

"Alright, y'all, give us a minute and it'll be on to the next adventure." Marlin looked amused at my expense, too.

"Copy that," Lightning said and shot his leadership within the club a smarmy little salute.

We went out into the hall, which was clearing, batches of men in Kraken and Sacred Hearts vests waiting for the elevator down the hall. Reaver waved at us from the back of the pile and Lightning threw him some chin.

"Hey, Lightning!" A big, tall man with graying blond hair in a long tail down his back waved from beside Reaver and Doll. A diminutive woman around the same size as Doll, only more delicate with long auburn hair, held the big man's hand and my first thought was a crude one – *how do they even fit together?*

We went over and joined them and the introductions were made. "Trigger, Sunshine, this is my girlfriend, Honor."

"Hi," I said and Sunshine smiled up at me. Her eyes were this peculiar golden color, like an eagle's.

"Hi," she said brightly.

"What's the plan?" Lightning asked.

"We're all heading out to the Busted Wheel for dinner and beers," Trigger replied.

"Nice!" Lightning said.

"Yeah, no official ride, just every man for himself, riding in a pack here or there. Nothing formal," Reaver said.

"Cool." Lightning looked to me. "You ready for some food or…?"

"We can go now." I said with a grin.

"Right on, let's go." Reaver bounced on the balls of his feet and I laughed. He seemed to have this wonky highly keyed energy that was pretty fun, to be honest.

THE RIDE back across the bridge, over the water, and the wind in my hair, was just what I needed to put all of the funny business with Pyro out of my mind. As the warm spring air washed over and through me, it took with it all the tension and worry I'd been carrying without realizing it.

It seemed that the club really was on my side in this which made me wonder – just how long and how bad had things with Pyro been for the lot of them to reach the point that they no longer defended him and would instead take up for me – a near perfect stranger?

It worried at my mind a little bit and I realized just as we pulled up into the driveway and into the copse of trees surrounding the big neon and enamel looking sign for the Busted Wheel that I had far more questions than answers about it all. I really would like to ask Lightning.

The music up here was near deafening and there were several tents outside the place, like a pop-up farmers' market for bikers selling all sorts of things from stickers and patches to tee shirts and leathers, all the way down to a stretch of tarps out on the ground under a row of like six of these pop-up tents with all kinds of new and used bike parts on them.

There was even a tent with tables set up and rows and rows of displays of knives, which Reaver lit up like a Christmas tree when we saw that. Trigger was like, "Ope, we lost him!"

"Yes, you did!" Reaver called, towing Doll along with him laughing.

"You can't find us in like the next hour, call search and rescue!" she shouted back at us.

"Will do!" Trigger called back at her, shaking his head and grinning.

"Reaver and his knives," Lightning said ruefully, and Sunshine giggled.

We ran into Charity and Galahad who were with Rush and Bailey from the Sacred Hearts. Rush was a big dude, and Bailey screamed "horse girl" from her cowboy boots to her country blouse to the belt buckle she was sporting with its horse's head and wild horses tooled into the leather.

We joined them in line for the food trucks they had set up in like a grotto as the live cover band started to play from the big stage set back into the woods.

The place was an absolute *carnival* of all things biker, and it was an absolute spectacle to see. Like, it was totally nuts but in a good way.

We got some food, and some beer in plastic cups, and found some seats at a long picnic table with some more Kraken and Sacred Hearts.

I listened to everyone joke and laugh, telling stories, and all of them doing everything they could to not only include me, but top each other for the wildest tale, like they were trying to impress me.

Before long, Bailey and I started talking horses and traded stories, comparing horse life back where I was from to thoroughbred life in Kentucky.

"I would *love* to see your farm," I said.

She positively beamed and said, "You and Lightning are welcome anytime! I'd love to show you a few of our real promising yearlings. I have a real good feeling about at least two of 'em. I'm talkin' real strong contenders for the triple crown."

"That would be awesome!" I said and the conversation naturally ebbed and flowed.

Still, it was crowded, and the darker it got, the absolutely wilder it got. It was going to be really easy to get overwhelmed real quick.

When I hit my limit, I spoke up and cuddled up to Lightning. I said, "How about that raincheck before Reaver and Doll get back to the room?"

"Well ladies and gentlemen!" he declared immediately. "It's been swell, but the swelling's gone down. Time for me and my lady to turn into a pair of pumpkins."

"Aw, you sure?" Reaver asked with a wink.

"You just go on and take your time coming back to the room," Lightning said and Reaver laughed. Doll's eyes sparkled knowingly.

Lightning got up and took my hand, and I stood with him.

"Don't wait up, Daddy," Reaver said with a wink, and Lightning gave him the finger, laughing.

We walked back out to the bikes and I could feel myself starting to relax with every step we put between us and the crashing music and stifling crowd, even as more people were arriving in droves.

"How about a walk on the beach when we get back? Sort of finish shaking off the crowd?" Lightning asked and I smiled, grateful.

"That obvious, huh?" I asked.

He gave a shrug. "Kinda, and that's okay," he said.

The ride back to the hotel was pleasant but also still jam-packed with bikes and people. We ended up riding in a pack, whether we really wanted to or not, and that was okay, but I was definitely overstimulated.

We skipped going upstairs in order to bypass the building and go straight for the beach around the side. It was much more open. While there were some people, it wasn't crowded by any means and there was enough space to really finally open up and *breathe*.

"I have questions," I said as we took off our boots to step into the sand, tying the laces together and slinging them over our shoulders or over the back of our necks.

"Shoot, it's just you and me now. You know you can ask me anything."

"I don't want to sound indelicate, but… just how long has Pyro been this way that everyone was willing to take my word over his from the jump? I mean, you guys barely know me," I said, as we worked our way through the tough boggy dry sand toward the much easier to walk along wet sand.

Lightning huffed out a breath and said, "Wow, I didn't know what to expect, but that wasn't it. Um, it's been building for a while, now."

"What happened? Do you mind my asking?"

Lightning shook his head.

"No, I don't mind. As much as I hate to say it, it's a tale as old as fucking time. Pyro was hooked up with this chick for a long, long time. Like, they were solid – or so we thought. But then she cheated and dumped him, and shit just went real toxic real quick out of nowhere."

"Ah," I said nodding.

"We all thought it was her, but man, he just really took this nose-dive and got real fuckin' bitter. He started up drinking hardcore, and no matter what we've tried to do to support him or get him right, he's just been spiraling so hard. It really sucks to see. Like, Cutter seriously has the patience of a saint at this point."

"Yeah?" I asked.

Lightning nodded. "They've been best friends since for like fucking ever. Business partners for almost as long with the salvage thing, but Pyro has really been dropping the ball there, too. Not showing up to work or showing up too hungover or even drunk a few times to really work. He's been going through pussy like it's going out of style and like it's all wrong, you know?"

I nodded and said, "Meaningless hookup culture?"

"Yeah, but like these chicks aren't good chicks, either, you know? All drama and strung-out or grifter types."

"Yeah, I think I know the type," I said. "Women can suck too."

"Exactly," he said and took my hand.

"Enough broken promises and not showing up or saying shit out of pocket. I don't think he's been in anyone's good graces for a real long time. After a long enough time with an established pattern of behavior, it's not out of reach for any of us to believe what he did with you. Honestly, I think this was a long time coming and this is just the straw that broke the camel's back."

"Why though?" I asked. "I mean, why me?"

"You're not the first waitress The Plank has had. Cutter and Zach haven't really been able to keep 'em. We knew something was up, and that maybe it was Pyro, but none of 'em was willing to speak up. I knew you needed a job and I also knew coming from the truck stop, you weren't likely to take any shit. Plus, I was hoping you would know I would look out for you and protect you if some shit went down. I just didn't expect for it to be *that* soon or *that* in your face, you know?"

I wanted to be upset, but I could totally tell by the look on Lightning's face, he legitimately wasn't trying to use me as *bait* for Pyro, or whatever. He was genuinely hoping to kill two birds with one stone, getting me hired on at The Plank. One, get me a job which I desperately needed, and two, help his club and his friends by getting them the waitress their bar desperately needed.

There wasn't anything conniving or ill-intentioned when it came to Lightning. Not at all. I felt that down to my very bones.

He looked a little worried. Wincing, I said, "That came out really bad. You aren't pissed at me, are you?" he asked.

I stopped in my tracks and turned to face him. Smiling, I touched the side of his face and leaned in to kiss him.

He smiled against my lips and hummed in appreciation, putting his arms around my waist, and hugging me to him.

"Not mad," I whispered against his lips. "I know that's not what you had in mind when you pitched the job to me and me to Cutter."

"It wasn't at the forefront of my mind, no, but I'd be lying if I said it hadn't crossed it."

"You're lucky I trust you," I said with a wry smile. "And that I said something."

"I'm glad you trust me," he murmured. "I don't want to do anything at all to fuck that up. I really like you and I feel this really real and tangible connection with you that I don't think I've ever felt with anyone else before in my whole fuckin' life."

I rested my forehead against his and closed my eyes, those words so freely and honestly spoken doing something to me.

"I feel something similar," I confessed. "More than just chemistry, like a lot more. I just am not very good about talking about it, I guess." I laughed a bit nervously and he chuckled.

"We don't have to talk about it. We just have to keep believing in each other enough to be honest and communicate. Even when we might disagree or are afraid. Disagreement isn't a bad thing, but know, even if I do disagree with you, I will *always* have your back. Okay?"

I nodded and I felt the seriousness of his words as though he'd just made some sort of solemn pledge.

I swallowed hard and made a confession I was afraid was something far too soon to speak out loud, but I took the leap anyway. "I want something with you like Mitch and Ruthie had. I want a love so pure-like that it makes other people's hearts ache with longing just to see it in action."

He pulled his forehead from mine and replaced it with his lips.

"Get out of my head," he murmured against my forehead. "I've been thinking the same thing since I first laid eyes on you on that beach in that thunderstorm."

I smiled and had to giggle a little as I said, "Don't think I didn't see you stash that rebar in the back of the crash truck with Rocco, you little electric psycho."

He laughed at me then and crushed me to him and captured my mouth with his.

We didn't stay on the beach, both of us opting to get back to our room to make use of it before our unexpected roommates got back from the Broken Wheel and their night out.

The trip back was a blur, the elevator ride a rush of kissing and fevered touching. Of hands disappearing beneath shirt hems and hands against flushed skin. My body reacted beautifully to every touch, kiss, light nip, and blush of warm breath against my skin.

"Fuck, won't this thing hurry up?" he growled against the side of my neck and it sent an absolutely delicious shiver down my spine.

"Mm," I moaned into his mouth as I darted forward to steal another kiss when the elevator beeped, came to a stop, and the doors finally hushed open.

"Whoa, nice," a masculine voice said.

"Make way," Lightning ordered and towed me out of the elevator between a Sacred Heart I hadn't met yet, with long straight black hair, looking decidedly Indigenous or Hispanic – sometimes even for me it could be hard to tell – and a woman with long wheat-blonde hair in a braid over her shoulder. Both were wearing riding leathers and both were grinning.

"Later, Dray!" Lightning called. "Nice to see you, Irish!"

"Good to see you, too, bud!" Dray called after us.

We scurried up the hallway, laughing and giggling. Lightning fumbled with excited shaking hands to get us into our room. As soon as the door clicked shut behind us, the passion and anticipation of getting one another out of our clothes exploded in a frenzy of movement, the sounds of kissing, and the whispers of cloth hitting the floor.

To be completely honest, that was a blur too. One moment, we were walking me backward toward the beds, our faces smashed together and our lips and tongues vying for dominance in the kiss and the next, I was on my back, Lightning kneeling between my thighs, rolling a condom down his length as I whimpered and begged for him to fill me.

He didn't waste any time, wrapping an arm like a steel band around my lower back while he adjusted his cock with the other. He slid right inside of me.

His head bowed and I reached up, smoothing my fingers through his soft hair and capturing his face between my hands, rocking my hips, and dragging his mouth to mine. I loved kissing him while he was inside of me. It never got old.

We rocked together in this ungainly and awkward yet unified rhythm. While it wasn't exactly porn-worthy, looking from the outside, it did *all* the right things for both him and me.

I loved that about him, that he wasn't afraid to get weird and awkward in the bedroom with me as we both chased that golden glow of euphoria that lit us up from the inside out like lightning flickering through the clouds.

We moaned, panting breathlessly, the warmth and electricity building between us, the thermal energy rising, lifting us into the clouds as though we had wings outspread and just *soared.* It was everything I could have ever asked for or wanted. It was, in fact, the absolute best sex of my fucking *life*, and I couldn't get enough of him if I wanted to.

13

Lightning...

God, the way she wrapped her arms and legs around me. The way she insisted I lie atop her, pressing her into the mattress, as she begged me for my full weight, my full length, for me to keep going and to move against and inside of her. It was more intoxicating than any drug, than any drink, ever created by man or fuck, even *God.*

She sent my mind, my heart, my body, all of it into this tempest of desire and, I don't know, *strength.* I never felt so sure of myself and right versus wrong. I never had ever felt like such a good man or as *noble* as I did when I was in her arms. It was something completely fucking crazy and so fucking good, it wasn't even funny.

I loved the way that every time I withdrew from her sexy, hot, and sweet body, her pussy clenched, trying to draw me back into her. I loved how she locked legs around me until they trembled and how even then she still wouldn't let go. I loved how she tangled her fingers in my short hair, and how she scratched me lightly with her nails, but never to the point of leaving any marks. She was so into me it was crazy, but at the same time, she was so *careful* of me the way I was careful of her. It was something unbelievably sweet and made her incredibly addictive.

God, the feel of her wrapped around my dick was something that I had absolutely no comparison for. It was sensual, sleek, tight, and just so perfect how we fit together. I knew that there wouldn't ever be anything like it again. That there was literally no one else out there on this fucking planet that I would be so in tune with. It just wasn't possible.

I loved her panting, her feral little moans, the way she tried to keep quiet. But then I would hit that one spot and she would lose herself so completely beneath me, her voice rising in this piercing sharp cry that was pure fucking sex and I loved that. I loved that I could do that for her and I loved so much what she did for me.

I gave a wicked little smile and worked myself inside her the way that I was learning she liked and I said, "Good girl. Now you work on coming for me, baby. I wanna watch you lose yourself in it. I love the way you fucking come for me."

Oh yeah, her heavy-lidded gaze heated by *several* degrees, her pussy clenching around me making me lose myself for a second, bringing a sharp cry out of me as I drove into her deeper, our bodies pressed tight. I worked like a motherfucker at making her take that shining fall from grace right back down into my arms where I would fucking covet and protect her until the end of fucking time.

"Ah!" she cried out and arched. In arching like that, she thrust her sweet pussy down onto me, our bodies practically melding into one being. Then there was that telltale little flutter and she was crashing back to earth like the lightning I so loved, hitting the bed, and bouncing slightly as the world exploded around me into colors and sounds too sweet to be real, as my whole body drew taut and I filled the condom inside of her. Her sweet pussy rhythmically grabbed and pulled, milking me fucking dry.

Holy shit, I loved the way we loved each other.

It was so fucking *intense.*

~

It was so late that it was early, and the soft moaning from the bed beside ours woke me. I felt my smile spread slow and even like a Cheshire cat, Honor warm and tucked tight against my body, but I didn't move. She stirred and I looked down to kiss her forehead to catch her looking up at me. Her dark eyes glittered in the dark, the blue-white light of the moon making her features just visible through the gauzy curtains covering the window.

Her lips spread into a slow smile to match mine and we fought not to giggle.

"Quiet, I'm trying to concentrate over here," Reaver said through gritted teeth, and Doll made a noise that was breathy and intense.

We couldn't help it. Honor and I burst into a fit of giggles and she buried her face against my chest just as Doll's voice raised int a crescendo of her orgasm. An orgasm for which Reaver praised her for.

He ignored us, but it was just about impossible to ignore them. Honor snuggled her nude body closer to mine, and I was vaguely aware of her pressing her thighs tighter together which just served to make my cock throb and stir at the mere thought of her arousal.

I kissed her forehead and waited for her to give me any indication she wanted to have a go, but none came. She simply laid her head back down on my chest and pressed her lips to my skin. I closed my eyes, breathed out, and tried very hard to go back to sleep, which was far easier said than done once I got riled up.

"Fuck yeah." Reaver sighed his own relief, and I snorted.

"You fuckin' freak, you," I said and Honor giggled all over again against me.

"Yeah, but I feel fuckin' good," Reaver said. I rolled my eyes in the dark, and Doll giggled as he tickled her and by the sounds of it, kissed the side of her neck.

Fuck me…

Sleep was a long time coming after that.

14

Honor...

I woke up ravenous the next morning, but poor Lightning slept deep. I lay still for a bit, looking back over my shoulder to the sleeping couple beside us. Reaver and Doll were absolutely out cold.

I pushed up into a sitting position and Lightning groaned.

"Mm, what's up, babe?"

"I think I'm going to go down for breakfast," I whispered. "I'm starving. Want to go?"

"Mm-mm. Need more sleep. Do you need me to go?"

I loved him for asking.

"No, no, baby, you sleep." I bent down and kissed him and he pressed his lips back against mine in a chaste kiss, but I could already tell – he was slipping back down into sleep.

I smiled, got up carefully, and slipped around the corner, taking up my bag and going into the bathroom.

I showered, dressed in jeans and a light tank, and braided my hair.

I pulled out my hat from the back of the bag and kneaded it back into shape from where it was slightly wrinkled or crushed. I put it on my head, running a fingertip along the beaded band and sighing at the slight pang of homesickness for the high desert.

I quietly put on my socks and my boots, made sure my phone was charged and with me so Lightning could find me when he got up, and slung my little purse over my chest on its thin strap.

With one final careful kiss goodbye, trying very hard not to wake him, I slipped out of the room and went for the elevator.

Downstairs, in the hotel's dining area for breakfast, I found a knot of familiar faces from Ft. Royal at one table. A dark head perked up and called out. "Oh, yay! Another member of the early riser's club!"

I smiled at Serenity and Charity made a moaning groan next to her, peeling her lip back from her teeth in a feral grimace as she brought her coffee to her lips.

"Char's an honorary member," Faith said with a faint smile. "She's not human until after her first cup."

I laughed. "Let me grab some food and I can come join you?" I asked.

"Love to see it!" Serenity perked up even more and genuinely looked excited. I was kind of excited too. I was really hoping to make friends among them.

I went and loaded up a plate and came back to the table, which was a pretty big one, sliding onto the bench half of the seating next to Charity. She smiled and winked at me, but still just made a mono-syllabic groan in greeting.

"Hayden still asleep?" Sunshine asked, looking at me pointedly.

"Doll?" I asked.

"Yeah," she said, smiling big.

"Oh yeah." I made a face and the whole table started laughing.

"Yeah, Reaver's a freak," Sunshine declared and laughed with us.

I shook my head, widened my eyes, and said, "Woo-ee!"

The table burst out into yet more laughter.

"Did *you* get any sleep?" Faith asked with a wink and I grinned.

"More than Lightning," I declared after taking my first sip of coffee.

"You guys are relatively a new thing, right?" Bailey asked. I nodded.

"A couple of weeks," I said.

"Well welcome to the covenant of the early risers." Serenity swept a hand out to take in the table of women.

"Which still totally blows my mind," Charity said, looking at Serenity cross-eyed. "Like, aren't you supposed to rise with the moon? Isn't that what all good goths do?"

Serenity gave her a little shove and said, "Dracula broke the mold when he made me, okay?"

There was more tittering laughter around the table.

"Jussy is usually here, too, but I think Radar and Atlas kept her up all night long."

"Oh, she finally give in to Atlas's charms?" Charity asked, bouncing her eyebrows. Serenity rolled her eyes.

"Every once in a while," she said. "She has to be pretty lit, but don't ever say anything about it. She's still got her hang-ups and gets real self-conscious about it."

"Like, has she met me and Hayden?" Sunshine rolled her eyes and more laughter burst around the table. I felt out of the loop but didn't let on.

"So, what's your story?" another woman who had to be with the Sacred Hearts asked. "How'd you and Lightning meet?"

"Oh, my God, Everett! Introduce yourself first!" Sunshine said. "My word!"

I realized where I recognized her from. She was the woman at the elevator the night before as we'd gotten off. The one Lightning had called Irish.

"Maybe we should just go around the table," Faith suggested.

"I like that," I said. "I'll go first. I'm Honor. I'm here with Lighting."

We went around and made introductions and Everett grinned and said, "No dodging the question, girl. Spill the tea. How'd you bottle yourself some Lightning? I didn't think that guy would ever let himself be caught."

I blushed and said, "Well, weird story that…" and I filled them in. The short version, leaving out a bunch of details.

"He is such a dumbass," Everett said, her shoulders shaking with laughter. "Leave it to him to spot this gorgeous thing on the beach and get himself fried by a lightning bolt."

"It was really scary," Charity said and she looked sobered. "Galahad and I lost him twice and barely got him back into sinus rhythm."

"Oh, wow… he made it sound like it wasn't that bad," I said.

"It was bad," she said. "Still won't stop him from doing it again."

I sighed and sat back in my seat and said, "He's got rebar in the back of the crash truck."

"Shit, you're joking!" Faith asked wide-eyed.

Sunshine shook her head. "That boy will never learn."

I thought about that for a moment, losing myself in the process, and finally concluded that no, he wouldn't, but that was just who he was. I didn't think I wanted to change that.

Was I scared for him? Yes, absolutely, but one of the things I adored about Charlie Boyington, AKA Lightning, was that he *was* this wild and free creature. Just like I wouldn't enjoy being caged; I couldn't cage him.

"Sorry, didn't mean to be a downer," Charity said and I shook my head and smiled.

I said, "No, you weren't. It's just very much so a part of who and how he is. As scary as it is, I wouldn't want to change it about him. I love that about him, actually. That he's willing to be that wild and free and to really *live*. Something about it, you know?"

There were a lot of nods of agreement around the table.

"So your grandparents you never met, but who weren't blood related in any way, left you a whole entire house and a car and everything?" Everett asked. "That's wild!"

"Yep." I took a deep breath and nodded, my eyes wide. "It's a little overwhelming, for sure."

"Lightning said you might be ready to make some changes," Serenity said and her tone was consoling. "When you're really ready,

I'm happy to help. I like flipping furniture, painting and changing up spaces and things like that."

I smiled and said, "Yeah, I've been meaning to talk to you about it. It's just it's been busy at The Plank and then this." I waved out a hand to take all this in and said, "It's been a little nuts."

"I promise it isn't always this bonkers," she said laughing.

We chatted over our hotel breakfast and coffee. It wasn't bad, the fare ranging from sausage, eggs, and bacon, to make-it-yourself waffles, to oatmeal, and a wide array of cereals.

Some of the older weekend biker types started filtering down in the last hour of breakfast and my phone buzzed at my elbow around an hour and a half of my being down here.

Lightning: Where are you? Are you okay?

I smiled and it was only slightly devious.

Me: I'm downstairs with a bunch of the girls having breakfast. They're closing down soon. Do you want me to bring you something?

Lightning: God, yes. Eggs and bacon and toast if they've got it?

I texted out my joke and hoped that the sarcasm would make it through the internet this time.

Me: AND toast? Getting a bit needy, are we? Would you like it cut into triangles or straight across?

Lightning: I can't believe this even has to be said… triangles. Always. Like, WTF, baby? Thank you!

I laughed, glad that it had and loving that he gave as good as he got. Making ready to get up, I stuck my phone into my back pocket, a bunch of the girls having diverted from their talking to look at me.

"Lightning's up. I'm going to bring him some breakfast," I said.

"Awwww!" a bunch of them chorused and we all busted up laughing.

I loaded him up a big plate and went back upstairs, knocking on the room's door.

Doll opened it sleepily a moment later and hobbled slightly back to bed. Guess Reaver'd given it to her good.

I could hear the shower cut off as I nudged the door shut behind me.

I poked my head into the bathroom, did my best to straight leer at my man, and bounced my eyebrows. He dropped the towel from drying his face, caught sight of my creepy grin and made this half-surprised, half-laugh sound. He said, "You halfway scared the shit out of me!"

"Hurry up, before your breakfast gets cold," I said.

"Fuck, just thank you for grabbing it," he said.

"No, problem."

I went out and sat on the bed. He came out and dropped down next to me. I handed him his food and said, "I didn't know how you liked your shitty hotel coffee," I said. "So I just grabbed a bunch of options and threw them on this set of plates and brought it to you black.

"Aw, thanks. I actually drink it black most of the time if it's not too bitter. If it is, I add two creams."

"You know only psychopaths drink black coffee?" I asked.

"I thought you knew," he said with a wink.

I rolled my eyes and sighed gustily. "Yeah, well, I drink it with cream and sugar because I love myself."

He snorted around his second or third mouthful of eggs. Before he even had that bite down, he was shoving half a piece of bacon into his mouth.

"What's the hurry?" I asked laughing. "You can slow down!"

"Didn't know if you and the girls had made plans to do something down there," he said. "Didn't want to hold up the train if you had."

Aww, I thought to myself. *That's sweet.*

I shook my head.

"Charity said something about her and Galahad going to the Ponce Inlet lighthouse today, but Galahad wasn't even up yet as far as I know when I left to come up here."

"Gotcha," he said and twisted this way and that, looking for his phone. He scooped it up and shot off a text. "That sound good to you?" he asked.

"Yeah!" I said excitedly. "I already told you, I've never seen any lighthouses before and I was excited for that."

"Cool," he said and smiled at me, his eyes warm over his plate that still had a considerable amount of food.

"Ponce Inlet is nice, but the pièce de résistance is *definitely* St. Augustine's Lighthouse. That's the one about forty-five minutes north of here." Reaver's voice was rough with sleep from the other bed as he cradled Doll against his chest and smoothed a hand over her back. She was wearing pajamas now, and had answered the door in the long, sweeping oversized tee shirt thing that was clearly a women's night-shirt and not just one of Reaver's tees.

"Nothing beats Short Cliffs," she muttered against his chest.

"Where's that one?" I asked.

"Down south on the inner coastal, near you guys," Reaver said. "But that one we're personally biased in favor of."

"Ah." I nodded.

"Ponce Inlet today then, and then maybe St. Augustine tomorrow?" Lightning asked, looking at his phone and setting his food aside.

"You done with that, bro?" Reaver asked and Lightning nodded. I thought it was a little weird, and gross, but I passed the plate into Reaver's grabby hands as he sat up, Doll making a protesting disgruntled noise at him and cuddling back down into the bed.

A knock fell at the door and I jumped up. "I'll get it."

"It's Galahad and Charity," Lightning told me, but he was already up and pulling his jeans on.

I opened the door and Galahad looked up, half of a buttered English Muffin hanging out of his mouth as he shoved his wallet closed and back into his back pocket. Charity waved over his shoulder.

"Hi, guys, come on in."

"Hey-yo! Nothing! How's it hanging?" Reaver called.

"It's Galahad now. Has been for years," Galahad declared. He went over and clapped hands with Reaver and half pulled him off the bed into a hug.

"I just think Nothing is sexier," Reaver declared and Galahad laughed.

"For a tortured angsty phase that lasted as long as it did, it served me well, but I'm not Nothing anymore. I have everything a guy could want, so..." he looked back at Charity who had dropped onto the end of the bed and she glowed under his smile, which made me smile. Then

I caught Lightning grinning up a storm in my direction and I melted all over again.

"Bad news for you, though, bro," Galahad said, turning to Lightning.

"Aw, yeah? What's that?" Lighting asked.

"It's the flea market in Daytona today," Charity answered.

"Aw, shit! That's right!" Lightning declared.

"Ponce Inlet was supposed to be Sunday's cruise. The Ride to the Light," he said.

"Oh, shit, that's right too, damn!"

"Okay, so we're going to the flea market today?" I asked, perking up.

"Yup," Lightning declared.

"Right on!" Reaver crowed.

"Shower," Doll grunted from where she was hunkered down at his hip in their bed.

"Tactical shower," Galahad said, looking at his watch.

"Copy that, bro. We'll probs see you out there. I'm sure our crew is riding together. You know how these planned runs go." Reaver bounced on the balls of his feet.

Galahad nodded. "We'll see you there, man."

They did that clasping handshake hug thing and Galahad and Charity turned to us and said, "See you guys in a minute." His and Lightning's phone went off in unison.

"Fifteen-minute warning, alright, bet. See you in a bit," Lightning said as he checked his phone.

He had a tee on from bike week of last year and was shaking out his socks before putting them on.

"You bringing your hat?" he asked me, looking up at me. I nodded.

"Sun is beaming down fierce and I have no idea if this flea market is indoor, outdoor, or what to expect," I said and he nodded.

"No, if you weren't, I was going to suggest that very thing. Just hang onto it for the ride over if you can. Don't want you to lose it."

"Oh, don't you worry about that," I said. "I'll lose this hat over my dead body."

He nodded and got up after tying off his last boot.

"Wallet, keys, sunglasses, room key," he muttered, sweeping each item in turn off the TV stand.

"Hold on to this for me in your bag?" he asked and handed me the room key. I opened up my purse which held all my cards and credentials and just had enough room left over for my phone and for my own sunglasses. I slipped it into an open credit card slot.

"Got it," I told him, closing up the purse and patting it.

"Sweet, let's roll. See you guys around today," he shot back to Reaver who looked up from where he was sweetly trying to coax Doll out of bed.

He looked up grinning and said, "Bet on it!"

We waited for the elevator, holding hands, and Lightning asked, "Your phone charged?"

I nodded. "Yes, it's at like ninety-six percent, why?"

"Good," he said. "If we get separated at the flea market, I want to be able to text or call each other."

"Why would we get separated?" I asked and he grinned.

"Bike swap meet is going on at the same time on the same grounds. Girls tend to get bored and break off to check out the regular flea market and then we meet up again."

"Ah." I nodded.

"We usually do this kind of thing, a planned group activity two to three times during the week and then we sort of split off and do our own thing. We usually all just end up meeting up anyway because we all like doing the same things." He laughed and I smiled as we stepped onto the empty elevator which surprised me.

I would have expected some of the girls to come up from downstairs, or even more of our crew or the Sacred Hearts to be waiting to catch it down.

"Hold up!" we heard from outside and lightning fast, Lightning stuck his hand out to catch the closing doors so whoever it was could board.

"Thanks," Zach said breathlessly, boarding with us, his jacket dangling from one hand.

"No problem," Lightning said.

We rode in silence for half a second. I finally broke and said, "Hey, thanks for yesterday," I said.

"For what?" he asked.

"For saying what you saw. I really appreciated it."

"Hey, I would have said something right then when it happened but I wasn't even really sure I'd seen it, you know? It was busy as fuck. When I looked Rocco's way and saw he didn't see it and you were acting like nothing just happened, I almost had myself convinced nothing did. Something like that happens again, never be afraid to speak up to me in the moment, okay?"

"Okay," I said nodding.

"We're a team in that kitchen and serving area." He held out his fist and I bumped it just as the doors whooshed open to Pyro standing right there.

I looked over and met his watery blue-eyed gaze, his eyes glassy with not enough sleep, a heavy hangover, or worse… with whatever he was on.

His brow crushed down in a scowl in my direction and he stalked off toward the lobby doors and out into the lot.

"Man, he's being an asshole," Zach remarked.

"Mm-hm," Lightning grunted unenthusiastically and I looked at him. His jaw was clenched and he was *mad*, I could see it. His green eyes, the best that I could describe them? Glacial.

I didn't shudder, or shiver, but I wanted to. Then he turned those green eyes on me and it was like I was the sun or something. His gaze thawed and his smile was like the sun had just come out from behind the clouds.

"It's gonna be a good day," he said to me like it was a promise. I couldn't help but smile as we stepped off behind Zach to let the small knot of people get on to go up.

"It's always a good day when I'm with you," I told him, throwing my arms around his neck and kissing him soundly.

"Yo, bro? Where is your fuckin' head at?" Galahad called, laughing. When we looked over, he held his cut out from his body. Lightning looked down and turned fire-engine red.

"Got that room key, baby?" he asked as I laughed.

I fished it out for him and he said, "Be right back." He threw open the door to the stairwell.

"Yeah, you better take those stairs!" Marlin boomed and I laughed and shook my head.

How the hell had he forgotten that? Hell, how did I let him? I thought to myself.

15

Lightning…

I hated that I couldn't be sure whether Pyro had been giving my girl a shitty fuckin' look or if it'd honestly been directed at my dumbass for coming down without my colors.

I still couldn't fuckin' believe I'd left 'em hanging in the closet of our room like I was some dumb fuckin' prospect but, you know? Shit happens, and the way Honor's ass filled out her jeans? I had plenty to fuckin' distract me, okay?

The ride over to the Daytona racetrack was painfully fuckin' slow, but that's sort of what you had to expect during bike week, on the first Saturday swap meet and bike show.

The bike show was on the track itself and was pretty overrated if you asked me for the ticket prices they wanted to charge to get in there. The club had pretty much universally decided to fuck the official bike show this year in favor of just hitting the flea market and the biker swap meet happening outside of it.

The plan was to go to the flea market and swap meet as a unit, hang there and kinda disperse and do what anyone wanted to do individually, and then to fuck off on our own or in smaller groups to do lunch or what have you. We'd all sort of meet up at the bar of choice that night.

We didn't have a bar of choice for tonight, though. We had the entire fuckin' week to ride, explore, or do whatever, so ain't none of us pressed. We didn't have to be up each other's ass all the time like citizenry seemed to expect out of us. We just rode as a club to a few things here and there for the pride and pageantry of it, but most of the time, you could just find us doing our own fuckin' things.

Honor and I didn't really have a whole lot of set plans aside from club plans and obligations. We were a little too free spirited for that. There was plenty to do and plenty of our people out doing things, so we'd agreed to just do what sounded good in the moment.

We threaded down the dirt track into the field parking single file once we'd reached the gate, and whew, we were sweating by the time we got to the cover of the trees. The sun was beating down fairly fierce and there wasn't really a breeze today. I was glad Honor had her hat and glad I had mine, the plastic snap back around the handlebar behind the fairing and tucked down to where it wasn't in my way of the gauges.

One of the nice things about bike week was all the motorcycle-only parking and that they didn't make us vie for parking among the cages. We followed the parking attendant's waving hand to the left and crept carefully over the dried grass and the slick clippings they'd left down after they'd mowed the field to make it into parking. *That* part was annoying.

I couldn't tell you how many bikers had gone down because of grass clippings blown into the road.

We parked and some of the guys bitched out loud about that part. Just about as soon as Honor's feet touched the ground after dismounting, Serenity was there wrapping both her arms around Honor's one. She was gleefully saying to her, "Come on! Me and Jussy are going to find the orchid stand!"

"Fuck!" I heard Stoker cry from behind her where he was locking up his saddlebags. "You can have *one!*" he said. "We're on the bike, baby. I can't get a dozen pots of orchids home safe!"

"I bet I could hold one for the ride home," Justice said, sticking out her tongue playfully at Stoker.

"I'll hold one too," my girl pitched in, grinning.

"Plus there's the crash truck," Charity said casually.

"Shit, man, you've enlisted reinforcements!" I called out and a bunch of the guys were laughing.

"She knows she can have whatever her heart desires, but she's gotta figure out how to get it home!" he called, but Serenity, Charity, and Justice were already dragging my girl away in the direction of the garden and outdoor stuff tents that were closer to the low buildings of the regular flea market.

"Hey! Kiss!" I demanded and I went running up, my hat flying off as we finally *did* get a good gust of wind. I ignored it and got my kiss first, Honor holding her hat to her head as she leaned back over Serenity and Justice's arms that they had locked behind her back as they tried to sweep her away.

I gave her three chaste but quick kisses and waved her off with the girls.

"You guys are fuckin' cute as shit," Radar said, and I turned to him and Stoker grinning at me. All I could do was grin back.

"Heard what Pyro pulled," Galahad said, looking after Charity and he turned to me. "I'm behind you."

Stoker nodded and Radar just shook his head as we started strolling toward the bike swap meet. I bent and snatched my hat off the ground and put it back on my head.

"Yeah, I didn't want to ruin everyone's fuckin' vacation dealing with it now," I said. "It can all be dealt with back home."

All three of my brothers nodded in agreement.

"Thanks for that," Stoker said. "You know how violence and bully shit sets Ren off. If she caught wind of it, I'm afraid it might make her nervous, waiting on the other shoe to drop."

Radar glanced back in the direction the girls had gone and said, "With that lot? Ren'll probably know by the end of the day."

Stoker swore. "Right, you're right," he said.

"If it comes up," Radar sniffed, "just tell her on the down low nothing's gonna happen where she's gonna see it. It's nothing to worry about until after we get back to town."

Stoker nodded and said, "You have no idea how anxiety really works, do you?"

Galahad snorted and laughed and Radar grinned.

"Jussy's my woman. I'm afraid PTSD and CPTSD is more my wheelhouse."

"Ah yes, anxiety's never-ending font," Galahad declared.

"Good point," Stoker said as we started hitting the bike-related stuff.

"I'm so damn mad I forgot my colors upstairs, man," I said.

"Why? Happens to the best of us and it ain't no big deal," Radar declared.

I looked up to Cutter, Marlin, Zach, and Pyro walking in a knot up ahead of us by a good distance.

"Doors opened and Pyro was standing there. I *swear* he gave Honor the shittiest goddamn look, but I can't be one hundred percent sure because I was standing there with my dick in my hand with not having my colors on. So it could have been about that, you know?"

"Anyone with you?" Radar asked.

"Zach, actually."

"Want me to ask him?"

I shook my head.

"Nah, I'm just going to let that one go. As it is, just talking about it to you guys, I'm feeling like I'm coming across paranoid and vendetta–ish. Like I'm just out to get him or looking for more shit to pin on him because I'm butthurt."

"Nah." Galahad shook his head and ran a hand back through his dark hair. His had that slick blue highlight when the sun hit it, a natural black, unlike Stoker's long black hair which was almost the fucking absence of light itself from the hair dye he used.

"Pyro's been so shitty, I think he's honestly worked all our last damned nerve raw," Radar said.

"You ain't lying," Stoker grunted.

Radar looked up at him. "What beef you got with him?"

"Nothing as direct as what Lightning has," Stoker said. "But you know how he's been with his shitty remarks and biting commentary on just about fuckin' *everything*?"

Galahad scoffed. "Who hasn't fuckin' noticed or been on the receiving end of that shit lately?"

"Exactly," Stoker said. "It fucks with Ren's head something fierce when he does that shit. Especially when someone tells him to knock it off and he doubles down on it."

"See, now that's a problem," Radar said unhappily. "Why didn't you bring that up before now? You know the captain wouldn't like it if he was upsetting one of the girls."

"Serenity insisted it's her trauma and her trigger, and that she needs to be the one to manage it and not expect Pyro to do it for her. Says it'd be entitled of her. That and she also worries that asking Pyro to quit it will only just make it worse and make her a target. She doesn't want that either."

"Sounds like therapy is working, but she still has a long way to go," Galahad said, his brow furrowing over his black wraparounds.

"That's what she said," Stoker said grinning.

I smiled and nodded. "That's fucking awesome," I told him.

"Yeah," he said. "I'm proud of her."

"I don't know," I said, my mind clicking elsewhere and on a different track. "His attitude is so fucking bad anymore, I don't honestly anticipate getting through bike week without his ass getting handed to him or the club getting into a fight."

"Yeah, I'm worried about that, too," Radar agreed. "Captain's been keeping him on a short leash and is pretty prepared for that eventuality at this point."

"We let him get away with too much," Stoker said and I looked over at him.

"Sometimes I worry about that, too."

"Shit, I'm still surprised y'all let me get away with a bunch of my bullshit for as long as you did," Galahad said with a sigh.

"That was different, man," Radar declared, knocking his shoulder into my left one. I grinned, passing it on and knocking my right shoulder into Galahad's. It was a thing that we did.

"Your wife died," Radar went on. "And you didn't know about the cheating. Pyro's girl was an unfaithful piece of shit *and* she left him right before shit got way more toxic than…" He groped for an analogy. "Than a rattlesnake's bite."

I lifted a shoulder in a shrug and tilted my head. Radar gave me a look that said, *shut up.* I laughed some.

"Shit was already that fuckin' toxic and then some," Atlas said from behind me and I jumped.

"How long you fuckin' been back there, man? You scared the shit out of me!"

The guys had a laugh at my expense. It didn't bother me, though. I snuck up on these boys far more than they got me.

"Oh, hey, I'll be right back," Galahad said. He split off from the rest of us and made a beeline to one of the tents selling the motor oil we most of the time liked to use in our bikes.

"Deep discount," Radar said and we all sort of veered in that direction.

I dropped the conversation we'd been having about Pyro and hoped that Honor was having fun with the girls.

16

Honor…

We didn't make it but just inside the doors of the first building when we stopped.

They had bike week tee shirts of all kinds, in all different designs, and they were *stupid cheap*. Like buy-three-for-less-than-twenty-dollars cheap. You know we all had to stop for not just ourselves but our men as well.

Problem was, I didn't know Lightning's size. I mean, if I had to guess, I would say a large, but maybe he would want an extra-large? I didn't trust myself to make the decision and so I fired off a text.

While I waited for something back, I perused what was on offer and thought about what I knew about him so far and what he liked.

Hope, Faith, and Charity were huddled in a knot, making this look effortless, while Justice, Serenity, and I all did the same thing of rifling through *everything* and carefully putting it back as neatly as possible while we decided what for who. It was a striking difference, but a fun one.

My phone buzzed and I smiled. "I was right," I said triumphantly. "It was a large."

"Yay!" Justice said, laughing.

"Now the hard part," Serenity said. "Choosing!"

"Oh wow, that's more than a little offensive," Justice said, looking over at me as I held up a shirt with a cartoon stereotype "Indian chief" complete with war bonnet and buckskins on a motorcycle that looked a lot like Cutter's.

"I think it's showing pride for Indian Motorcycles," I said wrinkling my nose a bit and turning it around. I called out, "Hope!"

Her jaw dropped at first as she looked like it was gross but then as she registered the bike, it dropped open for a completely different reason. She called out, "If you're alright with it and you wouldn't completely fucking hate looking at it, I kind of want to get it for Cutter as that's almost his exact bike on it. We *never* find Indian motorcycle stuff."

"Size?" I asked her.

"Extra-Large."

I checked the tag on the tee I held and it was just a Large.

"Gray or Black tee?" I called.

"They got orange?" she asked.

"No, but they have red!"

"Black!" she called.

I threw her a black extra-large and she squeaked in glee. "You're sure you're cool with it?" she called and I smiled.

"I really appreciate that you asked, but yeah. It's just a tee shirt and honestly, I have some really fucked-up squirrel-brained stupid shit to sort out between me and my culture."

"How's that?" Faith asked curiously, quickly following up with, "Never mind if you don't want to talk about it. It's honestly none of my business!"

"No, it's fine," I said. "I'm half white on my mother's side, and my dad died when I was young. Like when I was so young that I can't even remember him. Anyway, my mom was… a mess. She let me see my dad's mom and we lived on the rez and all that. But any time she got pissed off at my granny or the aunties for anything, the only thing she could do was rescind access to me. Which she did, a lot, and I do mean often. So I have these big gaping disconnects and holes in my upbringing when it comes to my indigenousness. It's something that I wrestle with, but right now, with the whole big move and connecting with my white ancestors and the new house and the inheritance and the…" I held my hands around my head and made a noise like an explosion as I moved them out like my mind was blowing up, which honestly, it was. Like it was a lot… a lot, a lot.

"Wow, yeah, your trauma Bingo card is a little full," Hope said dryly, and I laughed across the table at her.

"You going to get anything?" Charity asked me and I nodded.

"Probably on my way out. I'm one of those people who has to look at everything before I commit."

"Oh my God, me too!" Serenity cried. "I really like these three, though, so I'm going to do what I don't normally do and take the leap early."

I nodded and she went up the line of tables and stopped at the kiosk to pay.

"We all have our fucked-up traumas," Justice said, looking up after Ren, as I heard everyone call her.

"Yeah?" I mused.

"Oh yeah," Justice said. "My ex-husband tried to kill me," she said. "Then he tried to have me literally assassinated from prison."

"Holy fuck, that sounds like it belongs on one of those true crime shows!"

"Well, it is, except for the whole tried to have me killed from prison part. Nobody knows about that part except me and the club. They handled it and Radar and Atlas kept me safe. But all the stuff that happened leading to him going to prison? I've got both a *Dateline and* a *20/20* episode out there about it and a couple of others have reached out. The money is good and it helps to talk about it, but I hate how much they fuck up the reenactments when it's one of the other shows that does that sort of thing. Anytime there's a new one, we watch it at the club and throw popcorn at the screen when I say they got something wrong. It helps me get through them to watch with everyone."

Serenity had rejoined us. "Yeah, we do the same thing every time there's a documentary about Rachel Alice Morgan," she said to me and I frowned.

"Who's Rachel Alice Morgan? A friend of yours? Why does that sound so familiar?"

"It was my high school, before my boyfriend at the time shot it up and killed a bunch of people," she said succinctly.

"Oh, God! I'm so sorry, you guys!"

"Don't be," Serenity said.

"We not only survived, we're thriving," Justice agreed.

"Oh, are we comparing trauma scars?" Hope asked, coming up. "Oh, Faith wins, hands down."

"I don't know if I even want to know," I said honestly.

"I was sold into a sex trafficking ring and was stuck there for three years," Faith said matter-of-factly. "You have no idea how long it took me to just be able to say that out loud." She turned to her sister, Hope, and said, "And it's not a competition, Hope."

"That's right," Charity declared. "Trauma is trauma."

"Meh, I just served overseas and spent three years looking for Faith."

"I almost got kidnapped by the same sex trafficking ring but Hope and Cutter and the club rode to the rescue. I got to kick the guy in the balls, though," Charity said.

I looked from one to the other to the other of them as they all sort of just looked at me sort of, I don't know, expectantly?

"My mom disappeared when I was like sixteen and my stepfucker kicked me out of the house. I'm pretty sure he killed her, but I don't have any proof."

"Okay, this is just our black humor, but hooray, she's one of us!" Hope said, throwing up her hands and I giggled right along with them.

"Seriously, that's heavy, though," Charity said. "Thanks for sharing with us."

"Like, it seems like *nothing* compared to what a lot of you have been through – for real," I said.

"Pfft!" Hope waved me away on that. "Faith is right. It's not a competition. The point is we've all been through rough shit and we all support each other through trying to deal with it. We like you, Honor. This little trauma dump was the fiery rite of passage. Welcome to the fold!"

I laughed and said, "We're all so weird."

"Hey, that's the way we like it." Serenity grinned.

"Damn straight," Justice said, throwing an arm around Serenity's shoulders.

I nodded. "I'm good with that."

We all burst out laughing. Hope put her arm around me, and the other around Faith and asked, "Where to next?"

The flea market wasn't like anything I'd ever considered a flea market before.

For one, it was located in these low, long, prefab buildings that reminded me almost of the livestock buildings at a State Fair. My mom had taken me to one when I was a kid to see all the animals and 4H and what have you.

The buildings had been networked together into a sprawling maze, and were made of wood beams and skeletal structure, roofed correctly, but had corrugated metal walls.

The nice thing about them was that about every ten feet or so they had a fan mounted from the rafters, blowing down the walkways between stalls and regular signs that said *Misting System is City Water.* So, I guess when it got *really* hot, there was a misting system. That was nice. Today the fans did just fine, though, in cooling the place and I realized pretty quickly that unlike the flea market I'd pictured with desperate people trying to hock their shitty broken stuff, these vendors actually had a lot of really nice things.

One thing I didn't even hesitate or think twice about was stopping at a stall full of phone cases. I bought like three of them for my outdated phone, and only spent like fifteen bucks! I felt pretty good about that score.

"Oookay ladies, we're here!" Faith sang out and there was some excitement out of the others.

"Where's here?" I asked, looking at the green painted door with the windows set in it. This shop was unlike the rest as it was contained and you had to go inside.

"Weed shop," Serenity said with a shrug.

I groaned and said, "I miss getting high every once in a while. I know, I know! Not what you would expect out of an addict's daughter but I'm careful with my alcohol. Weed is a different animal. I won't do anything harder."

Hope snorted. "Honey, you work for a biker bar and I happen to be fucking the owner – ain't nothing stopping you. I guarantee it."

I stopped and thought about it for a second to rounds of tittering laughter and I was like, "Holy shit, you're right. The owners at the truck stop would have cared a lot if they knew I did it, but yeah... everything is different now."

"You're free," Hope said and waved her hands out like some kind of demented Willy Wonka.

"They got edibles?" I asked. "I haven't smoked since my grandma died of lung cancer. Watching her on oxygen?" I shuddered. "No way. I'm very careful with my lungs."

"They have the *best* edibles," Charity said pouting, hooking her arm with mine. "Unfortunately, mine and Galahad's job *very much cares,* and we get popped for randoms. So no more for us but I'll be happy to be your guide."

"Amazing," I declared. "Let's go."

We went inside and the girls knew right what they wanted. I didn't want to spend too much, but the edibles here were stupid cheap. I ended up with a pack of ten gummies that were only like twenty-two bucks and a dose was only a half a gummy. Charity swore that I would really only need a quarter of each one and I'd be good. I didn't have a super high tolerance so essentially forty gummies for twenty-two bucks? Shit, that would last me a *long* time and was an absolute steal.

"This is the only place we've found these ones, so far," Faith said as she tucked her two packs away. "They help me sleep. I don't dream on them which I like *way better* than the fucking pharmaceutical my psych put me on."

"Oh, that Amberverse shit?" Hope asked.

"Eugh, yeah, that shit fucked you up. Zero out of ten, do not recommend."

"Worked great for me, but yeah, Faith had some bad reactions to it and went completely crazy. She started talking in tongues and shit. Scared the hell out of all of us," Serenity said.

"Yeah, we don't touch that anymore," Hope said making a face.

"It was terrifying for them, but I don't remember a thing. Seeing how scared they were and Marlin was though?" Faith shook her head. "Yeah, I don't want to do that again."

We perused a stall where a woman made rings out of old antique silver spoon handles, and matching pendants out of the bowls, if they were detailed too. Charity, Serenity, and I were enamored.

I ended up buying a bracelet made out of a serving spoon handle that had horses and a desert scene that had Shiprock in the background. I was absolutely giddy to find it and had to have it even with its fairly hefty seventy-something dollar price tag.

We were back at the tee shirts, where I had made my selection and was waiting in line when Lightning slipped up to me and put his arm around my waist.

"Hey, baby."

"Hi!" I crowed and put my arms around him in an enthusiastic hug.

"What'd you find?" he asked, looking at the tee shirts, but I had to show him my real treasure in the bracelet. His eyes lit up and he held my hand, peering at my wrist carefully.

"That's Shiprock in the background," I said pointing.

"No shit? This piece was meant for you, baby. Good find!"

I beamed and showed him the two shirts I picked out for him and the one I picked out for me.

"I'm going to take some scissors to this," I said. "Go full 80s rad neckline and sleeveless. Serenity is going to help me."

"Oh, yeah. She's good at the rockstar scissor fashion thing," he said. "You getting along okay with everybody."

"Honor's great," Serenity said behind us, Stoker with her, his arm around her shoulders with a couple tees hanging out of one of his hands.

I smiled at her, and Hope and Faith waved us down from over the table. "Hey, we're meeting up with our boys and getting lunch!" she called.

"Alright." Lighting waved at her, then asked, "Wait, Charity and Galahad going with you?"

"Nah, man," Galahad called from down the table. "Our plans are still good!" Charity waved and beamed from Galahad's side.

"Ooo, plans?" I asked a little excitedly. "What plans?"

"We're gonna find food," Stoker said from behind us.

"Wait, where'd Jussy go?" I asked, looking around.

"Radar and Atlas spirited her away. She's cool," Serenity said and I nodded.

"Sorry I missed saying goodbye," I said.

"You did. She tried. You were pretty absorbed in what you were doing." Serenity grinned and I felt myself blush.

"Well now I feel like an asshole," I declared.

"Don't," Lightning said, taking his arm from my waist and putting it around my shoulder and dragging my temple to his lips. He knocked off my hat which I made a mad grab for and caught before it got to go too far. Luckily, it would have just hit the table full of clean tee shirts and not the dusty concrete floor.

"I just took the asshole crown," he said, laughing as I put it back on my head. We got up to the register and I paid for the shirts. He said, "Aw, thank you, baby! Dressing me all sorts of snazzy already."

I laughed and shook my head and he winked at me. "I've got lunch," he said.

"Deal," I said, agreeing.

"So where are we going?" I asked when we got outside and started the steady walk back to the bikes.

"There's this place up in St. Augustine that Stoker looked up. Some seafood restaurant," Lightning said.

"Oh! Is it Robichauds?" Serenity asked excitedly.

"Yeah, I think that was the name," Lightning said. I have never seen *anyone* get so excited over a place to have dinner but Serenity literally squealed and jumped up and down for literal joy. Like she wrapped her arms around her man and looked like she was ready to cry she was so happy.

"What in the whaaat?" Charity asked.

"Shit, a reaction like that out of Ren only means one thing," Lightning said laughing.

"It's so *haunted!*" Serenity crowed. She laced her fingers together and it was like she was struggling to get herself back under control. I have *never* seen *anyone* explode with such unbridled glee in my life over someplace being *haunted* before.

"Are you sure your last name isn't Addams?" I asked, laughing.

"Right!" Stoker asked. "I've been asking her that practically since the day we fuckin' met!"

We laughed about that and reached the bikes in pretty good time.

"Hey, will the lighthouse still be open by the time we get there?" I asked.

Serenity spazzed once more and I laughed and asked, "Haunted, too?"

"Yes!" she cried.

"We have all week, ladies. Let's not get ahead of ourselves," Galahad said, laughing.

"Okay." Serenity stuck out her bottom lip and pouted slightly, but Galahad did have a point. We didn't want to do it all at once, otherwise what would we have left to do?

Traffic getting to the freeway was a pain in the ass, but once we hit the open highway, things got much nicer.

Robichauds was on a main drag, but there was also an alley behind it that had street parking. It was much more affordable than the lots that were around, especially since the boys could fit all three bikes into a space meant for one car with the way they backed them to the curb so carefully.

"Hey, look." Charity pointed at an old Victorian house and we looked up at the shingle hanging out front.

"Ooooh!" Serenity was transfixed.

I asked, "You wanna?"

"Oh my God, can we?" she exclaimed.

"Can we what?" Galahad asked. and I pointed above our heads. The shingle was for a ghostly walking tour.

Stoker started laughing.

"Fuck yeah, let's do dinner first though. It looked like there was a wait."

"You can buy tickets online," the woman at the podium up on the porch called.

"Thank you!" Serenity called.

"No problem!" she called down.

We went up the street and let ourselves in the back gate to the garden patio of the restaurant, following the roped off path to the hostess stand.

"How many and inside or outside?" she asked.

"Six and whichever comes up first. We aren't picky," Lightning declared.

"It's going to be around a forty-five-minute wait," she said.

"That's fine," he answered.

"What's your phone number?" she asked.

He gave it to her and she said, "You'll get a text when your table is ready. Your entire party must be present to be seated. You must arrive within five minutes of the text, otherwise it will go to the next people on the list."

"Sounds great, thanks!" he said.

We slipped out the gate right by the hostess station to the front side of the block and got out of the crush of people. The benches out front were taken up by mothers and old folks, and we looked up and down the street.

"Wow, there's not much to look at, is there?" Charity asked.

"Looks like there are a couple of shops to poke around in that way. They're close enough, right?" Charity asked.

"Yeah," Galahad said. "Come on."

We went through one boutique with overpriced old lady clothes, but the next shop down? Well, that was a good one! Right up us girls' alley. It had all sorts of handmade soaps and scrubs and even some stuff for the boys in the way of handmade shaving creams and oils.

We killed plenty of time in there smelling everything and even made some purchases. The last one of us was checking out when Lightning got the text from Robichauds.

"Perfect timing!" he crowed and we were back down the street and seated in no time.

Serenity regaled us with all kinds of stories about the history of the building right on up through who it was and how they supposedly haunted the place.

"What about out there in Shiprock?" she asked. "You guys must have all sorts of crazy things out there. Aren't there skinwalkers?"

"Shh!" I hissed and I looked around us.

"We don't say their name. We *never* say what they are out loud," I cautioned.

"Oh, shit," Serenity said. "I'm sorry."

"What should we call them, then?" Stoker asked.

"Anything but that," I said.

"I've heard them called Flesh Pedestrians," Serenity offered meekly.

"Listen, I'll tell you my *one and only* experience with one later, in the light of day. Not right now and definitely not around so many people or at dusk or in the dark." I shuddered. "Even what you just called them is almost too much for me. You do *not* want their attention. Trust me."

"What are they?" Lightning asked, looking over me concerned.

I shook my head.

"They're like a Native American witch from what I know," Charity said. "But I think our curiosity can wait. I mean, look at her, she's shaking."

I was, too, the ice rattling against the inside of my glass as I raised it to take a drink. I swallowed the cool sip I'd taken and said, "Yes, but they traded their humanity to do dark works and the ability to do unnatural things. They're utterly *terrifying*. So, if we could drop that one for right now, that would be great. I mean, they could be literally anyone, could take any shape and you *really* don't want their attention."

"Wow, sounds nuts," Galahad said.

"Like I said, I've seen one and it was the most terrifying thing of my fucking life."

"I'm sorry I brought up a bad memory," Serenity said.

"I appreciate your patience, and like I said, I don't want to be stingy with my story but at the same time – time and place."

"No, I get it. I can wait, but I'd really love to hear it," she said.

"Me, too," Stoker said.

"Me three," Charity echoed, her sapphire eyes alight with curiosity in the flickering candle flame that was at our patio table.

We'd spent long enough at the flea market that it was getting on toward evening by now, the sun getting low, and the patio cast in deepening shadow.

We ordered our food and each got a drink from the bar in addition to our sodas. We were scrolling through our phones looking at the tickets for the ghost tour up the street.

"I mean, we'd have to wait a little bit after getting out of here to do the nine thirty, but if we try to book anything earlier, we'd have to rush our dinner and I'm fixing to enjoy this," Charity said.

"You speak truth," Galahad declared.

"I'm good with nine thirty," Stoker said.

"You good with it, babe?" Lightning asked me.

"Heck yeah! White people ghosts are far less scary," I said.

We all shared a laugh.

"I want to make sure we all get to go together, so I'm just going to get all the tickets and y'all can just pay me for yours if that's cool." Stoker said.

"What's your money app?" I asked.

He gave it to me, made the purchase, told us the total for our tickets, and we all sent him the money individually from our phones or handed him cash out of our pockets according to who had what.

"Thanks, guys," he said, tucking the bills into his wallet and smiling at Serenity who once again seemed so excited she could cry.

"It's like a Goth Disneyland here for you, isn't it?" Lightning asked, laughing.

Ren laughed, leaning into Stoker. I don't think anyone at the table *wasn't* smiling; each of us delighting in her joy.

Dinner was *phenomenal*, the food so very good, the fish perfectly cooked and tender. Nothing dry, nothing over or under done, everything perfectly seasoned and delicious. We even had time and just enough room for dessert and when in Florida…

"The Key Lime pie, please," I said and the guys all cheered.

"Wait, is this your first one?" Lightning asked.

"It is, actually!"

"Hold up, hold up," he said when it hit the table. He pulled up his phone and said, "Smile for me, baby."

"Oh, no!" I cried, putting up my hands.

"Oh, come on!" the rest of the table chimed in. Blushing and giggling, I smiled for him, my first piece of Key Lime pie in front of me, and I let him take my picture.

He stared at his phone, softly smiling like he'd captured pure magic on the screen and I swear my heart melted a little bit.

"Excuse me! Can you take our picture?" Charity asked a waiter going by.

"Sure!" She took Char's phone and said, "Everyone say 'money!'"

"Money!" we all chorused and I liked that. It was way better than "cheese" but still had that 'ee' sound at the end to get the desired effect.

Charity sent the pictures she took to all of us, and I smiled at my phone and maybe got just a touch emotional.

I couldn't help but briefly think that this was probably the greatest blessing my grandparents I had never met had bestowed upon me out of everything they left behind for me. They put me in the path of Lightning, and some very special and wonderful friends. More friends than I had ever had in my life.

Wow.

17

Lightning...

She looked a little emotional staring at the group shot on her phone that I had just sent to her when I'd gotten it from Galahad. She rallied pretty quickly from wherever she'd gone, though, and took a bite of her Key Lime pie and the absolute sublimity of her expression was worth another snap, which I took without warning or any preamble making her nearly choke on the graham cracker crust as she started to giggle.

"Sorry," I said. "Your face, though."

"It's really good!" she said with her mouth full of the creamy citrus dessert.

We finished or dessert, some of us having a cup of coffee to keep us up and running and stave off the food coma that wanted to set in. I paid for mine and Honor's dinner and then we slipped back out to the alley road behind the restaurant and up the street toward the old house and where our bikes sat out front.

"This ought to be good," Galahad said and we went up onto the porch and inside to see what the gift shop held. There wasn't much worth anything in there, sadly enough – but it looked like Serenity came away with a book.

We went back out front since the little house was definitely crowded and stashed our purchases from the bath shop and the gift shop in the saddlebags of the bikes, making sure everything was secure as we waited for our tour guide to come out.

There were the six of us on the tour, plus two other couples for a total of ten. Our tour guide introduced himself as Orion and we struck out pretty much right away in the direction of the lit up old Spanish fort two streets away and catty corner from us.

He led us around the side and down by the water all the while telling us the macabre tale of two ill-fated Spanish lovers who had supposedly been walled up and forgotten oubliette style into the fort by the woman's jealous and angry husband.

The guys sounded like a douche. I thought it was interesting, though, that there were actual historical records of when the woman and the young soldier or maybe it was an officer guy, had gone missing. Felt kind of bad everyone bought the Spanish captain's line of bullshit about not knowing where boy-o doing his wife went but that his wife had sailed home to see her family.

Like, no one questioned it, and meanwhile, here's this couple walled up screaming where no one could hear them and dying this horrible death of thirst or starvation while they were shackled to a wall down there.

I guess it was a good long while before they were found, too. Well after the original perpetrator of their murder was dead and gone and well after the British had taken over the old coquina stone fortress.

He had us on the ground outside the fort, around to the water side and showed us where a cannonball was stuck in the crumbling rock and then took us over to a wall where he shone his flashlight. It was the wall that they'd lined prisoners against before they met the firing squad for execution and it was pitted still all these years later with musket balls and bullets from a bygone era.

Some super cool stuff.

We went up and around listening to the tour guide repeatedly warn us to watch our step and shit when it happened.

"Oh! Ugh, oh!" came from behind me a bunch of horrified gasps and sucking in of breaths as one of the guys from the other two couples tried to use a set of stairs that weren't there. He took an eight foot or better drop into what had used to be the fort's moat which was just mowed grass now.

"It's alright, I'm okay!" he called as Galahad and one of his buddies hoisted him up. He barely put one foot down before it shot right back up in the air, and yeah – he was not fine. I mean I'd heard him hit even if I didn't see it and he went down *hard.*

"I'm a medic. Sit down," Charity ordered. Galahad held a flashlight for her as the guy, a gangly balding fellow, put his ankle up on top of her thigh for her to have a look.

"Man, you're done," she said. "You're already swelling this bad and bruising? This is seriously likely broken. You need an x-ray, bad."

"No, I'm fine," he tried to argue.

"We're the trained paramedics, and we're saying you're not fine. You're done," Galahad declared. "You guys go on. We're going to help this guy out in getting back to their car," Galahad declared.

"Shit," the guy muttered. "Thank you," he said, admitting defeat and wincing. Yeah, that jolt of adrenaline wasn't even keeping the pain at bay – he was really fucking hurt.

"Alright guys," I said, knowing better than to argue.

The tour guide was sort of poleaxed as we all watched the girlfriend fuss behind him while Galahad and the male half of the other couple got on either side of him to help him along. Charity rolled her eyes and waved at us and off they went.

"I have never in like the four years I've run this tour, had anybody do that," he said.

We sort of half huffed a laugh and Stoker said, "Buddy, we've seen it all."

"Just about," I agreed.

Things went from bad to a little bit worse through the next story when he talked all about how the Spanish fucked over the local indigenous tribes and how a white doctor, who was supposedly the leader of said tribe's friend, took the dude's head and kept it in a jar after he died as some sort of specimen of the 'wild man' or whatever.

You could see the silent heartbreak in Honor's eyes as Orion pointed out the narrow windows of the fort and said visitors on the tour sometimes caught photographs of a severed floating head in them at night.

There was more seriously heinous stuff about warriors from tribes starving themselves to fit through the windows to try to escape only to break bones and shit in the fall and to be hauled back in to be executed, or worse, just left to die of their injuries real slow.

"You alright?" I asked Honor when we moved on to the next stop.

She just sort of silently shrugged. I stopped her and wrapped her up in my arms and said, "I'm sorry."

"Don't be," she murmured. "You didn't do anything. It's just… history," she finished lamely and I sighed.

Yeah, it was history… but man how we took for granted being on the side of the oppressors' vs. the oppressed, man. For a lot of us, it was just a grim and gruesome piece of the past to look at in fascination. For others it was like an axe wound to the chest leaving them bleeding out hundreds of years of rape, murder, and abuse that'd been endured by their ancestors and in a lot of cases, were still endured today. Like the more things changed, the more they stayed the damn same, man.

We broke apart and she smiled and said, "Thanks, I needed that hug after hearing all that."

"You're welcome," I said and we caught up pretty quickly.

"Everything alright?" Orion asked.

"Yeah, just a little overwhelming hearing stuff like that when you're part of the people that've received that kind of treatment and still do today," I said.

"Oh…"

That's all he managed to say, but at least he had the grace to look a little embarrassed. Serenity took Honor's hand and gave it a squeeze, looking at her with empathy and Honor gave a watery smile back.

"Well, I can promise there are no more indigenous ghost stories beyond this point," Orion said as we walked.

Honor smiled and nodded. "Thanks."

I could appreciate his trying too and so we carried on.

She did a pretty good job of shaking off the horrors from the fort and by the time we reached the next stop outside the perimeter of some old cemetery gates, you could barely tell anything had shaken her at all.

I got a text from Galahad that dude really had busted his ankle and was on his way to the hospital, and that he and Charity had gotten refunded for their ticket prices. Since they had been refunded, they said they were going to head back south and meet up with some of the others at the Broken Wheel or Iron Steed, they hadn't decided which yet, and they'd see us around.

I let the group know what was up and Stoker had gotten the same text as it was in the group text chat – which of course started blowing up but we just silenced our phones and ignored it.

The rest of the tour was pretty great. It had grave robbing, and angry old women, and an exploding corpse and touched on yet more bullshit colonizing with that last story. Honor patiently explained that Cuba was well within their rights to want their dead bishop back and that because at the time, he was buried, they performed burials quickly. Just because of the heat and the smell didn't make it alright that Americans buried a Cuban national in American soil against the wishes of his government and his family.

Orion just didn't seem to get it, and Serenity was getting irritated with him to the point she started correcting him on certain points about some of his stories. I had to laugh because what the hell? She already knew them! Stoker grinned behind her back and had this look of pride on his face about how smart and fantastic his woman was. I had to agree.

Even Honor was smiling at her antics. As Orion bid us a curt goodnight at the end of the tour and went on up the porch and into the house, we all fell out laughing.

"And that's on karma and having the night you deserve," Serenity said like she was quite proud of herself.

"Do you think he took notes or…?" Honor asked.

Serenity grinned. "We should send someone else from the club on one of his tours later this week and find out."

Stoker laughed like hell and I said, "I think he's rubbing off on you."

"We're rubbing off on each other," he said. He looked so happy he could die if he wasn't already some kind of dead already – I swear to God the motherfucker was legit some kind of vampire, and not just because of his whole goth metal shtick. I'd known dude for almost ten years and while I aged, he and Ren just seemed to stay the same.

"What 'cha feeling?" I asked my woman and she stifled a yawn.

"Is it bad I feel like a pumpkin?" she asked.

"Not at all. We still got a whole seven more days to go. We don't ride home until next Sunday."

"How does bike week go from a Friday all the way to a following Sunday and yet it's still only called 'bike week?'" Serenity asked.

"Don't think too hard about it, baby," Stoker said and she gave him a little shove.

We rode back to Ormond Beach and Stoker and Serenity split off from us, turning into the Iron Steed while I took Honor and myself on through to our hotel.

She was practically swaying on her feet, her modest bags of shopping from St. Augustine and the flea market earlier that day clutched in one hand.

We were alone in the room, but I could tell she was tired enough that there shouldn't be any bumping uglies, and truth of it? I was just in the mood to lie with her and hold her and soak up the cuddles. I mean, I was kind of a cuddle slut and always had been so… yeah.

We got into bed and she cuddled into my side and we just sort of spoke softly in the dark. About all sorts of things, really, but mostly I got to learn about her culture and I got to learn from her with a few well-placed questions, how I could have better supported her out there and maybe changed some of the narrative around Chief Osceola. We both didn't really know anything about him, and we decided that if we could find one, we'd pick up a history book about him to read together as there had to be quite a bit to him if holding him captive for that long was any indication. Hell, for what he had happen after his death to be what it was, he had to be a pretty righteous dude.

We fell asleep late into the evening and unlike the night before, we got to sleep soundly, only waking late into the next morning when Reaver and Doll came in.

"Where the fuck you been?" I grated and Doll smiled tiredly.

"Adult fun with Trigger and Ashton," she answered.

"Ah." I nodded.

"We're gonna crash for a bit," Reaver said.

"We're going to get up, grab a shower, and get out of your way," I told them. "We have some adventures to take today."

"Aw yeah? Have fun!" Doll declared.

The best part of my morning was getting to shower with my lady and kissing every inch of her in that shower.

It was a good start to the day, but we hit our first snag when we got downstairs.

"Aw, we missed breakfast," she said and sounded genuinely disappointed.

"Have no fear," I said and got out my phone. It was a Monday morning but there had to be someplace around here that was serving breakfast or brunch.

"I got something," I said after a minute, because honestly fuck the chain places. We were on vacation. I wanted something good that you just couldn't get anywhere else. "Let's go," I said and I took her hand and towed her out into the daylight.

We did brunch and I was glad the place I picked was a good one. Yeah, sure, a free hotel breakfast was better for the wallet, but you win some and you lose some and this place was both good and not terribly unreasonable.

We talked about what we wanted to try and do that day, and she said light house, which didn't surprise me in the slightest. I ruled out Ponce Inlet, because we had that scheduled for the ride to the light with the rest of the crew for Wednesday, so back to St. Augustine it was.

We ran into Stoker and Serenity again, headed the same way on one of the surface streets, and just naturally fell in with them at one of the stoplights. I figured out we were both headed to the lighthouse and stuck together for it.

The gift shop was one that you went into *before* you went out to the lighthouse to climb it, and Stoker and I paid for ours and our girls' wrist bands to go up.

Honor squealed excitedly and held up a biography on Osceola, and I gave her two thumbs up.

"Awesome!" I told her and the gift shop worker gave us the pro-tip to wait until we came back down to make any purchases.

Honor nodded and put the book back where she found it and told Ren there were several books about the ghosts of St. Augustine.

"I have a feeling after we do this, tomorrow is going to be spent on the beach, reading," Serenity said.

"Oh, that actually sounds fabulous," Honor declared and Stoker and I shot looks at each other.

We'd just been talking about maybe heading back to the racetrack to check out some bike drag races they had planned. This sounded like the perfect escape route to have some dude time without the girls feeling left out at all – but if they wanted to go with us, they were perfectly fucking welcome to, too.

The climb to the top of the lighthouse was brutal, even with all of us in pretty decent shape we had to stop and catch our breaths at certain landings and my calves fucking *burned* from the climb. Still, we all made it, a little sweaty and a little noodle-limbed from the waist down, but we made it.

The view and the breeze from up here was fucking worth it, though. I took pictures of all of us and snuggled in close with Honor, snapping selfies with the bright red paint of the top of the light behind us and out over that endless view.

"Wonder what's going on down there." Stoker pointed to treetops way down below us a slight way out from the lighthouse.

"Oh, that's the Gator Farm," the lighthouse volunteer cut in.

"Really? Is all that white birds?" Honor asked, shading her eyes with her hand, even with her aviators on.

"Yeah," the volunteer offered eagerly. He wore wraparound sunglasses under one of those fisherman hats with one of those neck flaps to protect the back of his neck. The cloth catching and ruffling in the breeze. He tugged at the cuff of his long sleeve moisture wicking material shirt over his cargo shorts and sandals, and I tried not to grin.

He was dressed like a quintessential boomer around these parts but he had to be Gen X. I just found it kind of funny.

"When the alligator farm went in down there, they sort of created this accidental rookery," he said going into lecture mode and you could tell he was enthusiastic about the topic.

"What's a rookery?" Stoker asked, and I was glad he did, because I was unfamiliar with the word, too.

"It's where birds group together with their nests and raise their young," Serenity said.

"Ah." Stoker nodded, and that was one of the things I appreciated about his girl. She never made you feel dumb for not knowing something she just filled in the information and moved right the fuck on. It was outstanding.

"Exactly right," the volunteer said. "You see, the birds feel safe building their nests above the gators because the raccoons and the like won't go near them and thus the trees are safe to make their nests and raise their babies."

"I seriously want to go," Honor said, staring down at the white birds far below us. "It sounds so cool. I've been in Florida I don't know how long now, and I still haven't seen a gator."

"What?" I asked and leaned out from her to take her in.

"True story," she said.

"I saw one just on Saturday," Serenity said. "Slipped from the shore right down into the canal outside town as we were headed to the Iron Steed."

"You mean a wild one?" Honor asked excitedly.

"Yeah, you don't see them all that often, but they're out there," Stoker said.

"Lucky," Honor declared and I was pretty much decided.

"You guys down?" I asked Stoker and Serenity.

"Heck yeah," Stoker said. "Let's do it."

"Rock on," I said.

We headed back down after that, and let me tell you, going down?

Much easier than going up. We hit the gift shop and Honor grabbed that book on Osceola, some of their discounted drinkware with the lighthouse etched on it, and a fridge magnet or two before we left.

"You gonna get those home okay, you think?" I asked her as we stowed them on the bike. "They didn't wrap them very well."

"Oh yeah," she assured me. "I brought a lot of lightweight stuff to wear and still had room in my backpack – I knew I was going to want to bring some things back with me. I confess, I am a bit of a whore for a good gift shop and now that I'm an adult, I can have whatever knick-knacks I want.

"You couldn't before?" I asked, sensing there was something there.

She shook her head. "Mom wasn't always amenable to buying them. Most of the time she just plain couldn't afford them and, well, Ramone, my stepdad, he had a habit of breaking shit when he got into a rage before he started in on us."

"Piece of shit," Stoker muttered before I could.

"Yeah," she said a little unhappily.

"Did you get everything you wanted?" I asked her.

"Yeah," she said with a smile, but I knew it was a lie. She'd been looking at the miniatures of the lighthouse and I sniffed.

"Be right back," I said and I ran back inside and got one of the middle-sized ones. It was only $14.99. I went back out and handed it to her.

"A tradition is born," I said. "If they've got 'em, we get 'em. You got all kinds of shelves in that house, time to start filling them with memories," I told her.

She looked so happy she could cry. I hooked a hand behind her head and pulled her mouth to mine over the bike and got to work stowing the new purchase in one of my saddle bags.

I didn't care how we would do it, but we would get it all back to Ft. Royal if I had to stop at a fucking post office and mail some shit ahead of us.

Actually, that wasn't a half bad idea, there.

18

Honor...

We spent pretty much the rest of the day at the Gator Farm in St. Augustine. We decided on the Iron Steed for beers and some dinner before we headed back. Just before we got to the driveway turnoff into the Iron Steed, Lightning and Stoker pulled over.

"No colors allowed at this place," Lightning explained and he and Stoker stripped off their club vests and stowed them in their bikes, carefully locking and securing them against theft or harm.

Holy *wow!* I thought as we turned into the Iron Steed. I hadn't seen anything like it before. It was like a legitimate biker bar, only on steroids!

You rode directly under these raised boardwalk deck things and parked quite literally *in* the bar.

Everything was pretty much outdoors except for the gift shop, which *yay* for them having one of those.

The ground level was a wide-open space for bikes, with a stage at the back, and I do mean a pretty big stage, where live music was being played.

To the left near the entrance was the line for food under cover, and a kitchen working in full swing and whatever they had on offer? It smelled delicious. Next to it, as you headed toward the stage was a sort of set back booth kiosk thing boasting real Montana silver jewelry, which I wanted to have a look there.

Past that, I didn't see much, but then there was some red-and-white circus tent round build thing tucked back in the corner, then the stage and as I swung my gaze, there was another food stand thing and then a nook with patches and a guy waiting to sew them on for you if you needed with several machines for doing so. Past him was a bar, and then there was a gift shop.

We went for the food first and got steak tips and gravy with mushrooms over a bed of smashed potatoes. Then we headed upstairs to where the deck was. All throughout this place was like *seven* different bars and every few feet up here were these trash chutes that went to trash cans down below.

It was fascinating!

"Hey!" Hope hollered from a stretch of table space that was built along the railing. There were stools all along it too, and it overlooked the stage and the bikes parked haphazardly down below.

Several of the other Kraken and some Sacred Hearts were standing nearby with beers in their hands pointing and talking about some of the bikes down below.

"You girls grab a seat, what do you want to drink?" Lightning handed me his food and licked some gravy off his thumb.

"Just a beer," I said.

"Fruity and girly," Serenity said without any preamble or shame. Stoker kissed her, a quick press of lips and Lightning winked at me.

"Coming right up," he said and he and Stoker joined the short line at the bar closest to us.

We went over and joined Hope, Faith, Charity, Jussy, and some of the girls from the SHMC. I recognized Everett, but not the tattooed woman next – no wait, I remembered now, that was Mali, and then there was Sunshine and Doll, who I hadn't seen before and a dark-haired woman that I didn't have a name for yet.

"I'm Hayley," she introduced herself as I took a seat beside her.

"Hi, I'm Honor," I said.

"Where you been all day?" Hope asked us.

I let Serenity talk, so I could eat. I was *starving.*

She was chattering excitedly about the days adventures and was saying, "God, I am going to feel that lighthouse tomorrow," when I chimed in, "You and me both, sister."

There was some laughter and Charity said, "You know what'll help with that?"

I was drawing a blank and said, "I'm having a stupid, you're going to have to walk me through it like I'm five."

She laughed and said, "Some of those edibles we scored at the flea market."

"Ohhhh yeah," I said.

"Wait, you got the good shit?" Reaver asked whipping around. "Some of the HHC shit?"

"Yeah," I said nodding and he pouted.

"Awww, by the time we got there they were sold out! I wanted to try one of those!" he looked crestfallen, like someone had just kicked his favorite puppy and he was still a kid helpless to do anything about it.

"Well it's a good thing you got a benevolent roomie who believes that sharing is caring," I said.

"Yay!" he cried and spun around on his bar stool almost falling off because they were the sturdy square metal kind that were just what they were, no swivel mechanism to them.

"What's he all excited about?" Lightning asked, returning with my beer. I handed him is food after taking it and setting it by mine and he set his beer aside by mine to start eating.

"Honor is most honorable and willing to share some of her gummies she scored yesterday that I couldn't. They were sold out when I got there."

"Ah," Lightning said knowingly, "The early bird catches the worm." He winked at Reaver who stuck his tongue out at him and we all had to laugh. How this grown ass man could look so little boy cute doing that shit was beyond me.

"What're we doing?" I heard behind me and jumped slightly. Pyro put his hands on my shoulders and I wrinkled my nose subtly at Lightning.

"Nothing man, just talking about going back to the hotel and capping off the night with a little edible consumption," Lightning said.

"Alright!" Pyro said. "Who's sharing."

Hope rolled her eyes, "I am," she said and I shot her a grateful look that I knew Pyro couldn't see because he was behind me.

"Hey, man. Could you not?" Lighting said and Pyro leaned down and squeezing my shoulders almost painfully hard said, "I'm not bothering you, am I Honor?"

"Actually, yes," I told him. "I'm trying to eat and that's pretty uncomfortable, would you mind?"

The glint in Hope, Faith, and Charity's eyes was one that practically *shouted* their pride. Justice was pointedly looking anywhere but at Pyro, and Serenity was trying to make herself small too, but she kept giving me furtive glances like she was glad I'd spoken up, too.

"You heard the lady, my friend," I heard behind Pyro and I craned my neck back as his hands wobbled on my shoulders because Cutter had clapped his hands on Pyro's and was shaking him forward and back.

Pyro took his hands off me, "Didn't mean anything by it," he declared but his blue eyes were giving me a freaking death glare.

"I'm sure you didn't, bud, but let the lady eat," Cutter said, winking at me over Pyro's head. A gesture that was speaking volumes without saying a word just how *over* Pyro's bullshit he was.

"We're gonna eat, have a beer, and check out the gift shop downstairs and probably head out. You guys come find us when you're ready to hit the beach," Lightning said and I was grateful he was going to get us away from Pyro but that certainly wouldn't stop him from crashing our little beach get together we had planned.

Fucking jackass.

I almost felt sorry for him. Cutter had him aside from everyone, hands still digging into his shoulders as he spoke low into Pyro's ear. Pyro turned and shot me a dirty look like his getting a talking to was somehow *my* fault and I glanced to Lighting whose jaw was tightening, a muscle in it ticking.

"You saw the sign, bro," Stoker said without looking at him, and I realized that the anger was radiating off of Lightning like heat from a summer sidewalk and just by standing near Stoker, Stoker had picked up on it.

I didn't say a word, but we had seen the sign when we'd rolled in:

No Club Colors

No Weapons

No Attitudes

No Dogs

I think Stoker was warning Lightning not to get into number three on that list. Lightning's green eyes met mine and I let my eyes tell him, *he's right*. He smiled at me, and my heart melted a little and I swear I felt my panties vaporize. I raised an eyebrow and hoped he picked up on my subtle hint that *damn* I needed him between my thighs before long and he raised both of his eyebrows back.

I winked and he said, "So yeah, finish your food and we'll check out the gift shop and get on out of here, how's that sound?"

"Like she's getting laid, the lucky bitch," Hope said with a wry grin and I saw Cutter poke his head up like a meerkat as it swiveled in Hope's direction and he homed in on her with laser precise focus.

"We'll ride back with you," he said promptly and our whole section busted up laughing.

That was good.

We checked out the gift shop, I bought another fridge magnet like I had at the Lighthouse thinking it would be fun to cover the whole thing in magnets from placed I've been to. We picked up a couple of tees with the Iron Steed emblazoned on them, and I got a shot glass to make drinks with for the glassware I'd picked up at the lighthouse, too.

We took off, Cutter as good as his word and riding with us back to the hotel.

We carried our things upstairs with us so I could pack them later but they were quickly forgotten with the things I purchased yesterday on the TV stand dresser thing as Lightning swept me into his arms and kissed me passionately.

My brain officially checked out, and I let my body do the talking at that point.

God his hands on my skin felt so good!

We peeled each other out of our clothes and fell onto the bed, but this time *I* was eager to drive. I took him into my mouth and he let out this feral cry that was both surprised and eager as I took him to the back of my throat.

I worked him in and out of my mouth and sucked him until my jaw ached from it and he just stared at me, eyes heavy-lidded with lust, hands gripping the sheets and hips bucking every time my tongue teased the places he liked.

I took copious amounts of mental notes on what spots sent him haywire and made sure to work him in such a way that I kept him on that fine, fine, edge without tipping him into satisfaction.

I wanted to see how long he would take it before he couldn't take it anymore, and the answer to that was longer than I expected but not as long as you'd think.

"Oh, fuck!" he cried, his hand working at the back of me, teasing between my pussy lips and rubbing my wetness up over my asshole in this tantalizing way I'd never experienced before.

"Stop, stop! I'm begging you! I need into that sweet tight pussy now, right now," he said rushing to get the words out, his desperation clear in his tone.

"Mmm." I giggled slightly, but it was deeper than that. The sound sultry and moaning, and barely tinged with amusement. A decadent and dark sound that I could hardly believe had come out of me.

He bodily threw me about in this sexy as fuck way, pressing my face to the bed as he got up behind me.

"Fuck," he swore and slapped my ass. I yipped and jumped and he said roughly, "Don't you dare fucking move while I get this condom on."

I nodded and closed my eyes, listening to him get ready for me and I swear to fuck that was some of the hottest sounds, the crinkle of the wrapper, the sound of the latex against his cock and the friction of his hand as he rolled it down and fit it snug to his base.

He knelt up, walking on his knees just a little awkwardly to position himself behind me.

"You're so cute, like a baby gira – ah!"

I threw my head back into his waiting hand that grabbed a fistful of my hair as he thrust all the way into me to the hilt.

"Fuck yes, the way you arch your back for me, that cobra spread of your hips," his other hand crashed down on my ass cheek on the other side and I cried out and clenched.

"Ooo, the things this pussy does to me," he growled and he set a rough pace that he slowly increased, working me up to taking each and every punishing stroke the way he liked to give it in the moment.

Oh, it felt so good. So very fucking dirty, so hot and so goddamn delightful. It seemed we were both in tune, both somehow in the mood for it, as I begged him, "Harder! Oh, God! Faster!"

He delivered, and demanded of me, "Tighten up that pussy for me baby," for which I obliged him.

I worked myself tighter, clenching up my pelvic floor for all I was worth, thrusting and wiggling my hips back to meet his every forward stroke until he was forced to relinquish the delicious stinging hold on my hair in favor of gripping my hips.

We fucked like animals, and yet he fucked me with *care*, checking on me any time I made a noise that sounded too much like pain over pleasure.

"You good?" he'd ask, smoothing a hand over my ass and my lower back.

"Yes!" I cried back.

"Touch that clit, baby. I want you to come and I'm not going to last much longer."

His voice was strained, and I knew he was telling the truth. My face pressed to the covers, I reached between my body and the mattress to touch my clit and he kept up the perfect pace, running over that spot inside me over and over and I was getting close, so very close, so maddeningly close, and then he did it, he drove deep but put this back-

and-forth wiggle into his hips swishing his cock back and forth inside me over that fucking *spot* and the sweet torture from both within and without sent my synapses firing, like lightning forking through the clouds as this devastatingly sweet orgasm hit me, my pussy tightening and rippling around him making him shout, as we both came crashing down together.

I came back from wherever my consciousness had been dragged to, pressed flat to the bed, Lightning's weight on top of me, his cock throbbing just inside my pussy which twitched in counterpoint to every twitch his body made. I could feel his cock softening inside of me, and I squeezed down cruelly, Lightning sucking in a sharp breath, his whole body spasming atop mine.

"Oh, that's so not fair," he groaned as I did it to him again.

"Hmmm," I hummed in satiated satisfaction.

"Fuck the things you do to me, woman," he murmured against my shoulder after pushing himself up slightly off of me. His cock slipped out of me and I shuddered, the sensation reaching up my back to stop where his soft lips pressed against my skin and then washing back the other way in a tingling echo.

"Goddamn that's good," I whispered and I heard him chuckle.

"Don't you move," he said. "I'll be right back."

"Oh, I'm not going anywhere," I said with a sultry laugh. "Not after the lighthouse and a fuck that good."

"Good girl," he said with a grin and I laughed, my pussy giving a delicious little thrilling throb at the words that were so fucking hot, you have no idea.

He cleaned us both up and got into the black bag from the flea market that held the edibles.

"How much on these?" he asked.

"You're supposed to cut them in half," I said, "but Charity said quarters will more than do you.

"You want a half or a quarter?" he asked.

"Mmm, gimme a half, I'm feeling adventurous," I said.

He grinned and took some out of the pack using a knife to cut them up for me and he came over with a long piece that was a half of one of the big squares.

"You know you better hope they get some more of this shit in this week, this pack will more than likely get gone if you take it down to the beach. I pulled on my bikini bottoms and raised an eyebrow nodding just as the door clicked. My eyed went wide and I doubled timed getting the bottoms up my legs while Lightning, with a wicked grin, just stood there naked.

"Oh! Shit!" Reaver howled from the door. "There was no Do Not Disturb out there, my guy!"

Lightning turned to face the door and *I* howled with laughter as he did the fucking helicopter with his dick at the doorway to a bunch of masculine shouts out in the hallway.

The room door slammed shut and Lightning fell onto the bed laughing with me.

We pretty much got dressed the rest of the way in a big hurry after that, Lightning munching down a half an edible while I went to get the door. Reaver and Doll were standing outside patiently waiting and both grinned at me.

"Lightning – 1, Reaver – 0," I declared.

Reaver tipped up his chin, looking down at me with a feral grin and declared, "Challenge accepted!"

"Did you just get me into a practical joke slash prank war with Reaver?" Lighting asked.

"Enforcer v. enforcer," Reaver said. "I like it!"

"You have no idea what you've done," Doll said, rolling her eyes and sitting on the end of her and Reaver's bed.

I said, "Half or a quarter of one of these? And I think we'll get through it."

She smiled and said, "Are they strong?" I shrugged. "Charity says they are, she said a quarter will more than do you. I just took the package recommendation which is half. You can wait if you want and I'll let you know."

"Nah," she said. "I trust Charity, give me a quarter."

"Can I have a whole one?" Reaver asked, grinning. "I got a tolerance."

"Sure," I said.

"Yippee!" he cried in a falsetto and it made him sound like a maniac.

"Just never make that sound again," I said laughing.

"No promises," he said scarfing down the green jelly Lightning handed him. "Ooo, watermelon! I expected that to be lime."

"Thank you," Doll said and took the quarter orange one that Lightning handed her.

"Cool, now we don't have to bring the pack down," he said.

"Yeah, that would be *gone* if you did that," Reaver affirmed.

"Want us to wait or you want us to see you down there?" Lighting asked.

"Motherfucker, you can wait!" Reaver said dropping his pants and helicoptering Lightning back.

"Oh, God!" I slapped my hands over my eyes and giggled like a ninny.

"Oh, shit, I think that shit's working fast," Reaver said grinning, toeing off his boots and stripping off his pants.

"I only just took it!" I said shaking my head.

"Maybe you're just that funny, darling," Doll said winking.

"Fuck yeah!" Reaver crowed.

We went downstairs with our beach towels and found a place in the sand to lay them out and take a seat, leaning back on our hands.

The sun was going down and the dusk was rising in that had to see in half-light that told me I was going to need glasses or contacts in my future.

"Man," Reaver complained. "Wish we were on the other coast."

"Why?" I asked.

"The green flash," Doll said.

"What's that?" I asked, brow wrinkling in confusion. "I've never heard of it."

I got an explanation about sunsets, light refraction, and the curvature of the earth and how it all came together in that one perfect shining moment that was the green flash and suddenly… "I can't wait to get home and see it, now."

"Promise, first night you have off from The Plank we'll sit down at the beach with a six-pack and watch for it," Lightning said and I smiled.

"I love the sound of that," I said.

More people found their way down to the beach including Cutter and Hope, a fire got started, even though I didn't know if they allowed them here, and oh, boy – did that edible start to take effect. It started with that full body relaxation sensation I would get with a good indica, but then the pleasant sativa mind high started to filter in.

Before I knew it, somehow a whole *couch* got brought down to the beach from somewhere and since this was my idea, I got put on it with Lightning, my legs across Doll and my feet in Reaver's lap. We were laughing and joking, Reaver rubbing my feet when a phone started buzzing and Doll pulled hers out of her bikini top under her beach coverup.

She made a disgruntled noise and rolled her eyes and rejected the call, turning off her phone and putting it back.

"Your mom?" Reaver asked.

"You know it," she replied with a sigh.

I got it, I mean I did, but the words were out of my mouth before I could stop them, the weed opening me up and making me juuust a little too honest.

"Man, I would give anything to talk to my mom again," I said.

"Oh, I'm sorry… did she die?" Doll asked.

Suddenly a lot of eyes from around the fire were on me. I shifted a bit uncomfortably with all the scrutiny.

"Not exactly," I said. "She, uh, she disappeared when I was sixteen, no one has seen or heard from her since so I just kind of have to assume by now that yeah… she died."

"Oh, my God! That's awful!" Faith exclaimed from nearby.

"My stepfucker kicked me out right after and I finished high school pretty much homeless bouncing from one tribal auntie's house to another just to finish and graduate without tipping off the school that anything was wrong. Sort of narrowly dodged the foster care system with their help so it was hard, but I guess the hardest part is honestly that I'll never know, you know?" I sighed and turned my head in Lightning's lap when he smoothed some of my hair back from my face.

He looked down at me with such love in his face it nearly brought tears to my eyes.

"How bad do you want answers?" Reaver asked quietly from the opposite end of the couch and I tipped my chin to my chest to look at him. He'd gone as still as a rattlesnake trying not to be noticed, the bonfire's flames suddenly flickering like the flames of hell in his icy blue eyes which had gone predatory as fuck.

Like a switch had been flipped.

"Be very careful what you say next, sweetheart," Cutter said from across the fire. "Whatever comes out of your mouth next will never get to be unsaid. You don't get to change your mind when he gets to looking like that."

I looked to Doll who had gone very still and was staring into the fire, too, but she didn't look anything like Reaver. She looked like a scared rabbit, frozen with fear, knowing that there was a rattlesnake just right there and she didn't want to get bitten.

"I…" I looked back to Reaver and I thought about it. I mean *really* thought about it.

He turned to look at me and the motion made him look more human as he swallowed hard and with an almost beseeching look in his eyes said, "I can't promise that you'll like the answer, and whatever the answer is, you can't tell a soul. It's just for you… and if your mom is gone? She's going to have to stay where she's at… but I can promise that I like you, and I'm willing to get those answers for you if you want them. You can take your time to think about it," he said. "I know you're high right now and might want to revisit things when you're sober."

I pressed my lips together and simply nodded and he smiled, and the ice cracked, and just like that he was the warm, caring, and goofy guy again… *and holy shit that was terrifying. What the fuck?*

I looked up at Lightning who smiled down at me and petted my hair soothingly as he gave me a wink, and I smiled back but I knew it was a fragile thing.

The conversation around the fire picked back up, and someone said something to make the others laugh but I felt as though I'd just been given a taste of something. Something dark, yes, but also… also very promising.

Answers…

I could finally have answers, and I didn't doubt for a moment that Reaver could get them… just at what cost?

"Would you go with him?" I asked Lightning quietly, because there was just something about the way he was looking at me.

"You couldn't stop me, baby," he told me. "I know how much it hurts you not knowing."

I swallowed hard and closed my eyes and wondered if I could do it.

If I could sign, seal, and have these two men deliver the horrors I knew deep down they were capable of to my stepfather Ramone's door.

"You saw a Skinwalker?" Dray asked from across the fire and I practically shot up and hissed at him, "Shhhh!"

Suddenly I was all the rage all over again with all eyes on me, only this time? I didn't think I was going to get away without telling the story in the dark… except this time, I think there was something scarier than even *that* sitting among us.

I looked back down to Reaver whose eyebrows went up.

"Oh, this I think we all gotta hear," he said and I took a deep breath and nodded, laying back down.

"Okay," I said, and I think Serenity let out a little squeal of excitement and I sort of felt bad we'd spent all day together and I'd forgotten to tell her like I'd promised. To be fair, though, she hadn't asked… but I think that was just because she was so very polite and she knew it had scared me something awful.

19

Lightning…

Considering how much she hadn't wanted to talk about it last night, the fact that she all of a sudden was willing to now, especially after full dark, outdoors, in front of a whole bunch of people? Shit, Reaver's spook factor must have outspooked a fucking skinwalker which was pretty wild if you asked me.

Trust me when I say I had a bloodlust and a thirst for violence, too – but Reaver? Reaver was some seriously next-level shit and even I couldn't touch that. Something about working an operation with him was pretty fucking appealing, though. I was always curious how he did things. I was always curious how other enforcers did things and how I matched up. Honestly, though – I hadn't ever felt anyone could give me a real run for my money until I'd met this fucking guy. Then I'd gone from no one could touch me to I wasn't even close to on par, I knew I was wholly outmatched when I saw it and I saw it when I watched hell freeze over in those icy blue eyes of his.

I was glad Honor took Cutter's words to heart and was going to take her time really thinking it through.

For sure, turning Reaver loose? That was something that had some serious weight to it and wasn't something that should ever be taken for granted.

"I was somewhere around thirteen," Honor said, her voice falling into a storyteller's cadence. "I was out at dusk, riding with Jordan Light Feather. We grew up together, sort of. Had known each other our whole lives. He was my cousin as far as everyone in the tribe was auntie, cousin, or other such relation. We had stayed out too late, and his mother was going to be mad – we weren't supposed to be out after dark. Everyone knew it was out there. There had been stories for generations, and each generation has one in it."

"A Flesh Pedestrian?" someone asked. "What even are they?"

"They are a man, or a woman," Honor said. "One who traded their spirit to work in dark and mysterious ways. Greedy, and awful people, they traded away part of their soul to creatures and beings older than time in order to work dark magic. To allow themselves to change shape – into man or beast, it doesn't matter. One could be sitting among us now, and you wouldn't know it… but that day? That day, I'll never forget because that day I *know* we saw one."

"Jordan and I were riding, like I said. He was riding his horse, and I was riding his mother's. She was a busy lady, working two jobs. One with the tribal police, and one on her days off from that, doing filing at the Indian Health Clinic. She couldn't find the time to ride so much anymore, so she asked me to go with Jordan and get her horse some of the exercise she needed and to keep her used to having someone in the saddle."

She swallowed hard and said, "We stayed out too long, looking for chunks of turquoise and for raw silver to take to Jordan's grandfather for his jewelry making, but he paid us good for it and sometimes that was money for food when my mom's check just couldn't stretch that far. So it was getting dark as we plodded along and I heard it, way away, it sounded so very far away; my mother screaming."

She paused for a moment and said, "Everyone knows, that the further away it sounds, the closer it is, so Jordan and I tried to ignore it and we kept going. He saw it first, up in the trail ahead. It was the most awful thing I have ever seen, standing upright on two legs, its body some sort of awful cross between a coyote and a mountain lion, but still somehow human. It stared at us with brown human eyes and when it opened its mouth full of fangs, like a mountain lion, I heard my mother's voice."

"Jordan threw his lantern that he kept, just in case of emergencies and the glass broke, and the fire touched it. It leaped for the rocks and scurried up it like a spider and we kicked the horses into a run. They were just as afraid as we were, and we didn't stop until we got back to Jordan's. We tearfully told his mother what we had seen and she called for the medicine man. He came and he cleansed us and gave us medicine bags for protection. I still have mine today."

It was quiet but for the crackling of the fire and the crash of the surf when a flashlight lit up the night and a voice called out, "You know there are no fires allowed on the beach here."

Everyone jumped and there were a few shouts and shrieks as the voice went on, "I'm going to need to see some I.D.'s from all of you."

A radio crackled to life and I swallowed my heart from my throat back down into my chest.

Honor's chest heaved and she looked down the couch at Reaver who was as cool as a cucumber and just a smiling away like not a damn thing had happened.

"I hate that you can be so calm after something like that," Doll admonished him, her hand pressed over her heart and her chest heaving.

Reaver just fucking laughed.

Fucking freak. Man, I wished sometimes I could be like him. I definitely was one of the dudes that had just practically screamed like an eight-year-old girl.

I looked over the back of the couch at the cop and called out, "Well played, man. Well played."

He grinned at me a wolfish grin and I heard Honor mutter, "This is why you never hear anyone say, 'fuck the fire department.'" The cop lost his fuckin' smile real fast and mine just grew. I had to laugh.

Guess who got the ticket for the fire on the beach?

Fuck it. It was worth it, though.

My legs were fucking *killing me* the next morning, but that didn't stop me from pulling on my clothes and going downstairs in search of Honor. I found a knot of ol' ladies at a table having breakfast and I asked them, "You seen my lady?"

Mali jerked her head at the back doors leading out to the pool and down to the beach.

"She went out to the beach, looked real thoughtful."

"Thanks," I told her and she gave a nod.

"If she wants me to read her Tarot cards for maybe some more clarity on the questions she has, I'd be happy too."

"Mali is really good," Sunshine said.

"I'll let her know, thanks," I told her and I went to find her and find her I did. She was on one of the lounge chairs pilfered from the pool area sitting in the sand, the book we'd bought on Chief Osceola open in her hands, but she wasn't reading out of it. No, instead her gaze was fixed, staring sightlessly out over the water as she was lost in thought.

"Hey, baby. Got some room for your ol' man on that thing?" I asked her gently from a few paces away.

I hadn't wanted to startle her, but I did anyway, damnit.

"Yeah," she said, scooting forward. "I was just thinking how nice it would be if you were here to hold me and to talk to. I'm glad you were reading my thoughts today."

I chuckled as I put a leg over the lounger and settled on it behind her, pulling her back into my chest. She sighed in contentment and I said, "You look like you were thinking awful hard just then. I think I can guess what you want to talk about."

"Yeah, you probably could," she said with a wry chuckle, but then she sighed and it was a heavy thing, filled with something like regret.

I held her a little tighter and murmured, "Talk to me."

She swallowed hard and said, "I want answers, but… but I'm

scared. I mean, wouldn't it make me just as bad if not worse than Ramone to essentially sign his death warrant like that?"

"No," I said. "Ramone did that all by himself by being such a piece of fucking shit to you and your mom that you already know, baby. I see it in your eyes when you talk about it. You already know he did something to your mom, hell – *with your mom*."

She nodded and sniffed.

"I know he did," she said. "And knowing that, do I really need to send someone?" she asked.

"Depends," I said sighing, already knowing the answer to this one, too: "You trust the cops back home to do anything about it?"

She scoffed, "No. They didn't even want to take a missing person's report," she said.

"Tribal or non-tribal?" I asked.

"Both," she said bitterly. "Tribal was sick of her shit, the white cops just didn't care."

I sighed and held her tight again, kissing her shoulder.

"I'm sorry," I whispered.

"Me too," she said and she took a deep breath. "I want answers. Real ones. Not these half-truths, unanswered questions, and guesses that I have now. I want real, solid, answers… and I don't think I care how you get them."

I nodded and said, "Consider it done. Won't be fast and it won't be easy, but it'll get done. I swear it to you, babe."

"So, do I have to tell Reaver?" she asked.

"No, I can do that," I said. "If he needs to hear it from you, he'll come find you."

She nodded, "I didn't realize he was so scary," she said.

"Only to the people who deserve it," I told her.

"Even Doll looked so frightened…" she trailed off and I could tell she was worried for her.

"Reaver's never so much as touched a hair on her head without anything close to adoration. I think she's just seen some shit firsthand; you know? She knows enough to be scared when he goes all spooktacular like that, but I know for a motherfucking *fact* she's never been on the receiving end of his psychopathy."

She relaxed into me and I rocked her back and forth a bit.

We didn't say anything. We didn't have to… and honestly? It was just nice to sit here in silence and hold her while she felt her way through some of these big, awful feelings. I mean, if I could feel them for her, I would, in a heartbeat – but I couldn't, so this was the very next best thing.

Serenity found us a while later and she was moving *slow*.

"Oh God," she said. "I think I'm dying."

Stoker set up a lounge chair for her next to Honor who laughed and said, "Girl, I feel you."

"Justice is going to come down and join us if that's okay," she said, settling into the seat Stoker had set up and turning her face up to his for a kiss. She had a small stack of her ghost story books with her.

"The more the merrier," Honor said and she sounded better. A lot better.

"You going to be cool if I fuck off with the guys for the rest of the afternoon?" I asked her.

"God, yes," Honor said laughing. "I want to walk more knowing we have Ponce Inlet's light house tomorrow, like I want to put a hole in my head."

I laughed and gave her a squeeze kissing the back of her head.

"Did you just kiss the back of my head?" she demanded. "No sir! You get your ass up come around the front and kiss me right!"

"Ooo, yes, ma'am!" I did as she ordered and put her hand over my boner.

"Yeah, I'm going to need that later, so save it for me," she said.

I wrapped my hand in the back of her silken hair and put my lips by her ear and murmured, "You know, I almost put my thumb up your ass while I was fucking you last night, but I didn't know how you would feel about that."

She pulled back and arched an eyebrow over the mirrored lenses of her aviators.

“Yes, please,” she told me and I gave her a feral grin. “Noted,” I told her.

“What was that about?” I heard Ren ask her as Stoker and I walked away, passing Radar and Justice on their way down.

I didn’t hear Honor’s answer, but Serenity laughed and that was good enough for me.

20

Honor...

"What was that about?" Serenity asked me.

"Pervy shit," I said deadpan, but I couldn't keep the smile off my face as I raised my book back in front of it.

Serenity's laughter was high and bright and my mood, which was already much improved, lifted that much more. After all, Lightning was right. Was I really unleashing hell on Ramone? Maybe. Had Ramone most definitely fucking earned it? Abso-fucking-lutely, and to that end, was I really being a horrible person or was I honestly just being an instrument of karma at this point? My moral compass was pointing west in Ramone's direction and it most certainly was telling me I was being the latter. How did I know? The sense of peace and solace I took when I framed it that way in my mind.

"Did Lightning tell you about Mali's offer?" Justice asked me as she settled into her lounge chair on the other side of me after saying her kissy faced goodbyes to her man.

"No, what offer, why?" I asked.

"Ooo, yeah!" Serenity declared. "Mali reads tarot cards and she's really fucking good at it. She said if you were having trouble deciding that she would be happy to read your cards for you to see if it helped bring some clarity."

"Huh," I said thinking about it. "I mean, I made my decision," I said. "Still, it'd be nice to see if the cards told me if it was the *right* decision."

"I bet she could do that," Justice said.

"I know she would," Ren answered.

"Cool," I said. "Next time I see her, I'll ask. I've never had my tarot cards read."

The day passed pleasantly, we read, and talked, and gossiped a little about club drama which is where I learned that as much as the boys thought club business was just that, club business and just for the guys to know… the women of the club knew *everything*. Mostly by eavesdropping and just comparing notes later.

"There's really nothing they can do to stop us from knowing all the things," Everett said dryly after joining us.

"Nope," Mali agreed.

She did end up reading my tarot cards, and my biggest takeaway from that reading was: yes, I had made the right decision but, according to Mali, I was a good person and it wouldn't be without consequence and that consequence would be some really big really earth-shattering feels.

I liked to think I was prepared for that, but you never really knew if you were until you got there and the whole world actually started crashing down… which was annoying. Very annoying.

The boys came back just in time for a late lunch/early dinner and us girls were all for it as we were absolutely starving. There was supposed to be this cool food truck grotto thing with bitchin' street tacos, and as it was taco Tuesday by all of our reckoning, that is where we decided to go.

"I need to make you an Indian Taco," I said as Lightning and I waited in line.

"Aw yeah, what's that exactly?"

"It's just like a regular taco only using Indian frybread for the taco shell. It's next fucking level shit, that's for sure," I told him.

"Uh, I may need to check this out," Zach said from behind me.

I narrowed my eyes, "You know how to make frybread?" I asked.

"No, but you do, and I already make killer fucking tacos. Shrimp tacos to be exact."

I gasped, "Oh my God, now I've had chicken and beef frybread tacos, but *shrimp* frybread tacos? Okay, yeah, I think we can make this team effort happen."

"If it's as amazing as I think it's going to be, you gonna entrust me with your secret frybread recipe?"

"Hold up there, Kemosabe," I said holding up a hand, "Let's not get ahead of ourselves."

Zach and lightning had a good laugh over that one and Zach said, "Alright then, we'll do it the once and you can be my Tonto in the kitchen."

"Does that mean I get off of waitressing duty that night?" I asked.

"Shit, that might be a problem," he said.

"Fuck that, I'll strap on an apron that night just to make this shit happen," Radar called from behind Zach and we laughed again.

"That's gonna be a sight," I heard Cutter holler from down the line and we had to all laugh all over again.

I loved hanging out with these guys. I really did… they were starting to feel like the family I had never had growing up.

Dinner was good, but not the greatness Zach and I were scheming up for The Plank. I did bring up that we were going to need a non-shrimp option that night because people with shellfish allergies and he was like, "Aw, yeah. Question is, Carnitas or Carne Asada?"

"Both, motherfucker," Radar said from around a mouthful of food.

Lightning's shoulders shook with barely suppressed laughter.

"Swear to God," Atlas grated. "You're like an honorary fat kid, but I don't know where you put it and still stay so cut, man. I eat like you and I'd be on that six-hundred-pound life show."

"I *am* an honorary fat kid," Radar said. "You should have seen me in junior high and freshman year. Then I got on the wrestling team and I've looked this good ever since." He flexed his arm and kissed his bicep and I just shook my head.

"You're ridiculous," Justice said laughing at him. "But you love me," he said, beaming at her.

"And don't let anyone tell you different," she said leaning over to kiss him to a chorus of 'awwww' from the rest of us and a harmony of giggles.

Lightning and I took a walk on the beach when we got back to the hotel, and even Reaver and Doll called it an early evening in anticipation of the Ride to the Light the next day.

We retired up to our hotel room and the boys made a snack run to the gas station across the street. We picked a movie on the hotel's television and watched it together from our beds while we chewed on Red Vines –fuck Twizzlers, they nasty – and just laughed and laughed at the antics on the screen.

Lightning and I slept soundly, too. If Reaver and Doll got to fucking in the middle of the night, we didn't hear it and that was alright by me. I wanted to recover enough to climb the light at Ponce Inlet the next day.

21

Lightning...

"Whoaaaa," Honor said from behind me, shading her aviators with her hand and standing up on the passenger pegs as we rolled to a stop. "This one is *way* different than St. Augustine's!"

"Sure is," I declared, shutting off the bike.

She hopped down and I leaned it onto its stand.

St. Augustine's had been this black and white barber pole paint job with a bright ass red top. Ponce Inlet's lighthouse was something like diametrically opposite. It was this painted brick red just a couple three shades darker than terra cotta. Like an old brick, but it looked good. Sleek and tall, she was only like ten steps or so short of being as tall as St. Augustine's light.

Like St. Augustine, you went into the giftshop first and got your wrist bands to follow through and be able to take pictures of and climb the lighthouse. We looked at everything in the gift shop and Honor picked out what she wanted to get and we went on through.

There were a bunch of Boomer RUB's out here being assholes, but they sort of chilled the fuck out in their shenanigans when the big dawgs that were The Kraken and The Sacred Hearts stepped on the scene. It was always funny to watch these fuckers act like big Billy

Badasses only to watch their nuts shrivel up and hide in their booty holes once they caught sight of our colors.

Some of them were the real type deal and treated us with a healthy respect but just like normal guys, but what it really came down to – at least for us, is that they treated our women with deference and respect.

If they didn't do that, then one or more of us was liable to catch a charge dangling one or more of these motherfuckers off the lighthouse. If they really pissed us off, we might even drop 'em if given the chance.

It was a good thing everyone stayed in their lane and nobody had to die today.

One of the other things we liked about Ponce Inlet over St. Augustine was just how the staircase was built. Unlike St. Augustine, when you entered Ponce Inlet, the stairs were this perfect spiral up to the top. It was a cool shot. St. Augustine had this landing that interrupted the spiral pattern and it just wasn't as cool.

We made the trek to the top, moaning and groaning and laughing at ourselves the whole way. Still sore from St. Augustine the day before yesterday.

"Remind me to give y'all some muscle relaxers tonight," Charity said, sympathetic. She and Galahad weren't faring quite as bad since they didn't walk the whole ghost tour.

"I kind of want to go back to the fort at St. Augustine when it's open during the day to see that secret room the lovers were walled into," Galahad said as we took in the view from the top of Ponce Inlet.

"Me too," Charity said.

They'd caught that part of the tour before dude had taken his step out into the ether and landed in the dry moat bed.

"I wish you guys had gotten to take the whole tour," Honor said.

"Me too," Charity said, "but duty called."

"May the rest of our trip be a lot less adventuresome," Galahad said.

"You mean quiet?" Pyro asked butting in with a wolfish grin.

"Shut up!" Galahad and Charity chorused.

"God," Charity muttered annoyed.

Honor looked sympathetic at her.

"What a dick move," some guy muttered nearby and we eyed him. He was wearing a bunch of veteran gear, so he most definitely got it.

"Agreed," Honor said, and I was glad I didn't have to explain the q-word curse to her. I didn't know if waitresses had the same superstition as military, first responder, or medical personnel, but apparently, she at least knew about it which fuck me – could she get any hotter?

We got what she wanted out of the giftshop after taking a gazillion photos both up top and down below like we had at St. Augustine and in the Gator Farm. There wasn't anything cool like that at Ponce Inlet. Just the lighthouse, that was it.

Honor and I took the ride back to the hotel where she went through everything, wrapping things carefully in her dirty clothes and putting them into the bottom of her pack, just taking the time to relax and chill out and make sure she was keeping up with things and track of her space to bring things home.

We took a midday nap, our energy flagging pretty hard mid-week like I knew it would, but it was a damn good way to spend bike week's hump day and overall there were no complaints.

It was fun hanging with Stoker and Galahad while we watched Serenity carefully cut Honor's bike week tee on her body into something suitably biker chic with Charity running commentary.

That night, we had a low-key dinner, just me and her, at this fancy bistro in town, and it was nice.

Reaver stopped me as he was talking to Dray in the lobby of the hotel, looking past me to Honor he said, "Hey, can I borrow your man a minute?"

"Sure," she murmured softly. I kissed her and said, "You got the key to the room, I'll be up in a minute."

She nodded and put on a brave smile, but she was smart. She knew this had something to do with those answers she asked for.

"What's up?" I asked.

"Just talking to Dray about my availability to swing out to New Mexico with you," Reaver said with an excited grin.

"Jesus Christ, would it kill you to *pretend* it bothers you killing people, even just a little?" Dray demanded.

"But it doesn't," Reaver said, straight faced.

"No shit," Dray said with a snort. "Yeah, absolutely you're good to go," he said, "I already talked to our P. back on the home front and he okayed it, he just asked you not wear your colors," he said to us. "I mean, you do whatever your club and president tells you to do," he amended toward me. "I'm just saying he prefers the Sacred Hearts colors not be involved.

"Oh, hey, yeah, no – this is personal," I said. "I had yet to run the particulars with Cutter, but I'm sure he'd want the same thing. That and it's just easier on a ride like this not having on any identifying whatever. I may have been born at night, but it wasn't *last* night," I said.

"So, when?" Reaver asked, bouncing his eyebrows.

"That's a good fucking question," I answered him. "I gotta get Honor home and I'm sure you've got your day job and shit. Can I get back to you guys on that by the end of the week?"

"Sure," Dray said.

"Awww," Reaver pouted.

"Dude!" Dray said, but he was grinning.

"It's just been so long, man!" Reaver cried.

"You're worse than an addict jonesing for a fix right now, it's creepy as fuck and you're scaring people," Dray said, still grinning.

"You say that like it's a bad thing," Reaver said with mock confusion.

"I'm going to have Trig put a fuckin' leash on you in a second," Dray warned.

"Hey, question if you don't mind me asking," I said to Reaver.

"Shoot," he said.

"How'd you get your Enforcer patch back? I thought that went to Archer for a while."

"Something like that, but then kids, wife, family." Reaver waved a hand in the air like these were foreign concepts even though I knew he had a teenager. "Shit got too complicated for him to be out there busting heads."

My shoulders shook with silent laughter.

"Word, well, glad to have you back filling the role that I swear to fuck you were born into," I said.

"Thanks!" Reaver beamed at me. "That has to be some of the nicest shit anyone has ever said to me!"

"Jesus Christ!" Dray echoed, but he was laughing this time.

"I'll be here all week," Reaver said with a wink. "No, really, I will."

I rolled my eyes. "Okay, well nice talking with you, but my girl's waiting upstairs. I promise, I'll get with you guys later on the particulars."

"Copy that," Reaver called after me.

Jesus Christ was right… a bit eager, much? I thought to myself as I waited for the elevator.

MY PHONE WAS SHRIEKING awful in the late-night hour. I groped for it on the nightstand as Honor whimpered and Reaver called, "Shut it off!" as Doll squished her face into his chest.

I picked it up and squinted, hitting the green "accept" button. Marlin's face white as a sheet appeared on the screen.

"Lightning!" he called and I could hear a commotion behind him. There were a shit ton of red and blue flashing lights behind him.

"What's going on, man?" I asked.

"You gotta come quick, man. The address is in the mass text, all-hands-on-deck. It's Pyro. They're taking him to the hospital. It's bad man."

"What the fuck happened? Where are you?" I demanded.

"The Iron Steed. They're loading him into the back of the ambo now, dude. All-hands-on-deck, hospital now. Church when we all get there."

"Ah, got it, copy, I'm on my way."

"Go by Radar's room and check and see if he's there. We haven't been able to raise him or Atlas."

"Will do!"

"Thanks, bud," he said and the call ended, the screen going blank.

"That sounds really fucking bad. You want me to go with you?" Honor asked, her face pinched as I yanked my jeans up my legs. I shook my head.

"No, baby, there's nothing you can do and I'm going to be riding like I stole it. You stay here. I'll call you as soon as I know anything."

"Okay," she said. I kissed her quick and called to Reaver, "You look after my girl!"

"She ain't going anywhere," he said. "But call us as soon as you know what's up."

"I will," I said as I went out the door, tee and boots in one hand as I shrugged into my cut. I went and pounded on Atlas's door and didn't let up until Atlas answered it, his hair mussed, wiping his mouth.

"Where's the fire at?" he demanded.

"We gotta ride, you me and Radar. Pyro's being taken to the hospital, address is in the group text. Marlin said it's fucking bad."

"Shit," Atlas declared and called back into the room, "You hear that?"

"Yeah."

"Should I go?" Justice's voice asked, concerned.

"No," I said. "Church when we get there."

"Ah, yeah, no, baby, you stay here. I love you," Radar said.

I heard the smack of lips and Atlas said, "Two minutes," and shut the door in my face. I took that two minutes to put on my boots and strip off my cut, holding it between my knees so I could throw my tee over my head and my cut back on over it.

We fuckin' *blazed*. Like I swear our tire tracks had flame licking off 'em. We got to the hospital listed in the group text in record time and parked outside the emergency department with the rest of our brothers' familiar bikes and fucking *ran* across that lot to the entrance.

Once inside, Cutter looked up from where he'd been hanging his head, his hands on his hips. Galahad looked over from where he'd been standing with Cutter, and Charity was with her sisters across the waiting room, crying her fucking eyes out.

"What happened?" I demanded.

"She and I were there. We had to work on him. Guys, it ain't good," Galahad said, his voice cracking.

"Okay yeah, but what fucking *happened?*" Atlas demanded.

"Just waiting on Beast and—" The doors whooshed open and Beast and Gator spilled in, Hossler right behind them. She immediately split off and went for the knot of girls. Serenity came out of a bathroom nearby and Stoker went to her and led her over to Hoss and them, talking low and comforting.

"Cap, what the fuck?" Radar said impatiently.

"Chapel." Cutter raised his voice and all of us followed him to the hospital's literal fucking chapel for some privacy, Hope coming and standing by as we went to take our fucking phones and keep them back in the waiting room with the girls that were here.

"I'll send Hoss if there's any news," she called and Cutter waved over his shoulder in acknowledgment.

Once in the chapel, Radar put his back to the doors and crossed his arms, keeping them shut.

"Alright, this is what happened for those of you that weren't there," Cutter said.

"Apparently, a bunch of the guys had been at the Iron Steed, enjoying some tunes and cuttin' up. and Pyro had tied one too many on. He was being loud, drunk, and annoying enough that some fuckin' poser took offense and started talking shit. Of course, Pyro being drunk and dumb as fuck as he's been lately, he started writing checks with his mouth. Now his ass could have cashed them if it was a fair fucking fight, but this wasn't that. This douchebag said something as Pyro was standing at the railing, watching the band. When Pyro turned around? This fucking meathead clobbered him with a fucking sucker punch. A fucking sucker punch that sent Pyro flipping over the rail.

"He landed in the dirt down below, *on his fucking head.* Of course, Galahad and Charity were there, thank fucking God, and they jumped into action faster than even the Iron Steed's security could. Of course, the Iron Steed's bouncers were fixed on ejecting Meathead and his jolly band of cocksuckers while trying to keep the Kraken from being unleashed on those motherfuckers in more ways than one."

"So how fucking bad is it?" Gator asked, looking up from the pew he'd parked his ass on, his elbows on his knees.

"Most likely a broken neck," Galahad said. "He still had a pulse, but barely." He shook his head. "Even if he survives, he'll be lucky if he's not quadriplegic," he said.

"Oh, fuck no," someone said, but I can't be sure who. I had this rushing and roaring in my ears.

"Where's the guy?" I demanded through numb lips.

"In police custody," Marlin said. "So untouchable."

"Wanna bet?" Atlas demanded.

"Stop," Cutter said and his voice had the bite of finality. "Ain't none of you motherfuckers fixing to get yourselves arrested to get at this guy. You know that'll just lead nowhere good and…" he swallowed with how the next words fixing to come out of his mouth made him almost sick to say 'em, especially with how the look on his face was. "And with how Pyro's been? Shit, I don't know that I can blame the lunk for taking that swing. How many of us have barely held off doing it lately?"

"That's different, man," Marlin said. "One of us is one thing, but ain't no one else get to without releasing the whole damn Kraken."

Cutter nodded and sat down. He put his face in his hands and fuckin' lost it. Ain't a single one of us blame him or say shit else about it because we all knew both he and Marlin were right about this.

We went in for a big group hug, all of us huddled in our fucking misery and worry, our fuckin anger at Pyro set aside for the moment as we waited to hear what was going on with our club brother.

"I guess he really cursed himself up in Ponce Inlet's lighthouse today," Galahad said quietly, sniffing, wiping at the tears on his face.

"I don't know what that means," Cutter said. "But the only reason he has even a chance of surviving this is because you and Char were there and hopped fuckin' to. So thank you for doing everything you could, brother," Cutter said.

"It was stupid anyhow," I said and I told him about what'd Pyro said at the top of Ponce Inlet, about the whole quiet thing.

Marlin nodded. "Yeah, karma sure came back to bite him on this one," he said grimly.

"She always have to be such a fuckin' bitch?" Gator asked.

"Apparently so," Atlas said soberly.

We decided unanimously that no one was going to do shit about fuck on this one, that the risk was too great. The cops had the guy and if he skated, or got out? Then his ass was ours. That decision made, we returned to the waiting room and the girls and plans were made to get 'em back to the hotel. Mostly just plans for Faith and Charity because Hope would fight every one of us to stay by Cutter's side and ain't none of us want *that* heat.

I took Charity while Stoker took Serenity and Radar took Faith. We rode back to the hotel and Radar was honestly the only one prepared to go back to the hospital. I volunteered to stay and let Rocco and Zach know what the fuck was going on.

Hope had had the presence of mind to get Pyro's keys and had ridden his bike to the hospital, so that was handled and in hand. Stoker had his hands full with Serenity, but Charity and Faith were going to be alright. They had each other to lean on.

I filled Rocco and Zach in on what'd happened and my ears popped. I could feel the impending storm rolling in and so I said, "Hey, man. Rocco, gimme the crash truck keys, would you? I think I'm gonna set up and see if I can't catch some bolts."

He took up the keys and said, "I'll come help you, but I ain't going out once the storm gets close."

I nodded. "Thanks, man."

22

Honor...

I paced the room, Reaver and Doll sitting up in their bed, the television on the late-night local news station where a helicopter was flying over the Iron Steed, shining a spotlight down into it and all the emergency vehicles as the police conducted their investigation into what the news was calling a bike week bar fight gone horribly wrong.

I made a noise of disgust and went to the window to look down onto the night darkened beach. We hadn't heard anything from anyone at the hospital yet and it was maddening.

Lightning flashed way out over the ocean and I sucked in a breath. I dragged my eyes back to the sand and that's when I saw him out there, Rocco walking along, handing him rebar as he thrust it down into the sand.

"Oh, shit," I whispered out loud. Charity and Galahad weren't here if something went wrong!

"What is it?" Reaver asked, bounding off the bed and batting the curtain aside. He looked down on the scene in the sand way below while I rushed to get dressed, not caring that Doll was staring at my tits wide-eyed as I pulled a tee over my head.

"He's going to get himself killed," I muttered. "Again!"

I rushed out the room and fuck the elevator. I thundered down the stairs and tried not to giggle hysterically at the irony of that thought.

I burst out the back door of the hotel's lobby and ran full tilt down the zig zagging walkway to the sand.

"Lightning!" I cried, the wind picking up and whipping my voice back into my face.

"Lightning!" I tried again, and Rocco turned to look.

"Goddammit, Charlie!" I yelled.

He looked my way then as I practically crashed into him and wrapped my arms around him tight.

He dropped his chunk of rebar and returned my embrace, burying his face in my hair.

"Okay," I said, coming to my own senses on this. "Let's hurry up and finish so you can watch from inside with me. You don't have backup and there's absolutely no dying on my watch!"

He smiled at me and handed me the pink fluttery plastic construction marking tape.

"Tie one on each one," he called over the increasing wind.

"Rocco, start driving them in too!" I called.

The three of us made stupidly quick work of it all and rushed back inside.

Rocco stood at the back door and said, "Now we just watch and wait?"

"Yeah, but can we do it from our room upstairs?" I asked, shivering and wet from the rain that'd started.

"Yeah, I still feel like this is too close," Rocco said.

"Not close enough for me," Lightning said. "But I'm happy to compromise for you, baby, since you helped me get 'em all out there."

I smiled and nodded and we all went upstairs.

"You motherfucker," Reaver said, grinning as he let us into the room. "You may be crazier 'n me with that shit!"

"Oh please, girls. You're both pretty," Doll said, grinning from their bed. Rocco reached into the bathroom and handed me a towel.

"Thanks," I said and we all sort of went to the window to watch the light show.

A knock at the door heralded the arrival of Zach who came in and stood with Reaver, Doll, me, and Lightning at the window. Rocco was in the room's wing-backed chair, holding the curtain aside to look down from where he sat.

"So, what's the story?" Zach asked.

Lightning filled us all in and the outlook was nothing short of grim.

"Fuck," Zach whispered, staring at him in disbelief.

"No shit," Lightning declared. "I went from wanting to kick his ass for intimidating Honor to hoping like fuck he somehow lives from getting his ass kicked on a fucking dime here. I feel guilty as hell and angry, but not even at this fucking guy. No, I'm mad as hell at Pyro."

He heaved a sigh and scrubbed his face with his hands.

"Hey, it's okay," I said and pulled him into a hug again. I held him tight as the sky flashed blue and then the boom hit and the rest was drowned out by the torrential rain hitting the glass.

"Holy shit," Doll whispered in awe.

"I think that was a hit," Rocco said, impressed.

"Nah, the glass would have shook. That was all in the clouds," Lightning mumbled against my neck.

"The glass did shake," Doll said, perplexed.

"He means from the flash of light, not the thunder and that was a good second delay. That was a mile off or so," I said and he drew back.

"You do listen to me," he said, forcing a smile.

"Of course I do. I love you," I said, grinning back.

"Awww," Reaver said and Doll swung her hand back to hit him lightly in the chest.

Zach snorted a laugh and Rocco cracked a smile, too.

"I love you, too," Lightning said, and he went back to hugging me, squeezing me even tighter.

~

We were pretty confident there were hits, but we weren't about to go down to collect until morning. It seemed the mid-week storm that Lightning had prepared for had not only arrived, it was determined to sit on us for a while.

Eventually, we slept, though none of us particularly well. We ended up going down for breakfast and found a good portion of the rest of the ol' ladies and their men there. There was no real news on Pyro other than he was alive, and in a coma. The prognosis wasn't good.

"Hope that sucker punch was fuckin' worth it," Marlin muttered before swilling down some of his coffee.

"Only thing that pisses me off is that he's locked up and we can't get him," Radar said with a gusty sigh.

"Guys," Stoker said gently as Serenity started to cry.

"Let's curb stomp all the talk of violence, boys. At least for now," Cutter said quietly.

Everyone sort of fell silent after that.

Bike week was pretty much over for the Kraken at that point.

I caught Reaver, Lightning, Dray, and Cutter talking quietly in a corner at one point and wondered if it was about my answers. When they all looked over at me looking at them, that pretty much was all the answer on *that* that I needed.

"Hey, babe, let's go upstairs and talk, yeah?" Lightning said, coming to me quietly. I nodded and took his hand and let him lead me to the elevators, our fingers laced.

"So what's going on?" I asked.

"I wanted to ask you if you trusted my judgment and felt comfortable riding home in the crash truck with Rocco or with Zach on his bike," he said.

I thought about it. "Is that so you and Reaver can take a ride together to…" I glanced over at our phones on the bedside table and cleared my throat. "Clear your heads?"

He followed my gaze and smiled and nodded. "Yeah. I feel like I've got no control in this situation and it's driving me nuts," he said.

I nodded. "A ride would do you good, then," I said.

He nodded.

"Okay," I said and he looked at me, catching my eyes with his.

"Okay, as in, *okay?*" he asked. I nodded. "Okay," he said and it looked like a weight had been taken off his shoulders.

"We safe to check for fulgurites?" I asked.

"Let me check with Radar," he said.

"Okay."

He checked with Radar who checked his phone and some weather apps.

"You're good," Radar declared, giving the thumbs-up downstairs.

With all the rain, we all sort of just ended up hanging out in the area with all the seating for breakfast.

Rocco just sort of appeared by our sides and said, "Let's go see what we can pull up."

"It's not quite *that* easy, but come on, I'll show you how," Lightning said.

We ended up with three fulgurites, one of them the biggest one Lightning had ever captured.

We took the rebar with its melted plastic flags back to the crash truck and carefully crated up and packed away the fulgurites in the back. When we went back into the hotel, it was to management essentially asking us to leave, both for the lightning stunt and for the whole thing where we took one of their couches out onto the beach.

Cutter stepped in to smooth things over but the day manager wasn't having any of it and was going full Karen, threatening to call the cops and have us trespassed.

She was in for a rude awakening when two entire floors checked out early on her. The situation went viral on biker tok. *More* people canceled the rest of their reservations, and a bunch of people canceled their reservations for next year. Especially when her ranting about safety hazards were blown off because who goes out and hangs on the beach in the middle of the night in a raging thunderstorm?

It was a bitter end for bike week, and the majority of us from the club decided home was better than this. Of course, Cutter, Hope, Marlin, and Faith stayed. They just managed to find other hotel accommodations.

I opted to ride home in the crash truck and took all of our stuff, from purchases to dirty laundry and whatever else with us.

Doll was taken care of, she said, and had no problem with Reaver riding off with Lightning.

"It'll only be a few days or so, knowing him. It's been such a long time since he's had a long ride by himself. He's long overdue," she said, hugging me tight.

"You need to come up to Kentucky to see the farm," Bailey reminded me, hugging me tight.

"I promise, I will just as soon as Lightning is home and we can plan it."

"Deal," she said.

Saying goodbye to Lightning was the hardest thing to do. He'd written down Ramone's last known address, but I'd already told him I wasn't sure he lived there anymore. He said he didn't care. It was something to start him in the right direction.

Now he was really going and I was scared for him.

"I'll be home before you know it," he said. I nodded, swallowing hard.

"We'll be fine," Serenity said. "All of us are off work for the rest of the week. We all agreed to pitch in and help Honor with the Pilchuck's house, sorting and cleaning and making it her own."

I smiled back over my shoulder and Serenity smiled at me, bright and sweet but mostly reassuring.

"That's great," Lightning declared.

"So hurry back to me, huh?" I said softly for his ears only. I palmed the side of his neck and stroked a thumb back and forth beneath his ears and he closed those bright green eyes I loved to look into so much; the set of his mouth telling me that he was committing this touch to memory and that he held it in his heart as such a very precious thing.

"Kiss me and I gotta go," he said and I pressed my mouth to his.

He held me tight and kissed me so strongly, so sweetly, and I felt myself go loose in his arms and realized I was swooning.

Damn if it wasn't hard to swoon when it came to Lightning. I mean, holy fuck he was so damn sexy and I felt like the luckiest woman alive based on that alone.

"Okay," he said, pulling back reluctantly. He walked me over to the crash truck, the passenger door open and waiting, Rocco behind the wheel and ready to go, and helped me up into it. He shut me in and I reached down to grab his hand and give it a squeeze before he turned and threaded his way through the bikes that were firing up to his.

"He'll be alright," Rocco said reassuringly as the flash and glint of Florida sun off motorcycle chrome forced me to put a hand up as the bikes with their riders swooped out onto the main drag and we began the four-hour-and-something journey home.

Home...

After all of this, it really felt like home and like I'd finally found some kind of family and the thought honestly made me sag back into my seat with such relief I couldn't honestly and accurately describe it beyond that and the words just didn't feel like it did the sensation justice.

"Homeward bound," I said a little stunned and Rocco's lips twitched into a smile.

"Homeward bound," he agreed, moving up and flipping on the truck's signal, turning smoothly out behind the long twin rows of bikes.

Homeward bound.

I kept turning the words over in my mind like a particularly pretty shell found on the beach.

23

L**ightning...**

Watching the crash truck turn out of the driveway and head up the road with my heart in it sucked. Knowing I was now free to do what needed doing, though? That I had a place to channel all my hopelessness and rage surrounding not only the whole situation with Pyro, but for every time Honor stared sightless and the sadness crossed her face? Oh, I was down like four flat tires – I couldn't even begin to put it into words how ready I was to fucking *go*.

"Let's do this," I said to Reaver and he got this damn grin on his face and a twinkle in his eye that you'd like to think I'd just handed a kid a twenty outside a candy store and told him he ain't need to bring me any change.

"You like this shit way too much," I said.

He winked and said, "You do too, don't lie. You just have a pickier conscience about it."

I thought about that a second and tilted my head in silent concession that he might actually be right about that.

We rode out behind the rest of his crew, following them a while up the interstate until we reached the panhandle at which point Reaver and I veered left to head west while the rest of his crew headed north on home. They didn't much feel like fucking with finding a new hotel and shit, and damn sure our crew would never darken that places' door again.

We rode all day and on into some of the night, stopping in New Orleans. Radar had called ahead for me. While the Voodoo Bastards had, ah, seen a change in leadership and all? That hadn't affected our club's friendship with 'em at all. After all, it'd been La Croix and Collier who'd been there in the clutch to help our boy Radar and that whole thing with his lady Justice in Texas.

It'd been a big fuckin' mess of her ex trying to finish the job of murdering her from where he'd been locked up in prison.

Yeah, his ass had gotten straightened out in a big way. She would never have to worry about him again – which is as it fuckin' should be.

"You sure about this?" Reaver asked, eyeing La Croix flanked by Hex and Saint as they came out of their clubhouse into the fenced-in front to meet us.

"Absolutely," I said.

"Lightning!" Hex called genially as they approached.

"Who dat?" Saint asked with a wink. La Croix was just his typically quiet self, those creepy fuckin' eyes of his, the whites blacked out around the dark brown iris just stared at Reaver, looking him up and down.

"I'm Reaver," he said. "Uh, Reaver Michaels since I got married and changed it. My original government name was garbage so, not trying to be cheeky or show any disrespect, that's just legit my name."

I laughed and said, "Sounds like you've had some trouble meeting other clubs/" Reave just leaned his forearms onto his gas tank and shrugged.

"A little, but usually that's part of the fun. But you said you liked these guys a bunch and I don't wanna piss in anyone's pond when I'm this tired and flirting with a bad case of monkey butt."

Hex and Saint traded a look over La Croix's head and both were laughing.

"Yeah, he's always like this," I said and Hex shook his head.

"Why don't you boys go on and park them things. We got a crawfish boil goin' on out back there – let's get you some grub an' go on and talk about it."

"Is that a Tennessee accent I hear?" Reaver asked curiously.

"Why yes, it is, son!" Hex grinned.

"Thought so." Reaver shot a grin back. "I'm your old neighbor from the north, Kentucky," he said.

"Aw right now!" Hex cried.

"Park 'em," La Croix said. "Tell Louie what you want to drink."

"He still prospecting?" I asked.

"Fully patched now," Saint said.

"No shit? Good for him, man!"

Reaver and I parked and brought our backpacks with clothes in with us. Louie was behind the bar and wearing his still pretty new cut and La Croix went to this redhead leaning on the bar and put his hand on her waist. She tilted her head as she listened to what he said and turned her pale green eyes to Reaver and looked him over. She nodded and slipped off toward the back after a polite nod at me.

"My ol' lady," he said and I felt my eyebrows shoot up into my hairline.

"Nice work, man," I said.

It was only then that La Croix graced me with a crooked smile.

"So what brings you fellas passing through our neck of the woods in the middle of the week like this?" Hex asked.

"What can I get you?" Louie asked.

"Water?" Reaver asked. "Been sweating our balls off on the ride."

"Same," I said. "Hit something harder later if you don't mind." Louie nodded and I looked to Hex to answer his question. "That is a long story, my friend. Let's go on out and get the hi's and introductions out of the way and I'll tell you."

"You know what, that sounds good, mostly because I'm dying to know… why y'all flying under the radar like that?" he gestured at us and Reaver grinned.

"My cut is with my ol' lady, headed back to Kentucky," he said.

"Mine's with our Sergeant At Arms headed back to Ft. Royal with him, but it'd be with Honor if she was officially my ol' lady. This is a personal matter we're on, and both of our crews asked we keep our colors out of it. We ain't have no problem with that. Just makes our life easier skating across as many states as we need to."

"Where you boys headed, anyway?"

"Shiprock, New Mexico," I said.

Hex gave a low whistle. "That's a ways from home for sure."

Louie gave us a pair of ice laden waters and we followed Hex, Saint, and La Croix deeper into the club through the garages and out the big bay doors to the *way* back. There we found just about the rest of the Voodoo Bastards crew in a ring of lawn chairs surrounding a big ol' fucking pot on an outdoor propane filled burner.

There were a couple of ladies and a teenage boy, too.

"Lightning, Reaver, that there is my ol' lady, Corliss," Hex indicated a deep dark brunette with pride. "And that there is Jessie-Lou. She's Collier's woman and Cypress' sister, but you ain't have to worry about either of them you cross her. She's born and bred swamp rat Cajun around these parts and she'll get you herself."

The teenage boy laughed and Jessie-Lou grinned but it wasn't altogether filled with humor. No, it was a touch feral.

"Nice to meet you, Corliss, Jessie-Lou." I nodded politely to both.

"Where's Alina?" La Croix asked in that deep bass rumble of his.

"Right here," the redhead from earlier said and she stepped out and smoothed her hands down the tops of her jeans-clad thighs.

"Y'all need paper towels in the women's room."

"Heh." Axeman laughed. "We need another damn prospect for this type of shit."

"Don't need one," La Croix declared.

"We are at max capacity," Hex agreed.

"I know," he said getting up, "I was just sayin'. I'll get 'em restocked, doll face. Sorry about that."

"It's no problem," Alina said. "I'd get 'em if I knew where you moved 'em to."

Introductions were made around the fire and Reaver and I were given seats.

"So, about this story," Hex asked, leaning back in his chair, lacing his fingers with Corliss's.

I took a deep damn breath and launched into the short version of Honor's story.

"Got a picture of this woman?" Chainsaw asked, his interest piqued.

I pulled up some of the pictures from our recent trips to the lighthouses and gator farm and shit and let him scroll through.

"Nice," he said, passing the phone to La Croix. The phone made the rounds all the way around the fire and there were mostly nods of appreciation and only a few shrugs or facial expressions of *not my glass of sweet tea,* which was fine. There was no disrespect there.

"She's pretty," Corliss said. "Navajo?"

"Her daddy's side," I said.

"Nice."

"So how do you figure into all of this?" La Croix asked Reaver and Reaver grinned.

"Honor said she wanted answers," Reaver said with a shrug. "I like her well enough. She seems like a sweet girl. A road trip sounded fun, so I asked if I could tag along."

"That's not it," La Croix said with a creepy smile.

"Okay, you got me, but hey," Reaver grinned like a motherfucker. "Mixed company and all of that. I'd rather not upset anybody."

La Croix's smile bloomed into a full-on grin and he nodded with something like a psycho's respect and I honestly couldn't figure it. Hex was clearly the motherfucking brains out of all of these boys and yet he was only VP and that just didn't make sense to me.

Still, not my crew and it didn't affect me none, so curiosity wouldn't be killing this cat today.

We talked about other things after that, ate some good food, had a few beers, hydrated some more, and I watched Reaver throw knives against Axeman who was throwing axes at a target back here.

"You're going to an awful lot of trouble for her, she the one or what?" Saint asked, taking a drink out of his bottle of beer.

I smiled and nodded, "From the first time I saw her in that fucking lightning storm on the beach back in Ft. Royal I just had this gut feeling, man. Rest of my crew was calling me crazy and thought she was some kind of a fuckin' hallucination or something from me taking that hit. Like a… I don't know, like the people you see when you have a near death experience or something."

"Ain't those supposed to be people you know, though?" Jessie-Lou asked. "Like loved ones that died before you or something?"

I nodded, "That's what I said."

Hex chuckled.

"Guess you showed them up."

I laughed a little and nodded.

"I guess I did," I said.

"Come on, Tater – it's time to get going," Jessie-Lou said getting up.

"Aw, mom!" Tate said turning from where he was about to give it a try throwing one of Reaver's knives.

"It's a school night, baby."

Shit, she didn't look old enough to be that kid's mom. I thought he was Cypress's kid, but it turned out he was just the kid's uncle. Talk about mind blown.

"Fine, just after this throw?" he asked.

"Last. Throw." She said and you could hear in her voice, she meant it.

"Okay, watch your stance…" Reaver said and the kid checked his feet. He didn't stick it, the handle of the knife bouncing off the target, but he tried.

"Alright, time to go," she said.

"I'll see you at home," Collier said kissing her. "I'm gonna walk these two out," he said to the rest of us and waved and there was a… there was a tension among the club surrounding us that there just wasn't before… *what the fuck?* I wondered.

"Everything going okay with you boys?" I asked Hex and he raised an eyebrow at me and said, "Everything's just fuckin' dandy here, partner – why?"

"No reason," I said knowing when to press and when not to press and Hex had clearly given off the unspoken signal that it wasn't time to press.

Axe said something and Reaver cackled and both Hex and my gaze bounced to them and then back to each other.

"Just how many psychos can you put in one space and not have a volatile reaction?" I asked.

Hex sniffed, "Shit, between your boy, Axe, and La Croix we got at least three and I tell you what – I feel like I'm sittin' on a block of C-4 just waitin' for the signal to set it off."

I grinned and hung my head nodding and said, "That's an accurate description if I've heard any," I said.

"He certainly ain't right, that one," Hex declared.

"You have no idea the shit that I've heard I said with a sigh, watching Reaver square up to make a throw."

"If you're talking about the time I skinned that cartel guy and nailed his hide to his homie's front door – yeah, that was real disappointing that one. The shock set in and he died way too quick." He made his throw and it hit dead center and I glanced around and realized there were no women or children present – thank fucking God, but at the same time? Reave had somehow just known that without even looking.

Hex leaned back in his seat and looked real thoughtful.

"You ever just pop a boner when they start screaming?" Axe asked looking around.

"Yeah, that shit gets a little awkward," Reaver said and I realized just now next level some of these dudes were. I mean, I *definitely* never went that fucking far. Everything I'd ever done had been for the good of the club and out of necessity – these dudes seriously just fucking got off on it and *whoa.*

"Yeah, half the time, La Croix and I don't even wear clothes. It's just easier to wash up and keeps DNA evidence off of 'em. Seal that shit in a plastic bag first, man. Gotta get with the times."

"Givin' away trade secrets?" La Croix asked with a wicked smile coming back out the bay doors.

"Alina and Cor are making up some cots for you fellas in the garage," he said.

"Score," I said.

"Just watch what y'all say – we keep this shit as far away from 'em as possible," Hex said and I nodded.

"Copy that," Reaver said. "Sorry – but going back to what you were just saying, ain't you gotta worry about *your* DNA getting on their shit?" He lowered his voice and La Croix smiled that ugly little smile again.

"Y'all ain't got gators up in Kentucky."

Reaver shrugged, "Got pig farms."

Axe looked a little impressed and said, "That about'll do it too."

"Freaks 'em out harder when you're naked," La Croix said and Reaver and him traded a smile and fuck me, those two were about on the same fucking wavelength with their particular brand of psycho – Reaver looked like he may or may not be sporting a bit of a chub just thinking about that shit.

Hex cleared his throat and I looked to the bay door as Alina and Cor – as Hex called her – came back outside.

"I'll have to remember that," Reaver said to La Croix and La Croix nodded once.

Hex and I traded a look and I sighed, "Just glad you're on my side on this one," I said.

"Aw, any time good buddy!" Reaver beamed at me and Hex laughed.

I shook my head and had to laugh too.

"I'm going to give Honor a quick ring and say goodnight before it gets much later," I said.

"Do it back here," La Croix said and I frowned but I nodded, looking around at the high cinderblock walls back here and realized the heavy gat was sord of around a corner. No direct line of sights to where we were all chilling… something was up, especially seeing as they set us up on cots in the garage and not the common room – which they had on any other occasion they'd put us up here.

"You guys good?" I asked Hex quietly.

"Right as rain," he said with a wink and I dropped it once and for all.

I called Honor, my phone ringing to the point I didn't think she'd pick up but finally…

"*Hello?*"

24

Honor…

"Hello?"

"Hey, baby… you doing okay? Rocco get you home safe?"

"Mm. Mm-hm," I stretched and rolled over to look at the bedside clock. "Oh, shit… I meant to take like a thirty-minute nap when I got home but I've slept hours! Where are you?" I asked. "Are you stopped for the night? Are you safe?"

His chuckle was darkly sweet over the line and he said, "Yeah, I'm good. We're stopped for the night here in New Orleans with some buddies of mine. I'm sorry I woke you up, I'll—"

"No! No, don't be. It's good to hear your voice."

"It's good to hear yours, too," he said. "You might not hear from me for the next couple of days, though, alright."

That troubled me, but I knew better than to say anything. I could ask all the questions I wanted to in person when he was home and it was just him and just me.

"Oh, alright… I mean I don't understand but I do at the same time, you know?"

Like he plucked the thoughts right out of my head he said to me, "I can explain when I get home to you, okay?"

"Sounds good," I said.

"Alright, I am going to go, though. I just wanted to say good night and I love you."

I smiled, those three little words warming my soul.

"I love you too," I said softly.

"Okay, go back to sleep," he said.

"Okay, sleep well when you do," I said.

"I will, baby. Bye."

"Bye."

I sighed, disappointed when the tone sounded in my ear that he disconnected the call. I pulled it away from my face and looked at the screen and our smiling faces from the top of St. Augustine's light house.

I suddenly didn't want my answers so bad, at least for a fleeting moment. All I wanted was to have Lightning here, and to be cuddled up talking softly.

There was still no news about Pyro and I felt guilty for not telling him that. Last any of us had heard that afternoon was that he was in critical condition and in a coma from the swelling on his brain. He had a skull fracture and two broken vertebrae with significant damage to his spinal column. He'd failed all the reflexive tests they'd given him for hands and feet and it looked like Galahad was right… if he survived, then he would be a quadriplegic.

Even though I'd only known him a short time, he seemed troubled and I felt bad for him even though he'd tried so hard to intimidate me and to be a jerk to me.

No one deserved this, and I was scared for him.

I know it was a shitty thing to think and I would never in a million years say it out loud… but death may or may not be the bigger kindness here.

To listen to everyone talk about him, it was a clear picture that Pyro was a super active individual – and to never sail, or ride his bike again?

I shuddered.

If it were me, I know I wouldn't want it. To be trapped in a body I had no control over, or to be a vegetable… no, thank you. I think I would rather die, but that's just me.

I didn't know if he had any say or left any instructions or however you went about these kinds of things. My guess was no… I mean, no one ever thinks it could happen to them, so why would they?

I got up and changed into some pajamas, my stomach growling. I went into the kitchen, fixed something to eat, and returned to the bedroom. I ate, reading out of my book on Osceola, and sighed.

Even he had died a slow and lingering death, an illness that had taken months to eat away at him before he'd died and knowing what I already did about after?

I closed the book and set it aside.

I didn't want any nightmares.

Problem was, I wasn't tired enough to try and go back to sleep – and so I went into the living room and tried to find something on the television – but that didn't work either. After an hour of scrolling, I turned it off.

Fuck.

25

Lightning…

The ride out to Shiprock was a rough one that we broke apart into two more days. Ten-hour days on a bike killed you, man – and Reaver and I were both sore as fuck when we collapsed into beds at the cheap hotel we'd checked into under assumed names.

It was the kind of rundown shithole that if you paid cash? They didn't ask questions.

At least it didn't have vermin, but it damn sure couldn't be called clean.

We slept practically to the next night which was just fine. What we had to do had to be done under cover of darkness, anyhow.

Ramone didn't live at the address Honor had given us anymore, but sure as shit, we found his truck outside the local watering hole that night. A beat-up old Ford that had a faded, cracked, and peeling bumper sticker proclaiming pride in their local junior high honor student.

Honor had told us her mom had put it there and Ramone and her mom had a terrible fight about it. Her mom ended up with a black eye, but the bumper sticker had stayed. She said her mom had said piece of cake – all she had to do was work him up a little so he'd smack her, and then she could get what she needed or wanted by way of apology.

Thank God Honor *had* been an honor student, it meant she was smart enough not to buy into her mother's bullshit that that was how relationships just work… which is how her mother had tried to sell it or spin it.

Thank fuck for the Pilchuck's steadfast determination, too. To give their granddaughter everything they could in death that they only wished they could give her in life.

To some degree, I didn't understand why it was so important for Honor to know… why she still clung to her mother's memory so hard but… but on the tail of that thought, I could honestly say my parents weren't any better and while my mom was still alive? I didn't talk to her anymore, but my dad? Him, I did the same thing too, put him on a pedestal sort of when if I was being honest to myself? He didn't deserve it any more than Honor's mom did… probably less for how he would beat on my mom when she pissed him off and how I'd remember him straight up screaming in her face one time that the only reason she'd been kept around was because he'd be fucked if she'd take his son away from him.

I still couldn't figure how the fuck my having a dick made me special to him, I definitely don't think if I'd been born a daughter that he'd have given half a fuck. I was also pretty sure that if I ever did one of them DNA test kits for home that I'd have half siblings popping up all over Florida and half the country – but it's not like I was dumb enough to do that. Shit, it was enough that some of those siblings had probably already been contacted by LEO's looking for my dumb ass for leaving my hair or spit someplace it shouldn't be.

No, the older I got, the more careful I had to get, and if it's one thing I could respect and defer to it was that Reaver far outstripped me in not only psycho, but smarts as well. Pride got a motherfucker locked up, and I was fixing to get home to my woman as long as possible and to that end while we sat on our bikes in a lot across the street from the bar, I told him: "Age before beauty, man – what's the play?"

He smirked and without looking at me let his eyes rove the lot across from us and said, "First of all, fuck you for putting it that way. Second of all, I think we can get in the back of the truck, get him when he's home, maybe."

"What if it's an apartment?" I asked.

"Won't matter, I've got a plan."

"Alright," I said.

"I don't see any cameras, but that doesn't mean there isn't one," he said raising the hood on his dark gray hoodie to cover his head.

"Yeah," I said unhappily, and did the same with mine. It was cold out here in the desert at night.

We jogged across the deserted street and lifted the tarp in the back of the truck to see what we would be riding with.

"Oh," Reaver said. "He's in construction."

"Ain't going to be a comfortable ride."

"No, but this kind of shit ain't meant to be comfy," he said climbing in and holding up the tarp for me to slither under.

It was a cold and long wait.

Finally, he came out of the bar, got into his truck, and lumbered on home. He was drunk as fuck and weaving all over the road but he made it. Thankfully it wasn't but a six-minute drive.

When it'd been still long enough, we slithered out from under the tarp and found ourselves in what felt like the middle of nowhere at a tin can of an old mobile home. We heard him hacking inside and Reaver and I nodded at each other and went to the door, knocking.

"What?" he drunkenly called out. "Who's there?"

"Housekeeping!" Reaver called in a falsetto.

The door opened and we rushed him.

It was an ugly win, but we got him duct taped to a chair and now it was just a wait for him to sober up enough to answer some fucking questions. Namely what he'd done to Honor's mom, and to have him take us to her.

It was just before sunrise when we got the information out of him. Took a few good pistol-whips and a threat or two and you could just *see* that Reave was getting off on this, the fucking weirdo.

Fortunately for us, Ramone could see him getting off on it too and it got him to talking a lot faster.

I didn't see what Honor's mom had seen in this greasy bloated little fuck. I mean, Ramone wasn't a big man, maybe five foot four with a big fuckin' beer gut and a chevron mustache. For a guy who was getting older, his hair was still thick, but his skin was weathered from too much sun and the whites of his eyes were yellowed, a telltale sign that his drinking was catching up to his ass. Likewise his teeth were stained with tobacco from chewing *and* heavy smoking – the trailer fucking *reeking* of it.

"I'll take you to her, I'll take you to her," he said finally and started weeping and Reaver said, "You damn well better believe you will."

We sat him between us in his own truck and I drove while he pointed. We weren't honestly that far out, stopped in the middle of nowhere in the early morning sun near an outcropping of rocks. Still, there was nothing as far as the eye could see in any direction.

"Get out," Reaver ordered him and waved Ramone to his side of the truck.

I got out, taking the keys, and Ramone slid to my side and got out on my side of the truck. Reaver scowled and walked around to the back and pulled a shovel out of the truck bed.

Ramone said, "There," and pointed at a depression in the ground, however slight, just in the shadow of the rocks.

Reaver handed him the shovel.

"Start digging motherfucker," he ordered.

Ramone did a whole lot of crying and bellyaching as he dug up his wife's bones.

We stood by, waiting, watching, and soon enough he uncovered her withered remains from its shallow grave. Man, not even two feet deep… We were lucky with the coyotes and the other scavenger types out here that she remained intact.

"You motherfucker," I murmured and I yanked him up by the back of his wifebeater and he stepped out of the hole. He was out here in just his boxers, wifebeater, and cowboy boots. We had his wallet, his gun, and keys. Hell, his gun was the one I was using to beat the fuck out of him.

I got down in the hole and unclasped the dirty butterfly necklace from around the corpse's neck and slid the ring off her withered finger. I took the buckle from her belt, the leather disintegrating as I lifted it and the bones of her mummified corpse shifting some with that.

Reaver shoved him forward and Ramone stood shaking at the foot of the shallow grave, knees knocking and eyes wide with panic.

Reaver said, "Now I'm going to hamstring you, buddy. Let you get cozy with your wife down there, and then my friend and I here, we're going to tuck you in real nice for the long sleep." As quick as my name, Reaver's knife flashed and Ramone screamed as the blood welled on the backs of his legs from twin cuts that went fuckin' *deep*. He collapsed face first into the grave and was trying to crawl out and Reaver said, "Wing him, he might drown in his own blood before we get him buried. If you get him in the lung, the suffocation will at least be slow."

I shot him in the back, the report echoing off the rocks, the sound ricocheting and echoing through the clear blue sky.

Ramone couldn't scream anymore with the hole through his back. In like a dime and out like a pizza, his lung on his right-hand side shredded.

Reaver took up the shovel and looking like some kind of cyborg, face rigid, eyes icy, started to fill the hole back in. I went around to the back of the truck to see if there was another shovel or anything I could help with and I lucked out. In addition to the spade there was another shovel that looked less used, a transfer shovel is what those of us in the landscaping business called it.

I got to digging, and Reaver and I talked next steps. We would wait for nightfall to get the fuck out of here, wait until late. We would drive the truck back to the bar and leave it, get back on the bikes and head straight out of town. Were we worried about the bikes? No. They were back at the hotel. Once we'd spotted the truck, we'd taken them back to park 'em in front of our room. We'd gone out the window and had walked back to the lot across from the bar where this fucked up little adventure had begun.

We'd worn gloves, had kept our hoods up, and we would take a spray bottle of bleach to the inside of the truck when we parked it outside the bar that night. We'd retrace our steps back to the motel, would climb back in the window, and there would be no proof we'd ever left.

The plan went pretty much flawless. It'd helped that he'd lived in the mobile home with no neighbors. We buried his wallet and gun with him – we didn't need anything to connect us to this shit. I took Honor's mom's things – that was all. The keys we left in the bleach-soaked cap of the truck in the ignition.

Our room hadn't been touched when we got back to the motel. The bikes were fine. We showered, dressed in our clothes, and the fresh ones we'd bought in the last state on the way here we took with us, and set on fire two states over on the way back home.

We didn't stop back in NOLA, we took a completely different route, and now that the job was done, we would never speak on it again.

It was done. It was over. No questions answered, nothing to prove we'd even been… we were ghosts.

That was as it should be.

I wasn't looking forward to laying these old ghosts to rest for Honor. I worried for her… I knew it would be bad. By the time we were where we needed to be to turn on our phones and check on things, I had a slew of texts waiting. Among them, a shit ton of chatter in the club's group text about Pyro.

Cutter had called Pyro's next of kin – his estranged sister. She'd made it up to the hospital up there and she'd had him taken off the vent and shit. Said Pyro wouldn't want to live like this, which she was right. No one faulted her for that. Of course, Pyro never did know when to stop fighting… he'd started breathing on his own, but the doctors? They said they weren't confident he was going to come out of the coma. Said there was damage to the brain that was evident on the scans that said it was an extremely low chance. They could give him a while to see if he would pass, but if he didn't in some arbitrary timeframe? His sister was going to have to find a permanent full-time care facility to do round-the-clock care.

The messages from Honor were a balm to the soul after that news, and I couldn't wait to get to her.

It was a trial by fire for us, all of this grief and madness all at once, but fuck… if we could get through this storm? Shit what a beautiful life we should have on the other side. At least I hoped that would be the case. Silver linings and all of that.

26

Honor…

Stoker and Serenity came by the next morning just as they'd promised and I knew I was looking rough.

"Oh, honey," Serenity looked empathetic when I opened the door, squinting against the daylight.

"Sorry, I fell asleep right when I got home. I only meant to take a nap, but then Lightning called late and I couldn't go back to sleep and now I'm afraid my sleep is all fucked up. I didn't mean to oversleep but I guess I did."

"Shit, yeah, that definitely explains it," Stoker said. "Want us to come back later?"

"No," Serenity said firmly. "Look you just point and we'll do, but the only way to get your sleep schedule back on track is—"

"Yeah," I agreed and I had already stepped aside to let them in. "I know."

I shut the door behind them and turned to survey the living room and Stoker said with a wry grin, "Have a seat. I'll get coffee going."

"Coffee," my brain latched onto the word. "Yes, please, God yes…"

We caffeinated and Serenity went through a checklist of things she said would help get the house organized and would allow me to separate things for Goodwill, the trash, and the pile I wished to keep.

We worked throughout the day and Serenity was patient with my indecision on some things… some just didn't speak to me, but at the same time the way they were placed within the home spoke to the fact they had to Ruthie and that she'd loved them dearly. I'd had to wrestle with some serious guilt on putting certain items in the pile for Good Will or even the trash pile knowing that they may have meant something to Mitch or Ruth but that they wouldn't appeal to anyone else…

It was slow, and by the end of the day I would be lying if I said I wasn't discouraged. I felt like I could have gotten a lot more done, but I just… didn't.

It was even more stressful and frustrating not hearing from Lightning. Like, I wanted to message him, and I did finally at the end of the day when it was just me in the cavernous house alone. I wrote him a long, long, text about all that I'd done that day and my frustrations with how the progress went and I sat for a long time starting at the screen after I'd sent it…

I didn't get the little notification off to the side saying that it'd even been delivered, and when I chanced it? Yep. His phone had gone straight to voicemail. He'd turned it off.

I wished for him. I guess that you could call it praying but I didn't honestly know who I prayed *to*… I simply sat in the quiet of the night darkened space that was my bedroom now, and I wished for him to come back to me safely and I wished that he had no difficulties or complications in what he had set out to do for me…

I didn't wrestle with any feelings of guilt over what may or may not happen to Ramone. None whatsoever. I wasn't sure if that made me a bad person or not, and truthfully? I didn't really care if it did. As far as I was concerned whatever happened to my former stepdad at this point was going to be fucking Karma.

I knew… I just *knew* in my absolute *bones* that he had done something to my mother and I hated him for it.

So no, I didn't feel bad for that piece of shit, not one iota… I just worried about Lightning and his friend. I think I would continue to worry right up until he was home.

Home... I heaved a big sigh and looked around the master bedroom and thought about it.

Did this feel like home? No, not really… I mean, I felt no attachment to these walls or even this town… but you know what *did* feel like home to me? Or at least the closest I've ever felt to what the sensation of *home* should be?

Lightning.

Every time he put his arms around me, every time I laid my head on his chest and listened to the echo of his heartbeat… I felt like I belonged. I felt as though I was exactly where I was supposed to be… and *that?* I always sort of guessed that that was what home was supposed to feel like.

And so, I longed for that home back. I longed for Lightning to come back here and to give me that feeling of home and I doubly hoped and longed to be able to give him some good news about his club brother and friend in Pyro.

That was looking like it was going to be less and less of a possibility, though.

The last word on Pyro wasn't looking good. His sister, who was his next of kin and closest family member, had been called and she didn't seem to be giving her brother much of a chance… at least that's the way whoever had been on the phone to Stoker had framed it. Whoever had let Stoker know the information being passed from the hospital was mighty upset, but after Stoker had hung up, he'd sighed and tried to give us the news a little more gently. I think more for Serenity's sake.

"Pyro's sister has taken him off all the vents and life support, or whatever," he said.

"Isn't that premature?" Serenity asked.

Stoker shook his head, "The doctors say it's bad. If he starts breathing on his own at this point, it's not like he's going to wake up. He's just going to be in a coma and she's going to have to find long-term care. His body could keep going into old age, but he's not going to wake up – there's too much brain damage for that. Likewise, even if he did wake up? There's too much damage to his spine. He'll never walk or use his arms again and I know Pyro – he wouldn't want that. Gator just gets himself worked up and he just doesn't get it," he said.

"Was that who was on the phone?" I asked.

Stoker nodded.

"He's tore up. He was right next to Pyro when he went over, made a grab for him but it was mission impossible keeping him on the right side of the railing at that point. Dude rocked his shit too hard."

"Damn," Serenity murmured and I sighed.

"I wish there was a way to let Lightning know," I said unhappily.

"Lightning isn't ready to know," Stoker said. "When it cuts this deep, he does this kind of thing," he said. "Finds something to focus on and do until he's ready to deal with it."

"Oh," I murmured. I mean, I don't think I could blame him… I was similarly inclined if I were being honest. Disassociation had served me well on a number of occasions.

Still, I honestly didn't think he even realized he was doing it, and I now felt just a little guilty – okay, *a lot* guilty that he was out there doing all this for me to slay my demons and to lay some of my old ghosts to rest all in a bid to avoid his own problems and feelings and *ugh…* what a tangled web we all weaved without even realizing it, yeah?

"Hey, don't do that," Serenity said softly.

"Yeah, don't take any of this on yourself," Stoker said quickly. "Lightning's a big boy and he wasn't exactly wrong in his reasoning – there's absolutely nothing he can do about Pyro's situation and he'd be legit going crazy sitting or standing around waiting with nothing to do. Having a problem to solve and something to do is honestly the best thing for him."

Serenity smiled and said, "Confession time… we all are looking for something useful to do in the face of this whole mess, so thank you for providing it," she said sweeping a hand out and I laughed slightly and nodded.

"I didn't think of it like that," I said.

"We know," Stoker said with a smirk.

"Have you thought about paint colors for in here yet?" Serenity asked and I shook my head.

"Well start thinkin'," Stoker said kindly and picked up a box for the donation center and took it out to his truck waiting at the curb.

I settled into the work of getting things sorted a little better after that, but I still worried about Lightning and wished I could talk with him.

27

Lightning…

By the time I turned my phone back on, at the point where Reaver and I parted ways, it was to a slew of hundreds of messages in the group text with the rest of the club. I took my time, holed up in the last hotel room before I made the big push for home the next day and scrolled through the hundreds of messages, questions, and answers. Watching things get worse and worse for my club brother.

I swallowed hard at the last one in the chat from just a couple hours ago from Cutter, letting us all know as gently as he could via fuckin' text message that Pyro was gone.

It hit me like a blow to the center of my chest to the point that I put my hand over my damn heart like it'd been a physical thing, man.

I sniffed and was glad I was alone. I cried like a fucking baby. Not just because he was gone, but for all the times over the last couple to few years that Pyro could have reversed course on the litany of toxic bullshit he spewed and flung around himself like a monkey flinging his shit, and how he just didn't… I mean, *fucking hell*, what a goddamned *waste*.

My heart hurt for me, my surviving club brothers, *fucking Cutter,* man… and that was the rub. Cutter stuck by Pyro no matter fucking *what* and he damn sure didn't deserve this.

It was such a fucking *waste.*

When I was calmer and was numb over reeling, I picked up my phone again and went straight to Honor's smiling face and the unread text notifications that were waiting.

I swear, she anchored me without even knowing she did. Her litany of texts summing up each and every day we'd been separated were sweet. She sent pictures of empty shelves in the living room, and their plans to paint the ugly faux-oak entertainment center and to break parts of it off and to re-make it something cool. She sent pictures of Serenity's sketches and I had to admit, what they were doing looked cool.

The thing that made me settle into a space that would allow me to sleep for the ride ahead tomorrow was that she signed each and every one of her texts with how much she loved and she missed me.

"Same, baby… same," I murmured into the dark and sighed.

I wanted to call her. I wanted to hear her voice so damn bad… but it was *late* and I didn't want to wake her if she slept and she dreamed of me.

I would text her in the morning when I went to take off and then I would go straight to her.

Mind made up, that's just what I did. I went to bed and after a few hours of sleep that I only wished was restful, I got my ass up, into a cold shower to *wake my ass up*, and then I got ready to ride. I shot a text off before I got on the bike that said: ***I'm coming home baby. I miss and love you, too. I'll see you tonight. Please wait up…***

I knew it wasn't fair of me to ask, but now that the trip to New Mexico was in my rearview, the next big problem was laid out ugly in front of me.

I had to deliver the answers she so desperately sought, and they weren't the kind of answers any of us were hoping for.

Likewise, I knew she was worried about me. A woman as, well, *honorable* as Honor? I knew she knew I knew or I bet dollars to fuckin' doughnuts she thought she had to deliver the bad news about Pyro. She didn't know that we'd decided as a club a long time ago that when it came to shit like this? We'd all agreed that while text wasn't the best way to receive this kind of news that if we were scattered to the four winds when shit went down it *was* the most efficient way to receive it.

We'd all decided that we'd rather know, and I knew… and it fucking sucked, and all I wanted was to wrap my arms around my girl and hold her tight and have her hold *me* tight so we could get through our very separate but mutual pains on this together.

I rode all damn day and into the night and it was something like ten or eleven o'clock when I pulled up out front of Honor's house.

She was waiting for me on her front porch, a cooler between the two white rocking chairs, on the porch's floor, a bottle of some import beer open on the small round table between them. I didn't even bother with fucking with any of the shit on the bike. I simply got off, stretching while she raised her chin and looked on from her spot up there and I could tell, even from here, she was trying to be brave and stoic for me.

I smiled at her and unshouldering my pack, went on up. She got up for me, and her arms folded around me even as she just naturally fit against me.

"You don't have to feel like you need to tell me," I murmured into her hair, breathing her in. "I already know Pyro didn't make it."

"I'm so sorry," she breathed and she leaned back sniffing, her deep brown eyes brimming with tears as she smoothed the side of my face with her palm, as though trying to assure herself that I was actually here, that I was home.

"I loved all your messages," I told her. "Sorry I didn't respond last night. I wanted to, I just didn't want to risk waking you up from a time zone or two away, you know?"

"Oh, fuck," she muttered. "Wake me up," she demanded, pulling me in tight against her and holding onto me for dear life. "Always wake me the fuck up," she demanded, her voice rough with emotion.

"I've got you," I told her, nodding and luxuriating in the feel of her hair against my face.

"She's gone, isn't she?" she asked.

I held onto her tighter and murmured, "Yeah, baby. I'm so sorry."

She crumbled a little, a bubbling little sob and a sniffle escaping her. I stood back from her and heavy-heartedly dug in the front pocket of my backpack and pulled out the Ziploc bag with her mother's effects in them. She took them and turned them into the porch light and closed her eyes tight, hugging the items, still crusted in grave dirt, to her chest. She turned back to me and I got her, gathering her up and holding onto her tight as she wept years of pain, frustration, and her unanswered questions as to where her mother had gone onto me and I stood and took it, because she'd been waiting as long as long could be and she deserved closure before I did.

I could get mine at the upcoming funeral for our boy… she would never get a funeral for her mother. She would never be able to sit among her loved ones, supported and cared for, she would never be able to place her hand on her mother's casket and say a final goodbye as they lowered it into the ground, or wheeled it away for her cremation. She'd never be able to accept an urn or let her mother's ashes float on a summer's wind to carry her to a final resting place someplace beautiful…

No, all she was going to get was this moment right here. A few pieces of silver and my dumb ass with nothing to say, exhausted from the long ride to bring them to her. So, I let her have this moment and let her live in it for as long as possible until she was all cried out and as numb as I was the night before after my solo crying jag that I was grateful no one had been around to bear witness to.

It was a shitty homecoming, for sure, but one I'd expected to be a lot worse to be honest.

We sat on the porch and drank some beers, talking softly into the wee hours of the morning.

I answered her questions, gave her every gritty fucking detail I had knowing that she was strong and that she could fucking take it.

"So, did you kill him?" she asked, staring down into the bag in her hands with her mother's effects.

"Fuckin' slow," I affirmed. "Let him choke on a mix of his blood and the fuckin' grave dirt. I'm sorry, but we had to bury his fuckin' ass right on top of her."

"No, don't be sorry," she said with a sniff. "It's fitting that he should have to look at what he's done for the rest of eternity."

Her voice was velvet wrapped steel as she said it and I was proud of her. Her hatred of the man was palpable and her cheeks burned in the porch light with the passion of that hatred. It turned her beautiful in that frightening sort of way that women had when you knew they were so angry they had that effect of calm. I liked to call it *summoning the storm*, because that was exactly what it was. It was that calm before the storm. The kind that said she'd had enough and that lighting was off in the distance, flashing on the horizon, just behind her eyes.

Too many times I'd seen that look on or in a woman, and I never understood it. The way that dudes failed to recognize it, or how they just straight up *ignored* it.

It was stupid, it was folly… and I'd been lucky so far that like now – that ire wasn't directed anywhere at me.

She dragged her eyes from her mother's necklace, rings, and belt buckle in the bag and said to me, "She loved this belt buckle. It was the first thing my father ever gave to her."

"I think we can clean it up, give it a good polish and I know a guy that can put a new belt on it for you."

"I'd like that," she said.

"I would too," I agreed.

"Yeah?" she asked.

I nodded, "It belongs with you. On you. I don't think she ever meant to leave you, baby. Was she messed up? Yeah, people often are… they can't win for losing or they can't get out of their own way —" my voice cracked on that last part and I cleared my throat. "But that doesn't stop them from loving the people that they love and I think you were your mama's whole world when she had her shit together. At least from everything you've told me, I do."

She nodded, "When she had her shit together… which wasn't very often sometimes," she gave a bitter laugh.

We were silent for a long time and she finally asked me, "Did he say why he did it?"

I shook my head, "Just a bunch of bullshit excuses about how she pissed him off or how she was always pissing him off or whatever. Something about a smart mouth." I shook my head. "His inability to contain himself and walk away is what killed her. *He* killed her."

"He finally beat her to death, didn't he?" she asked quietly. "Like he always threatened he would any time they fought, any time, he did slap her around…"

I nodded, remembering the broken bones of her face, how the skull wasn't right at all under the caved in dried out husk of her skin…

"Yeah, he did," I said somberly.

"I hope he did die slow," she said. "I know that probably makes me some kind of awful—"

"No," I told her, threading my fingers through the spaces between hers. "No, baby. It just makes you human. That's all."

She nodded and swallowed hard.

"What happens now?" she asked.

"Nothing, unfortunately," I said. "The world keeps spinning on its axis, the night'll stretch into day, and the day will bleed into night, and time just marches right the fuck on."

I raised the back of her hand to my lips and pressed a kiss to her soft skin.

"Only difference is that you have answers you didn't yesterday, and Pyro won't be here in the morning… as much as it'll be different it'll be just as much the same and I hate it, but that's the fucking reality."

She nodded and said, "It's true… but, I mean, it's a shitty consolation prize, I guess but there'll be one difference."

I gave a crooked smile and said, "Living every day, the rest of my life, knowing that you're on this earth and in it? That's not a shitty consolation prize by any means, baby. You're the shit I've wanted and lived this long just wishing for… and now you're the shit I'll live for the rest of our lives. You make me smile, and laugh, and make everything about this life fucking bearable again."

She stared at me, open-mouthed, as I poured my fuckin' heart out at her feet and she said, "I'm so glad I fucking met you."

I don't remember who moved first. Hell, maybe it was the both of us. All I know is that we were suddenly both standing, mouths crashing into each other's like lightning into the fucking shore. I don't remember picking her up, I don't remember carrying her through the night darkened house or laying her down on her bed. I *do* remember her hiking up her long skirt, and I definitely remember getting my stiff cock out of my jeans and how could I ever fucking forget moving her simple black panties aside and burying my cock into her wet and waiting heat to the motherfucking hilt?

She groaned into my mouth as I stood at the side of her bed and drove into her. I wanted to take it easy, I wanted to give her soft and slow, gossamer kisses and silken thrusts, but I'd done myself a hell of a disservice the last few days.

I'd steeped myself so totally in death, and unlike Reaver and some other guys like Axeman and La Croix…. I didn't revel in it. I understood it to be a natural part of life – hell, of *this* life in particular, but I didn't revel in it. I had a healthy respect for it, but I didn't enjoy it, and after so much death and rot and decay of the human soul and condition I needed that breath of *life*.

I needed between Honor's legs, I needed her arms around me, I needed her whimpering and clinging to me like Ivy shuddering in the maelstrom, and I craved her feral cries and gripping cunt like nothing else!

I needed something life affirming, and I needed to hold on to life with everything that I had lest I be stripped of my fuckin' humanity, too.

I think she knew it, too.

By the sound of pain she made when I drove into her, and how her nails bit into my ass and she cried at me, "Harder!" despite it. By how she held onto me so tightly it was as though she wanted to pull me *through* her, and by how she bucked wildly under me when her orgasm hit her, and yet despite how I knew how over stimulated she probably was, how she let me drive into her that much more, that much harder, that green glowing spark of life tingling to life at the base of my spine, my balls tingling and drawing up tight, holding there for that beautiful perfect, shining fucking moment, before that life filled me out from my center, rocketing out along every nerve and fiber of my being and shit fucking *yeah*.

She was my glow, the sun on my face, the wind in my hair, the water that nourished my soul in that very moment and your boy couldn't ask for anything more.

We collapsed together, panting, and my cock twitched inside of her in counterpoint to every flex and spasm around it from her softly gripping little cunt and I suddenly felt like I could breathe again. The crushing weight of sorrow, the boulder of ruin sitting on my chest budging for me for the first time in fucking days.

I laid my ear over the thundering echo of her heart between her pert breasts as she lightly raked her nails along my scalp, her fingers twining through my short hair.

"I love you," she breathed and pressed a kiss to my forehead as I looked up at her words. I was rendered speechless in my worship and devotion to her.

28

Honor...

"You ever been to a biker's celebration of life?" Zach asked me, as we set up food along one end of the throne room back at The Plank. I shook my head.

Lightning and I had parted ways after the grave side memorial for Pyro as I took myself with Faith, Charity, Serenity, and Justice in Charity's Jeep back to The Plank ahead of the club. They were doing this strange procession through town, Pyro's bike riderless and on a flatbed trailer towed with a phalanx of the club riding around it. They were bringing Pyro's bike in here, putting it up beside Cutter's throne and roping it off. I couldn't honestly think of a better memorial... I guess if someone else passed, their bike would replace Pyro's and I didn't know the plan after that for his bike, but one thing I could say was that we all hoped that it wouldn't be replaced any time soon.

"Shit's going to get wild in here," Zach said. "A lot of drinking, maybe some drugs, some serious hard partying. Some clothes might come off – like it's no holds barred, the thing to remember? It's club only. If you see someone that's not club, you come find me or Lightning or any of the guys – hell, come find *me*. Anyone puts hands on you? Fuckin' let fly. We've got your back. No matter what? It's going to be all good and the most important thing? Ain't no room to be sad. It's about Pyro and *celebrating* his life. Got it?"

I nodded and he said, "Good."

"He makes it sound like someone's getting eaten out on the pool table," Justice said rolling her eyes.

"That may not be too far off the truth," Charity said laughing. "This place is about to be the Vegas of Florida. You didn't see shit, you didn't hear shit, you sure as hell don't say shit about anything that happens up in here. You just sit back, enjoy the ride, and most importantly? Do something you wouldn't ordinarily let yourself do – especially in public. That's how Pyro lived, and that's what we're here to celebrate. This is your one get out of jail free card to go buck wild."

"Shit, is this a biker funeral or a swinger's party?" Serenity asked with a grin.

"Yes." Faith said, deadpan.

"You've been to one of these before?" I asked.

"Not for any Kraken, no," she said. "But bike week a few years back a celebration of life went down at the Iron Steed and it was… *wow*." Her blue eyes were wide as she finished and I blinked.

"So exhibitionism, voyeurism, drunk until they puke, sex, rock 'n roll, and mayhem until everyone is exhausted." I ticked points off on my fingers and Charity nodded throughout them all.

"Shit, there are parties and then there's whatever the hell this is going to be," Justice declared, cheeks turning pink.

"You better get cool with a whole lotta shit real damn quick," Zach shouted. "That's them!"

It was hard to miss the low bass rumble of bikes making the turn down the block to head on up the way to The Plank.

They parked out front, backing bikes to the curb, and Cutter and Marlin wheeled Pyro's bike into the bar and over to the dais to the planks put there to get it up and on to the platform.

It was parked, the bar filling and packed to the brim with sun-drenched black leather and shouts and cheering, ear-splitting whistles as they got it into place and then *pandemonium.*

The music was cranked, the liquor was cracked and flowing, and before long, there was partying the likes I'd never seen before.

I joined Lightning and started drinking with him, and let me tell you, a game was played where everyone told a story about Pyro and the wilder it got, or any time the story told had something quintessentially *Pyro* involved? They drank. I couldn't hardly believe some of the stories, but at the same time? I could.

He sounded like someone that would have been really grand to know before the bitterness, heartache, and drug use had set in.

Things were kind of a blur after that. I remember looking up and Cutter had Hopes skirt up, her panties moved aside, as she straddled him in his throne, rising and falling, his thick long cock disappearing up inside her as several brothers looked on in appreciation and cheered them on.

I didn't think that they had it in them, but Serenity and Charity were *both* laid out on the pool table at one point, Heads near one another, Stoker's face buried between Ren's thighs, while Galahad gave Charity the same treatment at the other end of the pool table and a tally was being kept on the blackboard meant to keep score for a game of billiards.

It looked like Charity was up by two orgasms, I think Serenity was equal parts too drunk and having a hard time getting out of her own head to come as much.

"God, I want to bend you over the bar and fuck you," Lightning growled behind my ear sending shivers down my spine.

"When in Rome..." I murmured, tilting my head way back and pressing my mouth to his.

"Mm," he made this sound into my mouth that was half appreciation and half like he was trying to resist.

Faith and Marlin had disappeared and Justice was straddling Radar's lap, but Atlas practically had his tongue down her throat while she rode Radar's dick.

It was hot and heavy up in here, and I was catching the fever... still, I didn't know if I was precisely down for this level of public indecency even if it wasn't exactly public in the traditional sense of the word. I mean, it was quite literally *club only*. Even Zach and Rocco disappeared.

My thoughts were disrupted by the high, thin, breathy wail of *someone* having another orgasm. A cheer went up around the pool table in front of us and I had to guess it was Serenity this time.

"Come on," Lighting towed me out past the throne and onto the back patio where we found a dark and secluded corner by a giant plant in a humongous pot. He took a seat and got his cock out and I immediately fell on my knees to take him into my mouth, my mouth practically watering at the thought of having him there.

He grunted and let out a gasp and holding my hair back, watched me with lust filled eyes as I worked him in and out of my throat.

"Fuck yeah," he grunted and his mouth fell open in appreciation as he panted a little bit.

I loved that I could have this kind of effect on him and in my drunken haze I had the ridiculous thought of how I wished I could have him in my mouth and in my cunt at the same time – like that would be just perfect right now.

Of course, forget about the actual impossibility of those logistics, it just would feel so good and that's all I was thinking about.

I came up for air and to unlock my jaw and he looked at me, his green eyes heavy-lidded and drunk not just with alcohol but passion and I said it.

"God, I wish I could have you in my mouth and my pussy at the same time."

"Fuck," he swore, breath tight, his eyes dilating with a thought and he said to me, "How bad do you want a cock in that cunt while I fuck that pretty mouth of yours, because we can make that shit happen baby. You're feeling adventurous enough I'll call one of the guys over here right now for you. You only live once, and I fucking love you enough that I would fucking do it just to make you feel good."

I stopped and through the fog of booze and lowered inhibitions I *really* had to put my mind to it… I swallowed hard and said, "I want it, but… but I don't know if I really want to think about who is doing what, you know?" I swallowed hard and said, "Truthfully, I think I like it better as just a fantasy than a reality."

Lightning gave me a cocky grin, his cock throbbing and he said, "I have an idea, you trust me?"

I nodded, "Of course I do."

He got down off the bench and put his mouth to mine and kissed me. I closed my eyes and melted into him and that kiss, my hand gravitating and wrapping around his cock, stroking him still wet from my mouth in my hand.

He groaned into my mouth and shook something out, the motion of his arm and the snapping sound making my eyes pop open.

He pulled back and worked the bandanna in his hands, rolling it.

"I'm going to blindfold you, and I'm going to leave you for just a minute, and when I come back, I'm going to put this cock back in your mouth and I'm going to watch you suck it, while I watch one of my brothers fuck you nice and gentle from behind."

Holy shit.

"Why does that sound so *hot?*" I demanded.

"Because it is," he said laughing gently.

"Like, I'll never know?" I asked. "I'll never know who it is and this will never be spoken about again?"

"Never again, unless you get that itch and you want it – then tell me, and if shit's right…"

He arched an eyebrow and I could tell by the set of his jaw and the hard sparkle in his eyes that this was indeed a onetime thing, the stars aligned and the mood right but that it really never had to happen again if I didn't want it to, and that he was genuinely turned on by the thought.

I nodded carefully and he raised both eyebrows and I smiled and knew it was a wicked thing.

"Yes," I murmured, hushed.

"Good girl," he said low and deep and he tied the orange bandanna over my eyes, securing it firmly at the back of my head.

"You stay right there on your knees, baby, and you wait for me. When I come back, you be just the goodest little cocksucker for me."

I giggled and he went and all was still but for the throbbing pulsing of my pussy in time with the beat of the music through the cinderblock walls somewhere off to my left.

I heard movement a short time later and flinched when he lightly caressed my face. "Open that mouth for me, baby," he said and he guided his cock between my lips. I got up on my hands and knees and sucked him as he sat back down on the bench in front of me and he groaned.

"Aw, yeah… just like that, baby. Nice and soft."

"K, man. Go ahead," he said after a moment, and I tensed as my skirt lifted in the back, and whoever was behind me caressed my ass, around my panties.

I heard a grunt of appreciation behind me, but I had no idea who… there wasn't enough voice to match for me in my alcohol addled state.

My panties were swept down around my knees and I moaned around Lightning's cock in my mouth.

Fingertips teased at my slit and I arched slightly pressing back into them, because fuck that felt good. I heart a condom wrapper tear, faintly, and then a cock, not quite as thick as Lightning's pressed at my opening.

"That's it, that's good baby. Keep sucking, take that dick for me, yeah."

I gasped around Lightning's cock as whoever was behind me pressed himself inside of me, and I moaned, a deep and sultry thing as he struck as steady cadence, working himself in and out of me at a slick, even pace. His thrusts setting the rhythm of my sucking, as I heard Lightning suck in a deep, deep, appreciative breath as he watched me get fucked from behind even as I worked his cock deep into my throat.

"Oh, fuck yeah," he moaned. "Fuck that's hot. Put your thumb in her ass, dude. She fucking likes that."

A thumb slicked through some wetness where his condom covered cock disappeared in and out of my cunt and he worked it up over my asshole and I almost lost it right there. I don't know what magic fuckery this was doing to me, but he was hitting just the right place inside me, and I was panting trying so very hard not to come already – which had *never* happened. I had *never* come but for the one time, my *first* time ever, without having my clit played with.

The man behind me grunted, and I swallowed around Lightning's cock and he made a sound like *he* was close.

"Oh, man, that pussy's so tight," I heard behind me, and I lost it. I sucked in a breath around Lightning's dick, felt my pussy clench, and fucking hell I rode the passion and pleasure that flooded and overloaded my system, even as Lightning poured down my throat and I heard our mystery guest cry out. He slammed into me from behind and I cried out, the sound muffled by Lightning in my mouth and *holy fucking hell* that was good.

Lightning pulled himself out of my mouth and I felt the man behind me hold the condom on his cock and pull from me.

While he'd felt incredibly good, he just didn't fill me to completion the way Lightning did. Like, there was no comparison.

"Thanks, man," Lightning said over my head and I heard a familiar chuckle behind me.

"My fucking pleasure," whoever said, and I whisked the blindfold off. I just had to know.

Atlas winked at me as he tucked his cock into his jeans but I didn't get much more than a glimpse before Lightning was gripping me by the chin and dragging my mouth to his for a kiss.

"That wasn't the deal, baby," he whispered in my ear, playfully. "Now get up here and fuck me. I want that dripping wet pussy wrapped around my cock, no rubber, no barriers, because it's mine. Just like this dick is yours, and I'm not going to feel right until we reacquaint them…"

I groaned and whimpered as he helped me to my feet and pulled me to him, leaning back against the wall so I could straddle him and lower my juicy cunt over his throbbing, waiting, and already hard again cock.

A girl could get used to this kind of thing every once in a while…

EPILOGUE

L**ightning…**

I dropped the line into place around the mooring point to the boat deck of the *Reclaimer* and put my hands on my hips, sucking in deep fucking breaths. It was a fucking *workout* on this ship. I'd forgotten just how much.

"Nice work!" Cutter called down from the pilot house.

I just waved and he laughed at me, and I shook my head.

"Fuck me, that was a workout!"

"Ah, yup!" he called down as he steered us about to start hauling the yacht that'd started to go down back into port. Right now, it had several of our salvage airbags holding her afloat.

"That one put up a fight like a motherfucker!" Gator called over and I nodded again and went to grab a drink out of my water bottle.

Shit, it ain't even been a week after Pyro's funeral that Cutter hit me up to take his place on the *Reclaimer*. Cutter was sole owner of the business now that Pyro was gone. Some sort of default thing they had set up that if one died the other got the whole oyster.

Still, Cutter needed help, and I was the only one of the crew that had enough experience on the *Reclaimer* to even attempt to fill Pyro's shoes. Gator was in training as a deckhand to help out for when the baby came.

It was now six months out from Pyro's funeral, and about a month and a half after, Honor had gone to the doctor to get her shot. Surprise, surprise – she hadn't passed the pregnancy test to get it and it wasn't a few weeks after we got the news that she couldn't keep a fucking thing down.

We were down to one income while she dealt with what was proving to be a taxing fucking pregnancy, and I was alright with that. The captain paid me hella fucking good to be out here and I do mean more money than I'd ever fuckin' made in my life.

Honor and I were set, the house was just about remodeled where we needed it to be, the guest room turned nursery, and the whole place babyproofed to within an inch of its life. I'd moved the fuck out of my shithole apartment and we were going to be one big happy family of three just as soon as the kid was born.

We were hoping for a girl, but I would be cool with a little dude, too. We didn't do any of that gender reveal bullshit. We figured people went up to the last minute not knowing for thousands of fucking years. Why should we fuck with tradition on that scale?

Mostly, we just didn't want to fuck with any gender reveal bullshit, but we'd had a lot of fun fucking with people when we filmed a social media reel and the smoke bomb had popped off the back of the bike purple. We'd raised middle fingers to the sky and a caption'd come up: *you can fucking wait.*

We'd had a riot pranking the crew with it.

Faith, Hope, and Charity were going a little apeshit buying baby clothes for either a boy or a girl, and Serenity had tried talking Honor into a Goth nursery – but overall, everyone was just generally excited for the first mini-Kraken to be born.

Truthfully, Honor and I both were scared as hell about being good parents. That was, right up until Charity and Galahad had pointed out that our fear was our salvation.

"Hard to be shitty parents when you already love baby bean so much, and all you can think about is how *not* to fuck it up," Charity had said, and Galahad had looked at her in such a way it'd made me ask…

"You guys thinking about going there?"

At the time, I'd steeled myself from a bad reaction from Galahad, but he'd just smiled and Charity had said something about the appointment to have her IUD out was already scheduled.

I honestly was so fucking stoked. I wanted our kid to have a bestie growing up, and honestly, with how hard this pregnancy was going for my beautiful girlfriend? I didn't think a sibling was going to be in the cards.

I was honestly stressing the fuck out and scared as shit I would lose Honor, or worse, Honor and the baby if things got any tougher.

"You need me once we get back in?" I asked Cutter and he shook his head.

"Nah, you go be with your woman, send my love her way," he said.

I smiled and nodded and couldn't wait to get my ass back to port.

When I got home, Honor was waiting on the front porch, a glass of ice water at her elbow and a cooler with a few beers waiting at her feet for me.

"Hey, baby," she said her hands on her belly which was just barely starting to show.

"Hey," I leaned down to kiss her and she never disappointed on this front, her hands coming up to cup my face, her tongue plunging past my lips to stroke against my own as she hummed in satisfaction into my mouth.

I smiled against her lips and said, "I missed you, too."

"How was your day?" she asked, and I sat down with a sigh and caught the look on her face before she could school it away.

"Hey, talk to me…" I said softly. "What was that?"

She smiled and it was brittle.

"Same shit, different day," she said softly and I nodded, reaching out and taking her hand.

"I'm not going anywhere," I assured her and she smiled at me and my love for her got just that much deeper.

She was my best friend, and we shared everything and to that end, I knew already that her biggest fear was losing me. That something would happen out there and I wouldn't make it. That I would die, just like her daddy and leave her and baby bean all alone and I just couldn't seem to get through the pregnancy hormones just how big her and bean's extended family was with the club around her. That our child wouldn't have to grow up like she did. That everything would be okay, no matter which way the storm blew in.

"I love you," she said and I smiled at her and said, "Not a damn sight more than I love you."

She laughed slightly and I winked at our little ongoing game of one-upmanship in the how much we could possibly love each other department, and the honest answer?

Neither one of us could possibly love each other more than we both loved the baby she had growing in her belly.

"Can I?" I asked and held up a hand and she smiled and laughed happily and moved her hands away.

"Oh, hey, baby," I said and put my hand gently on her belly. "Sorry not sorry, kiddo, but I'm gonna be poking you in the forehead with my meat hammer later tonight."

Honor practically howled with laughter at that, and I grinned. I couldn't get enough of making my woman laugh with my ridiculousness. She sat back in her chair and her mother's necklace winked at the hollow of her throat.

She was so fucking beautiful to my eyes that it fucking hurt and I knew, fuck me, I just knew, this house was going to be one filled with love and laughter well into our old age where our kid was going to *want* to come home and visit as often as they could get away with and bring our grandchildren should they have them with them…

I know it's what my woman wanted and it's what I wanted too. Her dream was my dream was *our* dream…

ALSO BY A.J. DOWNEY

The Sacred Hearts MC

1. Shattered & Scarred

2. Broken & Burned

3. Cracked & Crushed

3.5 Masked & Miserable (a novella)

4. Tattered & Torn

5. Fractured & Formidable

6. Damaged & Dangerous

The Virtues

1. Cutter's Hope

2. Marlin's Faith

3. Charity for Nothing

4. Stoker's Serenity

5. Justice for Radar

The Sacred Brotherhood

1. Brother to Brother

2. Her Brother's Keeper

3. Brother In Arms

4. Between Brothers

5. A Brother's Secret

6. A Brother At My Back

7. A Brother's Salvation

Sacred Hearts MC Novella

Christmas with the Brotherhood

Indigo Knights

1. Her Thin Blue Lifeline

2. His Cold Blue Command

3. A Low Blue Flame

4. His Wild Blue Rose

5. Her Pained Blue Silence

6. A Cold Blue Call

7. Her Reluctant Blue Cavalier

8. Forged Under Fire

9. Under A Blue Moon

10. Sound of Blue Thunder

Sacred Hearts MC Pacific Northwest

1. Over the High Side

2. Wind Therapy

3. Apex of the Curve

4. Low Sided

5. Eating Asphalt

6. Hammer Down

7. Only Fool Riding

The Voodoo Bastards MC

1. Bourbon & Blood

2. Whiskey Shivers

3. Moonshine Lullabies

Paranormal Romance (with Ryan Kells)

1. I Am The Alpha

2. Omega's Run

3. Hunter's End

Indigo City Darker (with Jared KingPacal Lain)

1. Triple Threat

2. Double Shot

Standalones

Synchronicity

ABOUT A.J. DOWNEY

A.J. Downey is a Pacific Northwest girl living in an East Tennessee world who finds inspiration from her surroundings, through the people she meets, and likely as a byproduct of way too much caffeine. She specializes in real and relatable romance stories featuring that real-life kind of love that everyone craves.

Stalker Information:

Website
www.ajdowney.com

Sign up for her newsletter at
http://eepurl.com/dkQiIH

Facebook Group - AJ's Sacred Circle
https://www.facebook.com/groups/authorajdowney/

facebook.com/authorajdowney
twitter.com/authorajdowney
instagram.com/ajdowney
bookbub.com/authors/a-j-downey

www.ingramcontent.com/pod-product-compliance
Lightning Source LLC
LaVergne TN
LVHW010054110826
845155LV00028B/341

* 9 7 8 1 9 5 0 2 2 2 4 2 1 *